11TH HOUR WITNESS

AN ALEX HAYES LEGAL THRILLER
BOOK 2

L.T. RYAN

WITH
LAURA CHASE

LIQUID MIND MEDIA

THE ALEX HAYES SERIES

CHAPTER
ONE

THE STENCH HIT me like a sledgehammer as I ducked under the crime scene tape, my boots sinking into the mud with a wet squelch. A putrid cocktail of rotting flesh and landfill fumes assaulted my senses, churning my stomach with each breath. Dry heaves fought their way up my throat, but I swallowed them down, tasting bile. I switched to breathing through my mouth, though it didn't help much—I could practically taste the decay on my tongue.

The January morning was classic Houston—harsh and bitter one minute, deceptively mild the next. Steam rose from the disturbed earth as the weak winter sun tried to warm the ground, creating an other-worldly haze over the scene.

My gaze swept over the sprawling dump site, a sickly tableau of forensics teams in white Tyvek suits excavating the mass grave site. Yellow tape cordoned off the area in uneven rectangles, separating piles of refuse from disturbed earth. A blast of cold air whipped across the field, carrying with it another wave of that ungodly smell, and I pulled my jacket tighter around me, grateful I'd opted for pants and sensible boots instead of my usual courtroom attire.

Despite the number of people working the scene—I counted at least fifteen figures moving through the grid markers—there was an eerie silence over the whole place. It pressed down on me like a physical weight, broken only by sporadic police radios squawking and the wet sucking sound of boots trudging through mud. The scene reminded me of my first homicide as an ADA, but this … this was different. The scale alone made my chest tighten. I'd seen my fair share of ugly in this job, but this—this was a whole new level of grim.

A technician stumbled nearby, slipping in the mud, and the sound of retching followed. I didn't blame him. Part of me wanted to turn around, get back in my car, drive to the office and bury myself in paperwork, pretend I'd never seen any of this.

But I couldn't. Not again. Not after everything that happened with Andrews. Running away once had cost me enough.

Through the haze, I spotted a man who had to be the lead detective —mid-40s, rugged features etched with fatigue, his sharp eyes taking in every detail. He stood at the edge of the excavation site like a sentinel, feet planted wide to keep his balance in the treacherous mud, his dark coat flapping in the bitter wind. As I approached, picking my way carefully between evidence markers, I saw his gaze flick over to me, assessing. His jaw was clenched tight, a muscle ticking in his cheek. Couldn't blame him. A scene like this would get to anybody.

I squared my shoulders and headed over, trying to project a confidence I didn't quite feel. My boots slipped slightly with each step, and I had to fight to maintain my dignity. Sometimes I wondered how much more of this I could take before it ate me alive. But I'd chosen this. I kept reminding myself of that. Chosen to come back after everything had gone sideways with Andrews. Chosen to step back into this world of death and corruption and justice that never quite felt like enough.

"Detective Jason Turner?" I called.

He waited for me at the edge of the excavation site, his arms crossed tightly over his chest. A coffee cup sat abandoned by his feet, probably cold now. He nodded in greeting as I approached, his eyes exhausted yet alert, missing nothing.

"You must be the ADA," Turner drawled, extending a calloused hand. Up close, I could see dark stains on his cuffs—mud or something worse. I didn't want to know.

I accepted the firm shake, ignoring the undercurrent of dismissal in his tone. My hands were frozen despite my gloves, and his grip was almost painfully warm. "Alex Hayes. I'll be working this case along-side Robert Shaw."

A flicker of relief crossed Turner's weathered features, subtle but unmistakable. The same look I'd been getting from everyone since coming back to work, like they were all waiting to see if I'd crack again.

"That's a slice of good fortune," he said. "Shaw will bring good experience. You'll make a good team."

The implication wasn't lost on me—a fresh-faced prosecutor like me clearly needed the guidance of a seasoned veteran. I bit back the retort brewing behind my lips, tasting copper where I'd chewed the inside of my cheek. Ruffling feathers on day one rarely ended well. I'd learned that lesson the hard way more than once.

"I'm sure we will," I replied evenly, shifting my weight as my right boot slowly sank into the mud. "Mind bringing me up to speed?"

He pulled a small notebook from his coat pocket, the pages warped from the damp air. "We got a credible tip that led us to this dump site and the man we have in custody—Randall Pierce." Turner jerked his chin toward the dilapidated farmhouse cresting the hill above us. "He lives just up that way."

My eyes traced the path toward the ramshackle dwelling, its weathered siding barely visible through the morning mist following a set of deep ruts in the mud where vehicle after vehicle had churned up the earth. Crime scene tape fluttered in the wind, creating an eerie yellow line leading up to the house like some twisted version of Dorothy's yellow brick road.

Turner held my gaze with an inscrutable slate-gray stare, his breath fogging in the cold air between us. "We've pulled over twenty bodies from the dump site so far. Or pieces of them, at least."

I blinked, his words failing to penetrate at first, my brain refusing to process them. The wind died, leaving us in an unnatural stillness. "Pieces?"

As if on cue, two crime scene techs brushed past us, their Tyvek suits rustling with each step. Between them, they carried something wrapped in black plastic, roughly the size and shape of a human limb. The tang of decay clung to the air, creeping into my nostrils with grotesque intimacy. I swallowed hard against the rising tide of nausea, my gloved fingers digging into my palms.

Turner nodded, his mouth set in a grim line. "Yup, body parts scattered all over hell's half-acre back there. Biggest mass grave I've ever laid eyes on, truth be told."

Despite the roiling queasiness, I forced myself to survey the scene with a prosecutor's objectivity—taking stock of the chaotic sprawl of evidence markers, hazmat suits clustered around hastily dug trenches. My shoulder throbbed in the cold, a phantom reminder of my last big case, and I shifted my weight again to compensate. The rural stillness felt wrong somehow, the urgent shouts of law enforcement echoing for too long in the heavy air.

I swallowed again, my mouth dry as cotton. My chest tightened as the enormity of this case congealed into a sickening reality. Over twenty victims—potentially the most prolific serial killer in Texas history. The scope of it made my head swim, or maybe that was just the smell. Either way, I forced myself to stay focused, to breathe through it.

Inhale. Exhale. Just like my physical therapist had taught me during recovery.

"So, Pierce?" I managed, proud that my voice stayed steady. "What do we know about him?"

Turner raked a hand through his thinning hair before jerking his thumb toward the dilapidated homestead. Ice crystals had formed on the chain-link fence surrounding the property, glinting like tiny daggers in the weak sunlight.

"After we got the tip about bodies being dumped on the property, we pulled records. Saw the place was owned by Pierce. Brought him in for questioning, but so far, he hasn't said anything useful."

"Did he ask for a lawyer?"

"He hasn't asked for anything. Not even a glass of water."

"Great," I said with more sarcasm than intended, adjusting my stance as my boots sank deeper into the mud.

I'd dealt with guys like this before. They could be some of the hardest cases—the ones who just sat there, watching you with dead eyes, waiting for you to make a mistake. I looked up at the ramshackle house with its peeling clapboard siding, windows like vacant eyes staring down at us. A shutter banged somewhere in the wind, the sound making me flinch. My shoulder twinged at the sudden movement, and I caught Turner noticing my reaction.

I arched an eyebrow, deliberately casual. "Let me guess—you searched the premises and found enough circumstantial evidence to make you suspicious, but nothing iron-clad?"

A rueful chuckle escaped Turner's lips as he shifted his weight, boots squelching in the mud. "You've been around the block a few times, counselor. We found some, uh, concerning items inside the house. But you know damn well the judge is gonna want more than hearsay and spooky cleanup supplies to hold this bastard without bail."

Unconsciously, my fingers curled into a fist at my side, knuckles straining against skin. The all too familiar frustration burned in my gut —the same impotent rage that had compelled me to become a prosecutor in the first place. The same drive that had led me to chase Andrews down that hallway, despite knowing he was armed. Despite knowing how it would end.

But Turner was right. Without substantive physical evidence definitively linking Pierce to the makeshift graveyard, convincing a judge to deny bail would be an uphill battle. One I'd fought countless times before, with mixed results.

The wind picked up again, carrying with it that sickening sweet smell of decay.

"I hope forensics can work their magic on this one," I muttered, jaw clenched against both the smell and the memories threatening to surface.

Turner's mouth curved into a wolfish grin, devoid of humor. His breath clouded in the cold air between us. "Way ahead of you. I've got my best people sweeping every square inch. If the creep slipped up and left us so much as a fingernail, we'll goddamn well find it."

The crunch of gravel behind us announced a new arrival at the crime scene. Turning, I squinted against the glare of the rising sun as a Camry rolled to a stop. Lisa Cooper emerged, dark hair gleaming and heels not quite fitting our surroundings. I guess she didn't get the memo that this was a true field trip.

"Alex, Detective Turner." She greeted us with a warm smile, extending her hand to the detective. "Lisa Cooper. I'll be assisting the prosecution on this case."

"Cooper." Turner's brow furrowed as he shook her hand. "Your old man's on the force, isn't he? Worked Robbery for years before making major?"

Lisa's smile widened with obvious pride. "The very same. I'm a third-generation officer of the court, you could say."

"No kidding?" Turner's customary gruffness softened. "Well, it's a pleasure to have you aboard, Ms. Cooper."

With a polite nod, Lisa turned her attention to me. "I'm going to check in with the forensics team, see if they need an extra set of hands."

Nodding, I watched her stride away. When Lisa first started as a rookie ADA after law school, I had my doubts about her preparedness. Her optimism and earnestness seemed at odds with the harsh realities of our work. But I had looked past all of that because her mind was one of the sharpest I'd ever met. While things had been a bit rocky in our working relationship during the Martin trial, she'd proven herself to be an asset on subsequent cases.

In the time since I'd returned to the DA's office, I'd learned that she had a bachelor's in biochemistry, which was rare for an attorney. Most of us were afraid of numbers. Hence, our decision to go to law school. But more than once, I'd found myself relying on Lisa's scientific insights to explain things that would have otherwise sailed right over my head.

I refocused my attention as Turner gestured toward the dilapidated farmhouse up the hill. "Shall we take a look inside? There are still some techs working the scene."

I gave a terse nod. We trudged up the overgrown path in silence, ducking beneath the crime scene tape cordoning off the property. A few forensic technicians milled about, snapping photos and bagging potential evidence.

The house itself was unassuming from the outside—a simple clap-board structure with peeling white paint. But an undeniable feeling of dread washed over me as we stepped inside. Despite the bright sunshine filtering through the curtainless windows, the air was thick and stale, carrying the faintest whiff of something rotten.

My gaze swept across the modest living room, taking in the worn sofa and outdated TV. A stack of old newspapers lay scattered on the floor. So far, nothing leapt out as suspicious. And yet, that ubiquitous sense of wrongness persisted, raising the fine hairs on the back of my neck.

"Doesn't exactly scream serial killer's lair, does it?" Turner remarked, evidently picking up on my disquiet.

I shook my head, frowning as we made our way into the kitchen. "No ... I suppose not."

That's when I spotted the array of innocuous-looking grocery bags lined up on the table, each one carefully sealed. I arched an inquisitive brow at Turner. "What do we have here?"

He let out a weary sigh. "That's the long and short of it so far. Those bags, some rubber gloves, plastic sheeting. Nothing overtly damning, though certainly suggestive."

"I understand." I tore my gaze away. "I'm going to head back to the office while you finish up here. Lisa can stick around to liaise with forensics."

Turner nodded, his expression inscrutable. "Suppose you'll want to confer with Matthews and Shaw about keeping Pierce detained?"

"Yes. And given what we've uncovered so far ... you really think he's our guy?"

The detective's jaw tightened almost imperceptibly. "Absolutely."

There was an unshakable certainty in his tone that triggered a twinge of unease. Turner struck me as unflappable, steadfast—a consummate professional. Yet something about his conviction regarding Pierce's guilt felt odd.

Brushing it off, I turned on my heel to depart. But before I could take more than a few steps, Turner's fingers closed around my forearm with surprising force, halting me mid-stride.

"Look, Hayes ..." His eyes bore into mine with an unmistakable intensity. "I know your last case with Andrews was a real sonavabitch.

Heard you took a leave of absence afterward. Couldn't have been easy making the decision to come back."

The muscles in my arm twitched with the urge to wrench free from his grasp. Of course, he would bring that up. My agonizing personal demons laid bare for public scrutiny. A harsh chuckle tumbled from my lips.

"You could say that."

Turner's expression remained impassive. "Just want to make sure things between us don't get … compromised on account of it."

Don't worry, I nearly spat out the derisive retort clawing at the back of my throat. I've grown quite accustomed to compromising my principles in the name of justice.

But the words never materialized. Instead, I merely forced a terse nod. "Of course not."

As he released my arm and I strode away, the unbidden notion crept into my mind—the sole impetus for my return to this hellhole of a job.

Finding the truth about my mother.

If my own anonymous tipster was to be believed, those answers lay hidden somewhere in the bowels of the district attorney's office.

CHAPTER
TWO

I ENTERED the downtown courthouse through the revolving doors. The building smelled of polished wood and coffee. Footsteps of lawyers, clerks, and defendants clicked against the marble floors throughout the lobby. Fluorescent lights cast a harsh glow on the faded paint of the government-issued walls, their institutional beige doing little to soften the weight of justice that hung in the air.

I reminded myself for what felt like the hundredth time that I had chosen this life. I'd chosen to come back to the long hours, the stress, the political games, and the constant moral ambiguities. The stack of manila case files tucked under my arm felt like a physical manifestation of my commitment—or perhaps my burden.

Not that I didn't enjoy being an attorney. I mean, I'd worked too hard and sacrificed too much to hate it, right? The law degree hanging in my cramped apartment—paid for with years of student loans and late-night studying—was a testament to that.

The elevator banks were packed with a motley crew of legal professionals—some in tailored suits that screamed success, others in wrinkled blazers that spoke of overwork and exhaustion. Somewhere in between, I fit. A junior ADA with the faint hope that things would somehow be different this time. It was just that I didn't particularly like the work or the people I had to do the work with—or for.

I supposed if you'd never been in my shoes, standing in this temple of bureaucratic justice with its endless corridors and windowless conference rooms, it might not have made much sense. But there I was, anyway, another cog in the massive machine of municipal law enforcement, waiting to see what the day would bring.

Adjusting the strap of my bag on my shoulder, I passed the security checkpoint with a nod to a bored-looking guard. Even though I took a year-long leave of absence after the Martin trial disaster—I'd lost the case but somehow managed to get the mayor arrested on bribery charges—I still got to keep my office. I should have been grateful for that, I guess. Some poor, fresh-faced ADA had been unceremoniously booted to make room for my return. *Eat or be eaten, kid.*

As I walked down the hallway, the familiar walls pressed in on me, and I couldn't help but remember my friend Erin Mitchell, a federal prosecutor. She'd been the one to arrest the mayor, but it'd been my investigation that led her to him. My hard work. My sleepless nights. My gunshot wound.

No doubt Erin's promotion was fast-tracked because of that case. The mayor's trial, though? It was stuck in legal limbo, moving through the system like sludge. Now and then I got updates. Trial dates set, then delayed, pushed back again. Some circuits moved cases fast, like the Eastern District of Virginia, which they called the rocket docket. Cases were in and out in six months flat or they were dismissed. But as with all things, Texas did them its own special way. The third circuit often let cases sit and fester. The mayor's case was going to be one of those.

I found myself in front of Tom Matthews' office. Tom was still the DA, though maybe not for long. The seat was up for grabs soon, and everyone seemed to think he'd win re-election easily. To the public, he was the guy who got the real killer of Caroline Martin arrested and uncovered a bribery scandal run by a dirty cop that went all the way up to the mayor. Never mind that the trial was a total cluster. Never mind that I'd nearly had a mental breakdown trying to keep all the moving parts together. No, to the general public, Tom had done his job, and that's all they cared about.

I thought—maybe foolishly—that when I came back, I'd be greeted as something of a hero. But lawyers didn't celebrate other lawyers. It wasn't like we threw parties when one of us managed to do something extraordinary. There was always a bit of jealousy, an undercurrent of competition. When I walked back into that office after a year, no one acted like they cared. The reality was that they didn't. And that was fine by me.

As I turned the corner, I spotted Janice, Tom's assistant, manning her desk like a fortress. Janice was the type who acted like the gate-keeper to the underworld, but she really just enjoyed being difficult. I waved hello as I continued toward Tom's desk, but she caught me before I could slip by.

"Alex," she called out, her voice sharp. "Can we please stop with these impromptu drop-ins? You know Tom doesn't like being disturbed without an appointment."

That was a lie, of course. Tom didn't care at all. Janice, on the other hand, liked to feel in control.

"The issue is," I said, leaning against her desk with faux sincerity, "I always have vitally important matters to discuss. Imagine if something terrible happened because I waited to schedule a proper meeting."

Janice's lips thinned, clearly annoyed that I'd outwitted her. With a huff, she waved me towards Tom's door, muttering something unflat-tering under her breath.

I wasn't worried. If I ever needed to get back on her good side, all it would take was a venti caramel frappuccino and a buttery croissant from the cafe down the street. Janice could be bribed like anyone else.

Pushing open the door to Tom's office, I found Robert Shaw sitting across from him. Shaw was a fixture in the capital crimes division, his steel-gray hair and deep-set wrinkles a testament to decades of prose-cuting the worst of the worst. He was the kind of guy who had seen it all and had the calm demeanor of someone who had survived it. Although he'd run for DA back in the day and lost, he never seemed to hold a grudge about it. In fact, he'd remained one of Tom's most trusted people.

"Alex," Tom said, his voice steady but tinged with fatigue. "Join us. We were just discussing the Randall Pierce matter."

I sank into the chair next to Shaw, my muscles aching from the already-long day.

"Perfect timing," I replied, unable to keep the weariness from my voice. "I've just come from the crime scene. It's … a horror show, to put it mildly. Lisa's still there, working with forensics."

Shaw leaned forward, his brow furrowed. "Do we have anything concrete yet? Something that would be a slam dunk for denying bail?"

I hesitated, knowing my answer wouldn't be what they wanted to hear. "Not yet. We're still piecing things together." I paused and then chuckled dryly. "No pun intended."

Tom's face darkened and his fingers drummed against his desktop, a staccato rhythm of impatience. "Alex, we need something solid. Fast."

"I'm sorry, Tom, but I can't manufacture evidence." I immediately regretted my tone. These men had decades of experience on me, but sometimes their eagerness to close cases made me wonder if they'd forgotten the weight of what we did here.

Tom sighed, still tapping his fingers on the desk. "I want Randall put away."

"We're not even sure he's the guy who committed the crime."

"His house is near the dump site. It's a solid lead."

"Proximity to a crime doesn't make someone a criminal." My brow furrowed, and I struggled to keep the frustration out of my voice. "Let's try to remember it's innocent until proven guilty."

Both Tom and Shaw looked at me with barely concealed annoyance. Tom's look was specifically reserved for when I was being difficult. The knot in my stomach tightened, but I didn't care.

"The last thing we need right now is a repeat of the Martin trial," I pressed on, my words laced with frustration and tumbling out faster now. "We can't afford to put the wrong guy on trial for first-degree again. Not when I'm involved from the start this time."

I leaned forward, my palms flat on Tom's desk. "Let's make sure we're getting the right guy. We don't want to be halfway through the trial wondering if we're in over our heads."

The silence that followed was deafening. I could almost hear the gears turning in Tom's head, weighing political expediency against the pursuit of justice. Shaw, for his part, looked like he'd swallowed something sour.

"Alex," Tom began, his tone patronizing, "I appreciate your …

enthusiasm. You're great in court, which is why I want you on this case. But Robert and I have been around the block enough times to know when someone is guilty."

Shaw chimed in, his voice gruff. "We're sure Randall is the right person. We're moving forward with the arraignment and grand jury hearing as planned."

Tom nodded in agreement, his eyes locking with mine. "We've got enough to move forward. Let's not overthink this."

I scoffed. "Overthink? You're under-thinking it."

"Not in our opinions," Tom said, his tone brooking no argument.

A surge of anger rose in my chest. Without another word, I stormed out of the office, slamming the door behind me with a satisfying bang. Walking down the hallway, I questioned my choice to stay in law.

Why had I come back to this circus?

Outside, I took a deep breath, the cool air hitting my face as I walked down the steps of the building. The city buzzed around me, indifferent to the chaos I felt inside. Cases like these, they weren't just cases. They were a maze of political pressure, public opinion, and the weight of past failures. And right now, I was trapped in the middle of it all, trying to figure out which way to go.

CHAPTER
THREE

MARIA ALVAREZ, better known as Lola Star, had a knack for finding herself in trouble, and this time was no different. According to the report I'd skimmed on the way in, she'd been caught trying to meet up with someone she thought was a new client, someone she'd reeled in through one of her TikTok videos. What Maria had failed to realize was that this "client" had been an undercover vice cop running a sting operation. Apparently, Maria had upped her game since the last time I'd seen her—booking high-paying clients through social media, promising a "VIP experience." But her luck had run out, again.

The report detailed the setup. Maria had been trying to meet a man in a high-end hotel in Midtown. She'd shown up, dressed to impress, ready to close the deal. Instead, she walked straight into a trap. The vice unit had been watching her online activity for weeks, and this time, they had her dead to rights on solicitation, possession, and resisting arrest when she tried to make a break for it. I imagined her heels clicking fast against the lobby's marble floor as she bolted, and the inevitable crash of reality when the cops caught up to her.

I wondered if she even had a plan anymore. Every time she got caught, she was slipping further away, losing her edge, her street smarts giving way to desperation. Maybe she'd just been riding the highs of the next deal, the next hit, the next quick payday. It was sad in a way, watching someone circle the drain like that. But sad wasn't something I could dwell on. Not in this line of work.

She walked into the interrogation room deflated, her usual swagger gone. Eyes darting nervously around as the color drained from her face. Maria knew how interrogations worked, but something was off this time. I'd seen her strung out before, but this was new—Maria was scared.

I gave her a small nod. "Maria," I said, eyeing her across the table. "You know how this works."

Sitting down, her hands trembled as she tried to offer me a weak smile. "Can we just skip the lecture?"

"I don't think you're in a position to skip anything."

She sighed, rubbing her arms as if trying to calm herself. "I messed up."

"Yes, you did. Solicitation, possession, resisting arrest. Again. And you were offered rehab last time." Leaning back, I folded my arms. "So, what's your plan now? Same as before?"

Her eyes darted to the door. "Look, I know I said I'd go to rehab last time, but this time I mean it. I need to get clean. I can't go back to jail."

I raised an eyebrow, flipping through the file. "You already got your second chance, Maria. You know I can't cut the same deal twice. Not without something new."

"I'm serious," she said, her voice breaking slightly. "I'll do whatever it takes."

"Hey, you know the drill. If you take a deal, I can work on reducing your jail time, but there's no way you're getting out of this with just time served. This is your third strike."

Maria stared at her hands, fingers tapping nervously on the metal table. "What if I gave you something?"

I paused, narrowing my eyes at her. "What kind of something?"

Her hands stopped moving, and she glanced at the mirrored window behind me. "I don't know. I shouldn't have said anything."

"Maria, if you've got something worth trading, now's the time to speak up. What are you offering?"

Shaking her head again, more vigorously this time, a clear wave of anxiety washed over her. "No. I shouldn't be talking to you. I need Michael."

I blinked. "Michael? As in Michael Donovan?"

She nodded quickly. "Gotta be him. I shouldn't be talking to you."

Standing up, I pushed my chair back. Maria had just asked for a lawyer, which meant I was done here. "Alright. I'll make sure Donovan knows you're asking for him. But if you've got something, Maria, don't sit on it too long. This is your last shot."

I left the room and checked my phone in the hallway under the buzzing lights. No need to wait for Donovan—I knew what came next. Maria always called for him, and I always got ahead of things. I dialed his number, and after a few rings, Donovan picked up.

"Alex," he said, not bothering to hide his exhaustion. "What is it now?"

"Maria's in lockup." I stepped outside. "Figured I'd get ahead of things and give you a call."

Donovan cursed under his breath. "What's it this time?"

"Solicitation, possession, and resisting. But she's acting weird. More nervous than usual. She asked for you, but not before she mentioned something about bartering information."

"Information?" Donovan's tone shifted. "What kind of information?"

"That's the thing. I pushed her on it, and she clammed up. Said she shouldn't be talking and needed to talk to you."

There was a pause on the other end, and I could almost hear Donovan thinking. "You think she's got something worth trading?"

"She wouldn't have brought it up if she didn't think it was valuable. But you know Maria—she's not the most reliable witness."

"True," Donovan muttered. "But if she's sitting on something, it's probably the only leverage she's got left."

"That's what I figured," I said, crossing the parking lot. "I'll leave it to you to find out what she's holding back. Let me know if she's got anything worth bringing to the table."

"Okay, I'll head over there," Donovan said. "If she's got something, I'll be in touch."

"Thanks. I'll be waiting for your call."

I hurried to my car, wanting to escape the cold. Maria's odd behavior nagged at me. This felt bigger than her usual small-time crimes.

I slid into my driver's seat and dialed Lisa next, placing the call on the Bluetooth speaker. The Randall Pierce case was still hanging over everything, and with his bail hearing in an hour, I needed to know if there was anything new on the forensics front.

Lisa answered on the second ring. "Hey, Alex. Anything new?"

"That's what I was going to ask you," I said, pulling out of the parking lot. "Anything back from forensics on Pierce?"

"Nope. Shaw already called earlier, and I had to give him the bad news—nothing conclusive yet."

I sighed. "Did you talk to Turner about it?"

"No," Lisa said. "Turner's not exactly the sharing type. Why?"

"I'm going to swing by his desk before court. Maybe he's got something I don't."

"Good luck."

Hanging up, I drove toward the precinct. Old habits die hard, and I had to remind myself not to head toward Daniel Andrews's old desk. It still felt strange, knowing it was empty now. After his arrest in the fallout from the Martin and Thompson conspiracy, Andrews had eventually pled guilty to obstruction of justice and conspiracy charges. He was serving a six-year sentence in federal prison.

Every so often, I'd get a letter from him—rambling, half-apologies mixed with justifications for what he'd done. I never responded. What was there to say? The betrayal still burned too brightly, even if I couldn't ignore the part of me that missed his chaotic brilliance. Sure, he was a bull in a china shop, but his unpredictable approach kept things interesting. Turner, on the other hand, was his polar opposite. By-the-book to a fault, Turner made the precinct feel even less familiar.

When I arrived, Turner was hunched over his desk, flipping through a file. His workspace was as neat and orderly as ever, everything in its precise place. He glanced up when he saw me, giving a curt nod.

"Alex," he greeted, pushing the file aside. "Here to check in on Pierce before the hearing?"

"Yeah," I said, leaning against his desk. "Got anything for me?"

"Not yet," he replied, leaning back in his chair. "My team's still working on it."

The way he looked at me told me he didn't like me leaning on his desk. I couldn't bring myself to care, though.

I crossed my arms, frowning slightly. "Do you think the circumstantial evidence will be enough to get bail denied?"

Turner shrugged. "Depends on the judge. Depends on how good you and Shaw can argue. But I'm not worried. Pierce is guilty. We just need time to line everything up."

I raised an eyebrow. "How can you be so sure? We still don't have any forensics back."

"There's enough. He lives near the dump site, fits the profile. We know he did it."

A knot of frustration tightened in my chest. The same knot that formed when I'd spoken to Shaw and Matthews. "I feel like a broken record with this. Proximity to a crime doesn't make someone guilty. Without forensics or more definitive evidence, we're just guessing."

"We're not guessing," Turner said, his tone sharp. "He's our guy. We've looked at the evidence, and we've ruled out other suspects. This isn't the Martin case, Alex."

"I'm not saying it is," I said, my voice rising slightly. "But we can't be so sure without something definitive. What if we're wrong?"

"We're not wrong. We've got enough to keep him locked up. Forensics will back it up."

I stared at him, my mind racing. Why was everyone so convinced? Matthews, Shaw, and now Turner? They were all acting like Pierce's guilt was a foregone conclusion, but we didn't have any real proof yet. It didn't sit right with me. My father's conviction had taught me the danger of jumping to conclusions. It had taken years—too many years—for me to realize I'd misjudged him, blindly assuming his guilt without truly examining the details. It made me much more cautious now. I couldn't afford to overlook anything, no matter how small. The truth was in the details, and I wasn't going to let them rush past me again.

"I think we're moving too fast."

Turner gave me a hard look. "Trust me. Pierce is our guy."

Nodding, I left the precinct for the courthouse. Something felt wrong about this case. Maybe we were all too focused on Pierce to see we'd gotten it wrong.

CHAPTER FOUR

JUDGE MORLEY WAS A HARDASS, and everyone knew it. He rarely handed out favors and ran his courtroom like a military operation. Normally, that would be a good thing for us—especially given the absolute lack of forensic evidence we had to convince him that Randall Pierce should be denied bail. But today, I wasn't so sure. We needed everything to go our way, and with the way Shaw had been handling things, I wasn't optimistic.

Entering the courtroom, I spotted Shaw with the defense attorney, Marcus Ellis. Their friendly chat bothered me. Shaw always got cozy with defense counsel, but Ellis was different—he was sharp enough to make a judge doubt basic fact. He was the kind of attorney who could argue the sky wasn't blue and have the judge nodding along.

I walked toward the two of them. As soon as Shaw spotted me, he ended his conversation with Ellis, shooting me a quick nod before turning back toward our counsel table.

"Discussing anything interesting?" I asked as we sat down.

"Nothing that concerns you," Shaw replied dismissively, flipping through his notes.

I bit back the retort that rose to my lips. Shaw had made it clear who was taking the lead today, even though we hadn't officially discussed it. I had hoped we'd be working as a team, but it was obvious Shaw had already decided otherwise, that I was just along for the ride.

About to argue, the bailiff walked in, signaling that the judge would be arriving soon. I dropped it. For now.

Then Randall Pierce was brought in—tall and lean with cold eyes and slicked-back hair. He sat beside Ellis without a word, acting like this was just another day. The man's demeanor unsettled me, but I refused to assume guilt without evidence like the others had.

The bailiff called the court to order, and Judge Morley entered, settling behind the bench. His steely gaze swept over the room before the clerk announced the case.

"State of Texas versus Randall Pierce," the clerk read out.

Morley looked down at the paperwork in front of him and listed the charges—first-degree murder, multiple counts. His expression remained neutral, unreadable. He then asked counsel to introduce themselves for the record.

Shaw stood immediately. "Robert Shaw, for the State."

And then he sat back down. He didn't even mention me, which was just another irritation in a growing list of slights today.

Ellis stood and introduced himself smoothly. "Marcus Ellis, for the defense, your Honor."

Morley gave a brief nod, then gestured for Shaw to proceed.

Shaw moved to the lectern without even acknowledging my presence. I sat back, biting my tongue as he began laying out the circumstantial evidence. Proximity to the dump site. Pierce's suspicious behavior. It wasn't bad, but it wasn't strong enough.

I could see the judge wasn't impressed. Morley leaned forward, his face showing little emotion, but Shaw's reliance on proximity and vague behavioral claims wasn't going to cut it. There wasn't enough to paint Pierce as an undeniable flight risk or a danger to the community.

When Shaw finally wrapped up, Morley turned to Ellis. "Mr. Ellis, you may proceed."

Ellis rose from his chair, his confident stride making it clear he was in control of the room. Going straight for the weak points in Shaw's argument, He argued that the prosecution had no forensic evidence tying Pierce to the murders. Without it, the case was speculative at best.

"Your Honor, my client is a lifelong resident of this city. He has a stable job, a family, and no significant criminal history. There is absolutely no reason to believe he poses a flight risk."

Morley nodded. "Does Mr. Pierce have any prior arrests?"

"No, your Honor. Mr. Pierce has no prior convictions, nor history of failing to appear in court."

Shaw fumbled with his notes, flipping through and scanning each document for something, anything, but it was clear Ellis was gaining ground. The judge asked a few more questions about Pierce's ties to the community and any potential flight risk, but Ellis had all the answers ready, painting Pierce as a model citizen. The tide was turning, and fast.

Now I was growing frustrated. We were losing control of the hearing. Shaw wasn't fighting back hard enough, and Ellis was steamrolling over him. My fingers itched, and without thinking, I slipped my phone out under the table and quickly shot a text to Lisa. *Things aren't going well here. Do you have anything, anything at all?*

I didn't expect an immediate response, but my phone buzzed seconds later. I glanced down at Lisa's message. *Not forensics, but I went back through the evidence from the scene. Found something.*

My heart skipped a beat. *What?*

Her reply came fast. *A wad of cash and a plane ticket in one of the photos. It doesn't tie him to the murders, but it could help prove he's a flight risk.*

I swallowed hard. A wad of cash and a plane ticket—Pierce had been planning to leave. My mind raced as the judge looked over at me, clearly noticing I was on my phone.

"Ms. Hayes, is there something more pressing than this hearing?" Judge Morley asked, his voice cold.

I stood quickly, adrenaline kicking in. "Apologies, your Honor, but I've just received some new information that might be pertinent to this hearing."

Shaw shot me a glare, but I ignored him. We needed to turn this around and he wouldn't be able to do it on his own. "The crime scene unit found a large amount of cash and a plane ticket at Mr. Pierce's residence. While it may not directly connect him to the murders, it strongly suggests he was planning to flee."

The judge raised an eyebrow. "Do you have proof of this?"

"Yes, your Honor. I can show you the photograph right now."

Ellis stood, objecting. "Your Honor, this is highly unusual. The prosecution is attempting to introduce evidence through text messages. This is completely improper."

I shot back before the judge could respond. "This entire case is more than unusual, your Honor, given the charges and gravity of the situation. A plane ticket and cash indicate a clear intent to flee. If the defense is so confident in Mr. Pierce's innocence, they should have no issue explaining why these items were in his possession."

Judge Morley looked from me to Ellis and then gestured for me to approach. I walked up to the bench, holding my phone out for him to inspect the photograph. He stared at it for a long moment, then turned to Ellis. "Does the defense have an explanation for this?"

Ellis hesitated, but only for a second. "Your Honor, it's not illegal to have cash or a plane ticket. Many innocent people have such things in their homes. This is not evidence of guilt or intent to flee, as the State is trying to suggest."

Morley considered this, but I could see the wheels turning in his head. I held my breath, waiting for his decision.

Finally, the judge sat back and spoke. "Given the nature and the gravity of the charges, I find that Mr. Pierce has the means and apparent intention to flee the jurisdiction. Bail is denied."

Pierce was led back to lockup, showing no emotion as the guards took him away. As soon as the judge left the room, Ellis stormed over to our table, his face flushed with anger.

"This is not how we want to conduct this case moving forward," Ellis said through gritted teeth.

Shaw, ever the diplomat, raised his hands. "It won't happen again, Marcus. I'll make sure of it."

Ellis shot me a venomous look before turning on his heel and walking out of the courtroom. Shaw waited until the room was empty before he turned on me, his face red with anger.

Grabbing my arm, he pulled me aside, hissing. "Don't you ever pull that shit again. If you go rogue like that, I'll make sure Tom takes you off this case. Do you hear me?"

I yanked my arm out of his grip, fire rising in my chest. "The only reason Pierce is still behind bars is because of me, Shaw. So when you go running to Tom, make sure you tell him that."

Without waiting for his response, I stormed out, my blood boiling. I wasn't the same person I was before. I wasn't going to take shit from anybody.

CHAPTER FIVE

LISA'S NAME lit up my phone as soon as I left the courthouse. I swiped to answer, my heart still racing from the bail hearing.

"Did the judge grant bail?" she asked.

"No," I said, exhaling as I walked down the steps. "Thanks to your quick work with that photo, we managed to keep him behind bars."

"Good," Lisa replied, sounding pleased. Then she added, "You sound frustrated, though. What happened?"

"Where are you?" I asked, sidestepping her question.

"At the office."

"Meet me across the street at the coffee shop. I'll fill you in over caffeine."

"Two birds, one stone?" she teased. "Got it. Be there in ten."

I crossed the square, grateful for the mild weather. Winter was the only season I didn't mind in Houston, as long as I ignored the freezing mornings. The early hours were brutal when you were called to a body dump site at 5 a.m., but right now, the air was just brisk enough to clear my head.

By the time I got to the coffee shop, Lisa was walking through the door. We met at the counter, ordered our usuals, and found a quiet corner in the back, far enough from the morning crowd to have some privacy.

As we sat down, I couldn't help but feel a small surge of relief. It had taken time to get back to this—to having a normal working relationship with Lisa after the Martin trial had shattered my trust in almost everyone. Back then, I'd been paranoid, suspicious of everyone including her. I'd even questioned Lisa's loyalty because of her father's ties to the police department and a photo Erin had shown me during the investigation. But it had turned out neither she nor her father had been involved in the conspiracy with the mayor. After a few awkward conversations, we'd worked our way back to this—an easy, seamless partnership.

I took a sip of my coffee. Irritation seeped into my voice when I started, "Shaw has completely taken over the Pierce case. Barely let me breathe during the hearing."

Lisa raised an eyebrow. "Who did Tom put in charge?"

"No one," I grumbled. "Tom hasn't made anything official, but Shaw assumes he's in charge because he's senior. But as I saw today, seniority doesn't mean he's the right person for the job."

Lisa nodded. "Let me guess—he leaned on circumstantial evidence the whole time?"

I nodded. "And the judge wasn't buying it. The thing is, Shaw, Matthews, Turner—they're all so fixated on Pierce that they're not even considering other possibilities. If we don't act fast, the grand jury is going to indict Pierce, and this could turn into another Martin trial."

Lisa leaned back, thoughtful. "Why don't we look at the evidence ourselves while we wait for forensics? They should have something for us soon."

I shook my head. "The men won't like us looking into things behind their backs."

Lisa shot me a wry smile. "Since when have you ever cared about that?"

I grinned despite myself. "Fair point."

As we headed back to the office, I asked, "What cases have you been working on lately?"

"One domestic violence case, heading toward trial, and a new fraud case I just got word on this morning."

"How's the domestic case going?" I asked as we crossed the street.

"It's pretty straightforward," Lisa said, "but the victim's been wishy-washy about testifying."

I sighed. "That's always the hardest part with domestics. Without the victim's testimony, there's often no case. I hope she doesn't back out."

Lisa nodded in agreement as we entered the building. The elevator ride up to our floor was quiet until she broke the silence.

"So, what else have you been working on?" she asked.

"I'm waiting to hear back from Donovan about whether Maria Alvarez—Lola Star—is willing to trade any information."

Lisa gave me a sideways glance. "Maria Alvarez? What kind of information could she have?"

"Don't know," I admitted. "But something seemed off when I questioned her earlier. We'll see what comes of it."

As soon as we stepped off the elevator, Shaw intercepted us. "Alex, I need you in my office."

I sighed, then told Lisa, "I'll catch up with you in a bit," before following Shaw down the hall. He closed the door behind us, his face tense.

The office was all dark wood and muted tones, with shelves lined neatly with law books that looked more like decoration than tools of the trade. A sleek desk sat in the center, papers arranged in perfect order, as if even chaos needed his permission to exist.

"You went rogue in court today," he snapped. "That's not how we do things. I'm the senior attorney here, and I'm taking the lead on this case."

I crossed my arms, barely containing my anger. "If that's the case, then let's go to Tom right now and settle it."

Shaw hesitated, visibly backing down. "No, we don't need to involve Tom. Just don't do it again. The implications of this case are bigger than just Pierce, and we need to make sure we get the right verdict."

I frowned. "Bigger than just Pierce? What does that even mean?"

Shaw waved me off. "Just focus on the case, Alex. We can't afford any more surprises."

"I'm not promising you anything. If you have issues, set up a meeting with Tom, and we'll hash it out. But I'm not compromising my morals or losing any cases just because you can't accept help."

He sputtered, and I stormed out of his office, slamming the door behind me. By the time I reached my office, I felt like my head was going to explode.

Lisa was already there, waiting for me. I collapsed into my chair. "Maybe I shouldn't have come back to work after all."

Lisa shook her head, her expression full of sympathy. "This will blow over. It's just office politics."

"I don't know," I muttered, thinking back to Shaw's comment about the case being bigger than just Pierce. Was he talking about Matthews and his re-election?

The weight of the day pressed on me, but I tried to shove it aside. Shaw and his arrogance would have to wait.

We spread the case files and evidence photographs across my desk, the dim light from the desk lamp casting a long glow on the papers.

Lisa flipped open her laptop and pulled up a recording. "Let's start with the tip we got about the dump site. Maybe there's something in the wording we missed."

The audio crackled as she hit play, and the distorted voice filled the room. A standard anonymous tip line recording, the caller's voice altered to be almost unrecognizable.

"The bodies ... you'll find them near the old junkyard off of Route 5. They've been there for a while. It's bad. Really bad. You need to hurry." The voice paused, breathing heavily. "Check near the woods, in the ravine. There's more than one."

The recording clicked off.

Leaning back, I stared at the wall, replaying the message in my head. "There's something odd about the way they say, 'there's more than one.' Like they're hesitating. Almost like they're holding something back."

"Yeah." Lisa nodded. "It's like they know more but aren't ready to give us everything. Whoever this was, they had some knowledge of the bodies, but they're being cryptic. Maybe they were scared."

"Or maybe they were involved," I muttered, tapping my pen against the desk.

Lisa's fingers flew over her keyboard, pulling up the corresponding crime scene reports. "Okay, so we have a total of forty-four bodies found at the site. All of them female except for one male."

"Forty-three women, and one man?" I rubbed my chin. "That's got to mean something."

"I agree." Lisa scrolled through the victim identification process. "But we haven't ID'd all of them yet. So far, the male victim hasn't been matched with any missing person reports."

"Could he have been an accomplice?" I leaned forward. "Maybe the women were part of a trafficking ring, and the man was involved somehow, got killed when he was no longer useful."

"It's possible. For now, we can flag him as an anomaly, but we need something concrete."

We sat in silence for a moment, both of us mulling over the possibilities. The forty-three women, the lone male victim—the imbalance gnawed at me. It wasn't random, I knew that much.

Lisa pulled up the photographs next, flipping through shots of the crime scene. My mind wandered to the photo of the wad of cash and plane ticket. That tiny, overlooked detail had been the tipping point of the bail hearing.

"Can you pull up the scan of the plane ticket?" I asked, shifting gears. "Let's see where Pierce was planning to go."

Lisa opened the file and zoomed in on the ticket. "It's for a flight to Venezuela. Scheduled for today. I guess he missed his trip."

"Venezuela?" I frowned, tapping my fingers on the desk. "Why would Pierce be heading to Venezuela? He doesn't have any known ties there, does he?"

"Not as far as we know," Lisa replied. "But it's a pretty suspicious destination. Especially if he was planning on running."

I stared at the photo of the ticket, my mind racing. "But how could he have known he was going to be picked up yesterday? Some of those bodies were quite old. It doesn't make sense."

Lisa leaned forward, squinting at the photo. "Maybe he was meeting someone there?"

I shrugged. "Anything's possible. Maybe he had a standing flight to go just in case he ever got caught." I frowned. "Assuming he's really the perpetrator."

This was what I hated the most about investigations. The tendency to get tunnel vision. To make the evidence fit the suspect, rather than the other way around.

Lisa nodded slowly. "It definitely makes him look guilty.""We were both silent for a beat.

"Maybe it's not just about him," Lisa said quietly. "Maybe he was part of something bigger, something that spans beyond Houston."

The thought sent a chill down my spine. I glanced back at the photograph. We had Pierce, but every new detail made me wonder if he was just a small cog in a much larger machine. You don't just kill forty-four people for the hell of it unless you're extremely deranged.

"That seems likely," I said. "Otherwise, we're dealing with a certified psychopath."

Lisa's eyes flickered with understanding. "If Pierce is involved in something bigger, it could explain why Shaw, Matthews, and Turner are so focused on him. They want a quick win, but it might not be just about Pierce."

"Exactly," I said, a knot tightening in my stomach. "Shaw did say this is bigger than just Pierce. It could be political, or it could be something worse. But whatever it is, we're not getting the full story."

Lisa paused for a moment, then nodded. "Let's look at the missing persons reports again. Maybe the male victim was connected to Venezuela somehow."

We pored over files, matching missing persons reports to the dump site victims. The hours dragged on as we studied reports and photos. Every new piece of information felt like another clue that pointed in two directions.

I glanced at the clock. It was already after hours. "Let's continue tomorrow," I said, leaning back in my chair and rubbing my tired eyes. The rest of the office was empty and silent. "I can't focus anymore."

Lisa yawned, closing her laptop. "Yeah, me too."

Packing up our things, we headed out together. I drove home from work, my mind racing. The long drive to my dad's old house was a relief—since getting out, he'd been fixing it up, and it had become my refuge.

Just as I pulled into the driveway, my phone rang. I glanced at the screen—an unlisted number. My heart skipped a beat. I answered, and the same distorted voice from before came through the line.

"Pierce wasn't acting alone."

And then the line went dead.

CHAPTER
SIX

I MUST HAVE SAT in the car too long after the call. Before I knew it, my father opened the door and waved at me. Great, I thought, plastering on the fakest smile I could muster. Knowing I looked shaken, there was no way I could hide it from him. I wished I could tell someone about these anonymous calls. Better yet, I wished I could trace them, but neither option seemed like a good idea right now.

Ironically, if I were still working with Andrews, I might have told him about it.

I stepped out of the car, trying to pretend nothing was wrong. The smell of fresh paint hit me as soon as I walked inside. Dad had been at it with his renovation projects, keeping himself busy since he got out of prison.

"Looks good, Dad." I nodded toward the walls, but my voice sounded hollow even to me.

He eyed me, clearly not buying my casual tone. "What's going on?"

"Nothing, just a long day," I lied, hoping he'd drop it. But of course, he didn't.

"How about we talk about it over some chili?" he offered, already ladling out bowls.

Paint-stained fingers, as usual. He'd taken to cooking just like he had to fixing up the house. Kept him busy and gave him a routine. He passed me a bowl, and I sat down at the kitchen table, grateful for the distraction, but knowing what was coming next.

"How'd it go today?" he asked as he sat down.

Exhaling, I stirred the chili absentmindedly. "We had the bail hearing for Randall Pierce."

His eyes narrowed, clearly waiting for more.

I sighed, giving in. "Morley wasn't going to keep him behind bars, so I had to step in."

He raised an eyebrow. "You kept him locked up?"

"Yeah," I said, nodding my head. "But Shaw was pissed. He's been running this case like it's his personal project, and when I stepped in … let's just say, it didn't go over well."

Dad nodded, unfazed. "Sounds like a senior attorney who got outdone by his junior and was upset about it. Nothing new there."

I shrugged, feeling the weight of it all. "Maybe. I'm not sure it's that simple. The way this investigation is shaping up, I'm wondering why I even came back to work."

He gave me a soft smile. "You sound a lot like your mother, you know."

I looked up, caught off guard. "What do you mean?"

As he leaned back in his chair, sadness crept into his eyes. "She had a lot of frustrations with work too, especially when she started at the DA's office. Never thought she should've switched."

I knew so little about my mother, Since my father never wanted to talk about her. It had been a bit of a forbidden subject growing up.

"Switched?" I asked.

He nodded. "She used to be a defense attorney. But after w…e got married, she decided to switch paths so our careers would be more aligned, I guess."

"Dad," I said, my throat tight. "If Mom had stayed a defense attorney instead of becoming a prosecutor … do you think things would be different?"

"I've asked myself that same question." Staring into his bowl of chili, his expression was grim. "Maybe she'd still be alive if she hadn't switched sides."

When he trailed off, for a moment, we sat in heavy silence. Few things had driven us apart over the years. His refusal to talk about my mother had been one, followed by his arrest while I'd been in law school. That had closed the door between us. It wasn't until years later when I was working on the Martin case that I'd been able to figure out that he'd been framed for his crimes.

Finally, I broke the quiet. "What really happened, Dad? I've only ever heard it secondhand, because you never wanted to talk about it."

Sighing deeply, he set his spoon down. "It wasn't long after she became an ADA. She took on a case that consumed her. Coming home late, angry, frustrated. Said she didn't think the people in charge were looking closely enough, that they didn't have the right guy. Or maybe there were other people involved."

I swallowed hard, hanging on his every word. Each felt so familiar. He looked sad, his eyes distant.

"One night, she stayed late at the office," he continued. "I called her. She said she was on her way home, but... she never made it."

"What do you mean?" I asked, my heart pounding.

"She just disappeared, Alex. Driving home from work and then just gone. No trace of her car, no accident. Nothing." He shook his head, his voice breaking slightly. "I called in every favor I could, had every investigator I knew looking for her. But we never found any trace of her."

I sat there, stunned, the silence between us louder than any words.

"What case was she working on?" I asked, my voice barely above a whisper.

"I don't know for sure. But I know it was a trafficking case. More like a side issue that she stumbled on."

I sat back, running my hand through my hair. A trafficking case. My mind raced with possibilities. Could it be connected to what I was working on now? I didn't say anything. Not wanting to get him wrapped up in my own suspicions. Not yet.

He broke the silence. "Listen, Alex, just... don't let this case consume you like it did her."

I gave him a weak smile. "I'll try."

The exhaustion hit me like a truck, and I pushed my bowl away. "I'm gonna get some shut eye. Long day."

He nodded, watching me closely as I stood up. "You know where I am if you want to talk."

Upstairs, in the quiet of my room, I pulled out my old journal. The one I used to write letters to Mom in when I was a kid. I flipped to the back, where I'd written the first message from the anonymous caller.

Your mother's disappearance was no accident. There are answers at the DA's office.

I picked up a pen and scribbled down the second message.

Pierce wasn't acting alone.

I stared at the words, chewing on the cap of the pen. Could the tipster be the same person who called in the tip about Pierce? Why hide their voice with me but not the police? Were they contacting Shaw, Matthews, or Turner too? Was that why they were so convinced Pierce was the guy?

I couldn't help but wonder if I was being manipulated. This anonymous caller could be trying to confuse me and derail the investigation. They could be the true perpetrator for all I knew.

I flipped through the journal, skimming entries from years ago—old letters to Mom. Some were innocent updates about my day, others were filled with anger, blaming her for leaving me. An entire childhood of unresolved feelings inked into these pages.

Shutting the journal with a click, I tossed it back in the drawer, shoving down decades-old feelings.

Out of habit, I checked my work email on my phone and saw one from Turner. He wanted to meet at forensics tomorrow morning. Said we should go together.

My eyes narrowed. As far as I knew, forensics still hadn't come back with anything yet. What was he up to?

I decided I wasn't going into this alone. I dialed Lisa, and she picked up on the second ring.

"Hey, Turner wants to go to forensics tomorrow. Can you meet us there?"

"Sure," she said. "But why? We don't have anything back from them yet."

"I don't know," I said, my voice edged with suspicion. "But I want you there, just in case."

"Got it. I'll meet you at the precinct in the morning."

Hanging up, I scrolled through the rest of my emails. Two new cases: petty fraud and possession. I rolled my eyes. Guess whatever status I had as the "big case" ADA was out the window. Looked like tomorrow would be another long day at the office.

CHAPTER
SEVEN

WATCHING the empty precinct parking lot from my car, I drummed my fingers and checked my phone. Lisa finally pulled up and walked over, tugging her jacket straight.

"What's going on?" she asked as we walked in.

I shook my head. "Not really sure. I haven't worked with Turner much before, so I guess we'll see why he's dragging us to the lab. Should be interesting."

She raised an eyebrow. "Interesting is one word for it."

Exchanging smirks, we made our way inside, where Turner was waiting. We exchanged stiff nods and mumbled hellos. Turner hated small talk, and today, so did I.

I really wanted this trip to be over and didn't feel like hanging around the precinct. The way everything happened with Andrews still felt raw, and this place a bit like salt in a wound.

"Shall we?" I asked.

Turner grunted. "Can't believe they moved things. Now we have to drive downtown every damn time we need results."

Turner was referring to how the city had elected to move all forensic operations to the Houston Forensic Science Center a few years back. It used to operate right inside the precinct.

"It's only a fifteen-minute walk," Lisa pointed out.

Turner grumbled. "No one wants to waste time walking."

We rode in tense silence to the building—a sleek, modern place, nothing like our messy precinct. Inside, white walls and humming machines surrounded us. Turner strode to the elevator, knowing exactly where we needed to go.

As the elevator doors closed, I turned to him. "So, why am I here? You usually don't drag the prosecution along for this kind of thing."

He gruffed, crossing his arms. "You're part of the investigation. Seemed like you should be here."

"Why not Shaw? He's the senior prosecutor."

Turner gave me a quick, dismissive glance. "Shaw's busy. Senior prosecutors tend to be."

I bit back a retort, shaking my head. As if I wasn't busy, too. As if I wasn't running around cleaning up messes every day. But I didn't say anything. No point in arguing with Turner when I knew it wouldn't go anywhere.

The elevator dinged, and we stepped out on the seventh floor. Turner led us down a narrow hallway, stopping at a door on the left. Pushing it open, he ushered us inside.

"Alex, Lisa, this is Sarah Milton," Turner said, introducing us to the woman working inside.

Sarah was tall and lean, with messy, short-cropped red hair and oversized glasses that made her eyes look way too big for her face. She looked like someone who lived in the lab, quirky but sharp.

"Hey there," she greeted us, her voice upbeat despite the sterile environment. "I've just about finished up with the knife."

Turner perked up. "How's it looking? Any matches yet?"

Sarah leaned over her workstation, picking up the blade with gloved hands. "I think we're going to get a hit on something. There's blood residue, and the pattern's consistent enough to link one of the victims. Lucky you brought it in when you did."

My eyebrows shot up. "Wait, what do you mean *he* brought the knife in?"

Lisa turned to me, frowning. "I didn't see any mention of a knife or blade in the evidence files."

Sarah hesitated, glancing at Turner. He quickly dismissed it with a wave of his hand. "It's in the record. Don't worry about it."

He turned back to Sarah. "Let me know as soon as you get confirmation. How long are we talking?"

Sarah glanced at the clock. "Shouldn't be more than thirty minutes. You're welcome to hang out here while I finish up."

Turner nodded, and we walked out into the hallway. The second the door closed, I turned on him.

"What the hell was that, Turner?" I demanded. "You're bringing in evidence that wasn't logged? If you're bending the rules, you could screw up this entire investigation. Ellis will have a motion to suppress on the judge's desk the second he gets wind of this."

Turner's jaw clenched, and he shot me a look. "I'm a detective. I can bag evidence and have it evaluated. Lisa must've missed it when she was going through the files. I wouldn't screw something like this up."

I narrowed my eyes at him. "Then why drag me here in the first place? Why not just handle this on your own?"

"I told you. You're one of the two prosecutors on this case. Shaw's busy, and you're here. Why wouldn't you be involved?" He leveled me a look and added, "I think you need to take a breath and ask yourself why you're jumping to conclusions."

I crossed my arms, biting back the urge to snap. "You need to stop acting like my past with Andrews has anything to do with this. I'm not paranoid. But I'm not going to let you or anyone else jeopardize this case by cutting corners."

"I thought I made it clear from the start that you shouldn't let Andrews get in your head." Sighing, he shook his head. "You and I are supposed to be on the same side here, Alex."

I didn't respond, not trusting myself to say anything that wouldn't escalate things. Maybe he had a point. Maybe I was too sensitive now.

Or maybe Turner was hiding something.

My phone rang, cutting through the tension. I glanced at the screen —it was one of the legal assistants from the office.

"Hayes," I answered, casting a glance toward Turner.

"Hey, Alex," the assistant replied, sounding flustered. "Uh, an emergency hearing has been scheduled."

My blood pressure began to rise. "For what case?"

"Something about Maria Alvarez?"

I pinched the bridge of my nose, trying to keep calm. "You need to give me more than that. What's the purpose of the hearing?"

"I'm sorry, the clerk spoke really fast, and I didn't catch all of it. Something about a protective order?"

"When is it?"

I could almost hear her gulp. "Thirty minutes."

I mumbled in acknowledgment and then ended the call, frustrated beyond belief. Turning to Lisa and Turner, I said, "I've got to head out for this emergency hearing. Lisa, can you stay and wait for the results on the evidence?"

Lisa nodded. "Yeah, no problem."

I ordered an Uber and stepped outside to wait for it, pulling up Donovan's number as I paced the sidewalk. He answered after a couple of rings.

"What's this emergency hearing about?" I snapped.

"I figured you'd be pissed," Donovan said, sounding almost amused. "I filed for an immediate protective order."

A protective order was usually reserved for situations involving harassment, threats, or violence, meant to shield someone from immediate danger.

"For what? Why?"

"I heard what Maria had to say, and I needed to file. The judge wanted a hearing because she's in lockup."

My mind raced. "What are you talking about, Donovan? What does she know?"

"I'd rather not discuss it over the phone," he said, his voice lowering. "The hearing will be private. I've asked the judge to seal the record."

"So what you're telling me is, you've thrown this at me last minute with no time to prepare?"

Donovan sighed. "I'm sorry, but it's what's best for my client."

I spotted the Uber pulling up. "Fine. I'll see you in court. But don't expect me to go easy on this, given the circumstances."

Donovan chuckled. "Don't take your frustrations out on Maria."

I hung up, not bothering to continue the back-and-forth. I wasn't in the mood for Donovan's games. Not today.

CHAPTER
EIGHT

EMERGENCY HEARINGS ANNOY JUDGES—THEY'LL do them if someone's in danger or needs urgent legal action, but not for legal games. Yet here I was, walking into the courtroom and scanning it as I approached the bench.

Judge Nelson was presiding—thank God. Nelson was known for being fair, although "fair" in the legal world really meant that this hearing could go either way. But if it had been one of the more unpredictable judges, I'd be sweating a little more. Personally, I would've preferred an in-chambers discussion rather than this formal affair. It would've made things a lot easier to hash out, especially if I decided I didn't need to object to whatever Donovan had up his sleeve.

I still wasn't sure what game Donovan was playing, which kept me on edge. The fact that he filed an emergency motion for a protective order on behalf of Maria meant something big was happening. Maria's information could be critical, or it could be another one of Donovan's ploys. I couldn't afford to underestimate either of them.

Maria was brought out. She looked rough—thinner and paler than before, with shadows under her eyes. Prison had already taken its toll. But something in her manner worried me. She wasn't the cocky starlet turned criminal anymore. Now she just looked haunted.

"Court is now in session," the bailiff announced, and Judge Nelson took his seat. He exchanged polite nods with me and Donovan.

"Good afternoon, Ms. Hayes," Judge Nelson said, his voice even and measured. The courtroom's fluorescent lights hummed softly in the background. Nelson leaned back in his leather chair, his black robe draped loosely around him. "Mr. Donovan, you've filed an emergency motion for a protective order. Why don't you explain to the court why this required immediate attention?"

Donovan stood slowly, taking his time as he buttoned his jacket. He always did that—little gestures meant to buy time, make himself seem deliberate. He straightened his tie before addressing the judge.

"Your Honor," he said with controlled urgency. "My client has information that could endanger her life if shared without protection. We're requesting a protective order before she proceeds."

As he spoke, I studied Maria. She sat frozen, staring past the walls, her hands clenched white in her lap. The vibrant Lola Star I'd once known had been replaced by this hollow shell. Whatever secret she held was destroying her from the inside out.

Judge Nelson leaned back, fingers pressed together, eyebrows raised. He glanced at Maria before fixing Donovan with an impassive stare. "What kind of information are we discussing?"

Donovan cleared his throat and looked to Maria, hesitating as if asking her permission. "It pertains to an ongoing investigation involving criminal activity—high-level trafficking, Your Honor." His voice softened, the gravity of his words hanging heavy in the air. "My client is in possession of sensitive information that could compromise her safety. We're asking for a protective order to shield her identity and ensure her cooperation without endangering her."

The room fell silent except for the clerk shuffling papers and the loud tick of the clock. "Trafficking" was the word no one liked to say out loud, the kind of crime that turned stomachs and made people look away. And yet here it was, dropped into the middle of a courtroom on a routine Thursday afternoon.

Nelson's eyes flicked to me, his sharp gaze locking on mine. "Ms. Hayes, your response?"

I stood, feeling the cool press of the wooden table against my fingertips as I steadied myself. I chose my next words carefully and kept my voice steady, professional.

"Your Honor, this is ... unusual. I've never been asked to agree to something without knowing the cost. Mr. Donovan is essentially asking for me to negotiate a plea deal without knowing what information we're being offered." I let the silence linger for a moment before continuing. "I understand his concerns, but this puts me—and the State—in a difficult position."

Nelson leaned back again, his fingers tapping lightly on the bench. He turned his attention back to Donovan. "To clarify, Mr. Donovan, you're asking Ms. Hayes to consider a deal ... without providing any details of what your client is offering in return?"

Donovan spread his hands in a gesture of helplessness, playing a role for the judge. I wasn't buying it. "Your Honor, my client's life is at risk. She's prepared to offer valuable insight, but we need guarantees that she'll be safe."

Maria shifted in her seat, her eyes darting toward Donovan before quickly returning to the floor. Her entire body tensed as though bracing for a hit. It was like she was trapped in a prison far worse than the physical one she'd been confined to.

I looked back at the judge, taking a breath before responding. "Your Honor, I understand the need for protection, but the state can't offer leniency without knowing the weight of what's being traded."

Nelson tilted his head slightly, considering my words. His eyes moved back and forth between Donovan and me, like a referee weighing two sides of a playing field. "Ms. Hayes, you're being asked to trust that Mr. Donovan's client is offering something of significant value. And yet, you cannot know what that is until it's too late to object?"

"Exactly," I replied, trying to keep the frustration from creeping into my voice. "I'm being put in an impossible position."

Donovan raised a hand slightly. "Your Honor, with all due respect, we wouldn't be here if this wasn't a matter of significant importance."

The judge sighed, his fingers still tapping on the bench, the faint echo of each tap almost louder than any words that had been spoken.

"This is a hard decision," he said finally, his voice heavy with thought. He glanced at the clock on the wall, then back at us. "I'm going to take a five-minute recess. I'll need to discuss this further."

The bailiff nodded and called for a recess as Judge Nelson stood and made his way back into chambers.

Slumping against the table, I let out a breath I didn't realize I'd been holding. Donovan stood near the defense table, his usual swagger somewhat muted.

"This doesn't seem like your style," I muttered, crossing my arms as I turned to him. "What's going on here, Donovan?"

Donovan gave me a look, half annoyed, half resigned. "You think I'm pulling something, don't you?"

I shrugged. "You usually are."

He smirked, but it didn't reach his eyes. "Not this time. Maria's scared, Alex. She's in way over her head, and if she's told me the truth, we all need to be looking at a much bigger picture than just her."

As I studied him for a moment, his usual smoothness was gone, replaced by something that almost looked like concern. Donovan was not playing the game today.

Still, I asked him, "What's the play, then?"

"There is no play," he said, running a hand through his hair. "She's desperate. And what she knows is big. I wouldn't be wasting your time otherwise."

I narrowed my eyes but stayed silent. Maybe he was telling the truth. Or maybe this was just another layer of the puzzle.

Before I could press him further, Judge Nelson returned to the bench, looking between us.

"After reviewing the situation, I've come to a decision." He glanced down at his notes before continuing. "I will grant the protective order, but with conditions. We will conduct an in-camera review of the information. This means I will review it privately, under seal, and the court will decide if it warrants further action. Based on this review, Ms. Hayes, you can decide whether a plea agreement is appropriate."

Donovan opened his mouth to protest, but Nelson cut him off with a wave of his hand. "This is the best I can do. I'm not negotiating without seeing the cards. Court is adjourned."

The gavel came down with a decisive crack, and Maria was led away, her eyes never once meeting mine.

Donovan and I stepped outside, the late afternoon sun bathing the courthouse steps in warm, golden light that felt at odds with my current mood.

"So, the Pierce case," Donovan said casually, shoving his hands into his pockets. "That's what's keeping you busy?"

"You know I can't talk about it," I shot back, pulling my coat tighter against the wind.

He nodded, grinning. "Of course not. But you always seem to find yourself in the middle of these headline cases. Guess it comes with the territory, huh?"

I sighed. "I'd kill for a nice, simple fraud case right now."

When he laughed, the sound echoed off the courthouse walls. "Be careful what you wish for."

I gave him a small wave as we parted ways. The courthouse steps felt heavier beneath me than they had an hour ago. I still didn't know if I could trust Maria's information, but I'd find out soon enough.

As I reached my car, my phone buzzed in my pocket. Lisa.

"Hey," she said. "Forensics is back. You might want to head over to the lab."

"On my way," I replied, sliding into the driver's seat and starting the engine.

Tomorrow was shaping up to be just as complicated as today.

CHAPTER
NINE

I ARRIVED at the forensics lab, the sharp scent of antiseptic cutting through the air as I pushed open the door. Inside, Lisa hunched over a table next to Turner. They were reviewing some reports, but from the way Lisa's brow was furrowed, I knew the results weren't what we'd hoped.

Lisa looked up when I entered, offering a small smile. "Hey, Alex. We were just going through the results."

"How bad is it?" I asked, stepping toward the table, a knot tightening in my gut.

Turner glanced up, his expression unreadable. He leaned back against the counter, arms crossed. "Not what we were hoping for," he said flatly. "Didn't get a match on the DNA from any of the bodies to Randall Pierce."

I stared at the reports on the table. No match. All that waiting, all that buildup, for nothing but more question marks.

"This doesn't make sense." I flipped through the pages, frustration gnawing at me. "We have multiple dismembered bodies, a suspect with no direct ties to said murders, and now no forensic evidence to even link him. So what are we supposed to do now?"

Turner shrugged, his eyes narrowing. "Look, I know the evidence isn't perfect, but I've been in this game long enough to know a guilty man when I see one."

Looking up at him, my eyes narrowed. "A guilty man? Really? Based on what, Turner? Your gut feeling?" My voice was sharper than I intended, but the tension between us had been brewing for days, and now I was in no mood to let it slide.

Turner uncrossed his arms and stepped toward me. "Yeah, my gut. And it's usually right."

"Turner, a gut instinct isn't going to convince a jury. It's not going to put Pierce behind bars, and it sure as hell isn't going to solve this case. You want to go to court and tell the jury you, 'just have a *feeling*'?"

Lisa glanced between the two of us, likely sensing the escalation. At the evidence table, she quietly flipped through the reports as she watched the exchange. Maybe I should have offered to make her a bag of popcorn.

Turner's jaw tightened; his voice low but defensive. "I've seen this before, Alex. Guys like Pierce don't leave easy trails. He's careful. That doesn't mean he's innocent."

I stepped closer. "I'm not saying he's innocent. What I'm saying is, we don't have what we need. We've got no DNA match, no solid evidence, nothing that ties him directly to these bodies. And you're sitting here, dismissing every other possible lead because your 'gut' says it's him?" I shook my head, my nostrils flaring. "That's not how this works."

Turner ran a hand through his hair, his frustration palpable. "I've been doing this job a long time, and you—"

"And me? I've been doing mine long enough to know that a jury doesn't care how long you've been in the field. They care about evidence, about facts, and about proof. We don't have any of those."

"You're overthinking this, Alex. I know what this guy is capable of. We've already got him on the dump site, and—"

"And what?" I snapped. "We have him at a dump site, sure, but we have nothing that proves he killed these women. Nothing. And if there's someone else out there—someone who's actually responsible—then that's who I'm going after. You want to play this by your gut, fine, but I have a duty to find out who's really behind this. If Pierce isn't the guy, then we're letting the real killer walk free."

"You think I don't know that?"

Unwilling to respond, the silence between us grew heavy and uncomfortable. For a moment, neither of us said anything, the hum of the lab equipment filling the space. Lisa shifted slightly, staying out of the direct line of fire.

"I'm not saying Pierce isn't involved," I finally said, my voice softer but no less firm. "But we can't put all our eggs in one basket. We need to explore other possibilities—other leads. If we don't, we could lose this case."

Turner took a step back and stared at me for a long moment, his expression hardening and jaw working, but he said nothing.

Lisa broke the silence. "Alex is right," she said, her voice calm but firm. "We need more. Pierce might be our guy, but without hard evidence, we're not getting a conviction. We need to keep looking."

Turner let out a breath, rubbing the back of his neck. He looked like he wanted to argue more, but he just nodded, the fight clearly draining out of him.

"Fine. Keep looking," he muttered. "But don't be surprised when I'm right."

Before Turner could storm out, the door to the lab creaked open, and Dr. Sarah Milton stepped in. She had a file in her hand and a hesitant expression on her face, like she already sensed the tension in the room.

"Sorry to interrupt," she began, her voice tentative. "I've got the results on the knife."

Turner's eyes lit up, his earlier frustration momentarily forgotten. "What've you got?"

Sarah flipped open the file, glancing between the three of us. "The knife came back positive for blood, but ..." She hesitated, dodging eye contact. "The results are inconclusive."

"Inconclusive?" I asked, stepping forward. "What does that mean, exactly?"

Sarah let out a breath and brushed a loose strand of hair behind her ear. "We couldn't definitively match the blood to any of the victims from the dump site."

"How is that possible?" Turner asked, his voice edged with irritation. "Blood is blood. Either it matches or it doesn't."

Sarah glanced at him, clearly trying to keep her professional demeanor intact despite the rising tension. "It's not always that simple. There are a few reasons why we can't get a definitive match. For one, the blood sample on the knife was degraded—likely from exposure to the elements, considering the condition the knife was found in. Environmental factors like heat, moisture, and bacteria can break down DNA over time, making it harder to extract a clear profile."

She paused, as if giving us time to digest the information. "When DNA degrades to a certain point," she continued, "the markers we usually rely on to compare samples aren't clear enough to make a definitive match. We can tell it's blood, but as for whose blood it is … we just can't say for sure."

"So what?" Turner asked, folding his arms against his chest. "We've got nothing?"

"We've got something," I said, not wanting to let the frustration turn into hopelessness. "It's just not the smoking gun we were hoping for."

Sarah nodded, her face a mixture of sympathy and professionalism. "Exactly. It doesn't mean the knife isn't connected to the case. It just means the forensic evidence isn't enough to prove it beyond a doubt. We'll keep running tests to see if we can get more, but as of now, that's what we have."

Sarah shifted slightly, the weight of the tension clearly getting to her. "I'll leave you guys to discuss. Let me know if you need anything else."

"Thanks, Sarah," I said, giving her a tight smile.

Once she left, the silence in the room was suffocating. Turner let out a heavy breath, clearly unsatisfied. He turned to me, his eyes dark with frustration.

"It's still Pierce," he said, his voice low but firm. "I know it is."

I shook my head, keeping my tone measured. "But we still need more."

Turner glared at the table for a moment before finally nodding. "Fine," he muttered. "Keep looking."

With that, he turned and walked out of the lab, leaving Lisa and me standing in the heavy silence.

Lisa exhaled slowly, leaning against the table. "That was … intense."

"Yeah," I muttered, rubbing my temple. "I don't know what his deal is, but he's too fixated on Pierce. It's like he's shutting out everything else."

Lisa raised an eyebrow. "Maybe it's just the pressure."

"Maybe." I gave her a sideways glance. "But it's starting to feel like there's something he's not telling us."

Lisa was quiet for a moment before nodding. "We'll figure it out. But right now, we need to focus on what we have."

I nodded, my mind still racing with the argument and the lingering sense that something wasn't right. But she was right. We had to focus on the evidence, not on gut feelings or personal vendettas.

"Let's get back to work," I said, flipping open the report again. "We need to figure out our next move."

CHAPTER TEN

I WAS DIGGING through old case files in the DA's storage shed on Friday evening. The place gave me the creeps with its flickering fluorescent lights and dusty corners, but at least I'd have some peace and quiet. No one else would be crazy enough to be here this late on a Friday.

I wasn't sure what I was searching for. That anonymous caller had claimed there was information about Mom's disappearance hidden in the DA's files. It was probably a dead end, but anything about my mother made me ignore logic.

My footsteps echoed in the otherwise silent space as I moved through the rows of cabinets. The files I'd pulled so far were dead ends. Every case I flipped through felt like a waste of time—old court pleadings, motions, things that had nothing to do with my mom or her case.

Finally, I found myself back at the busted filing cabinet. The same one Andrews had shot open the last time I'd been here. It had since been fixed, yet it still bore the scars of the incident. Yanking it open, I rifled through files again, hoping for something—anything—that might shed light on what I was supposed to find.

But there was nothing. No new clues, no hidden gems.

I rubbed my temples, ready to give up and leave this graveyard of old cases. As I shifted my gaze around the dimly lit room, I spotted it.

A box hidden under a heap of papers and binders, all coated in years of undisturbed dust.

Slowly I crouched down and tugged the box free, dusting off the top. It was labeled in faded ink. *Trafficking Investigation.*

My pulse quickened.

I flipped the lid open and began rifling through the files. At first, it seemed like just another case—pages of legal documents, reports, photos. Halfway through the pile I stopped.

The file label read, *Katherine Hayes, Assistant District Attorney.*

I froze. My breath caught in my throat as I stared at the page, the weight of it hitting me like a punch to the gut. This was it—what I'd been searching for, even if I hadn't known it. But why had I never heard about this? Why hadn't this case made headlines? Where were the arrests, the news coverage?

As I flipped through more of the files, each page revealed something bigger. Documents outlined a massive trafficking ring operating across Texas. My heart rate skyrocketed. It wasn't just small-time crimes. This was organized, powerful. And my mother had been right in the middle of it.

I leaned back on my heels, the files scattered around me, my heart pounding in my ears. Why hadn't this case ever seen the light of day?

Something wasn't adding up. Not with a case this big, with so much evidence.

I stuffed the files back into the box and hustled it out to my car, hiding it in the trunk. I'd need time to wade through everything, but I knew one thing—I wasn't letting this lead go cold.

This wasn't just another dead end. This was my mother's case, and it was far from over.

Driving home through the dark streets, I wondered how far this conspiracy went and why it had stayed buried. At home, I parked quietly. Through the window, I saw Dad asleep in his recliner with the TV on. I crept inside, clicked off the TV, and headed to the kitchen while his snoring continued.

I spread the documents across the kitchen table, the overhead light bright against the white of the papers. Dust rose as I flipped through some of the older sheets, pages yellowed and brittle with age. Most of it was routine legal work—pleadings, motions, discovery requests. Nothing earth-shattering.

Then, I found the first page with her name. *Katherine Hayes, Assistant District Attorney.*

I stared at the neat, professional script typed at the top of the document. It felt surreal, seeing her name on an official case document after all these years. She had worked this case. She had been close to something, something big, and then … she vanished.

I pushed the thought away and kept going. The next stack of papers was more mundane legal paperwork, interspersed with reports on the trafficking ring itself—names of suspects, locations tied to the investigation, notes from detectives who had worked the case. Some of the documents detailed shipments of people, routes used by the traffickers, coded conversations intercepted by wiretaps. Horrifying and brutal, but still not what I was looking for.

I paused when I came across a folder that looked like it had been shoved into the box haphazardly. Inside, I found handwritten notes in my mother's handwriting. I recognized it instantly, the familiar slant of the letters sending a jolt through me.

The pages were in no particular order. There was an address with a note that read, *Slim's base of operations? Women report being processed here before transport. Handles recruitment. Controls day-to-day. All roads lead back.*

I set it aside and kept going. The next page was a list of names. Random at first glance, and in no apparent order. Then I scanned down the page, my eyes grazing over names that felt both familiar and foreign.

Josephine. Whitaker. Cain.

Then one hit me like a freight train. *Randall Pierce.*

My breath caught. He was on this list—written in my mother's own hand.

What the hell?

I rifled through the rest of the folder, my pulse quickening, but there was no other mention of Pierce. No case report connecting him to the trafficking ring. No arrest warrant or charge sheet. Just his name, scrawled among others. It didn't make sense—had Pierce been involved back then? Was he part of the ring my mother had been investigating, or had his name come up later? And why had there been no follow-up on him in these files?

I spread the documents out again, flipping through each one more frantically, but it was clear this box didn't contain the entire case file. There were too many gaps—too many missing pieces. Something had been pulled from this investigation, either intentionally or through negligence, and I was only holding fragments of the story.

My hands landed on the pleading again, the one with my mother's name. As I studied it closer, I noticed something I hadn't seen before. There, at the top corner, was a docket number.

Docket numbers meant there were more filings. More documents. And if they weren't here, they had to be somewhere—probably in the office, hidden in the bowels of the DA's filing system.

I leaned back, my mind racing. Tomorrow was Saturday, and the office would be empty. No one would question me going in for a little extra work. I could use the docket number to pull the rest of the case files, to piece together whatever my mother had been working on before she disappeared.

I stood and gathered the files back into the box, careful not to disturb my father, still sound asleep in his chair. The box weighed down my arms as I carried it out to the car again and stashed it in the trunk, ready for tomorrow.

As I headed to bed, one name kept circling through my mind— *Randall Pierce*. Whatever was going on, Pierce had something to do with this trafficking ring long before his name had ever crossed my desk.

And now I had to find out how deep that connection went.

CHAPTER
ELEVEN

I WAS ALONE in the quiet Saturday office, with just the humming lights and ticking clock for company. I sat at my desk, staring at the screen, trying to pull the case docket linked to my mother's trafficking investigation.

I drummed my fingers on the desk as the system loaded. When the file finally popped up, my stomach sank.

"Damn it," I muttered under my breath. *Sealed*. Of course it was sealed.

I tried again, but the result was the same. Sealed. Locked away behind layers of bureaucratic tape, keeping whatever secrets my mother had uncovered from seeing the light of day.

I sat back, frustrated. Filing a motion to unseal was an option, but the last thing I wanted was to tip anyone off that I was looking into this. It wasn't exactly related to Pierce—at least, I couldn't prove it was yet—and trying to get a judge to unseal a case on a hunch wasn't going to fly. Worse, it could bring scrutiny I wasn't ready for.

I rubbed my temples, the tension building in my skull. There had to be another way to figure this out, but I wasn't sure what it was yet. I needed to think.

Coffee. Coffee would help.

I stood and headed for the coffee machine, desperate for a caffeine hit. The halls were empty as I made my way toward the breakroom, but just as I turned the corner, I bumped straight into Shaw.

"Whoa, sorry," I said, stepping back.

Shaw gave me his usual half-smile, the one that always seemed just a little too smug for my taste. "Working on the weekend?" he asked, his tone more amused than surprised. "You must be here working on the Pierce case."

"Yeah," I lied quickly, trying to keep my expression neutral. I definitely wasn't going to tell him what I was really digging into.

"Turner tells me you didn't get what you needed from forensics," Shaw said, leaning against the doorframe of the breakroom. "But don't worry. I don't think that's going to kill the case."

I stared at him, incredulous. How could he brush this off so easily? "You don't think not having any forensic evidence is a problem?"

He shrugged. "Forensics are nice, but they're not always necessary. I've seen worse cases still come together."

I could feel my frustration rising, especially after what I'd found last night. My mother's note had Pierce's name on it—he was connected, I knew it. But Shaw and Turner seemed to be ignoring every other possibility. And for what? A gut feeling?

"I think he's involved," I said, trying to stay diplomatic. "But we don't have enough to get a guilty verdict, not for something this big. Not for a crime this heinous."

Shaw waved it off like it was nothing. "Cases like these have a way of working themselves out. Trust me, I've been doing this long enough."

Crossing my arms, I didn't bother to hide my irritation. "Please, spare me the lecture. We need evidence, Shaw. Not gut feelings."

He raised an eyebrow, clearly not used to being called out. "Alex, you've got the suspect. Don't let yourself get distracted by looking for something else when the answer is right in front of you."

That's what it felt like—Shaw and Turner were actively refusing to consider any other suspect. And I didn't get it. Why were they so dead set on Pierce, even with the lack of solid evidence? It was like they were willfully ignoring the holes in the case.

Before I could respond, the coffee machine sputtered and gurgled, but it was clearly not working. Perfect.

I let out a groan. "Of course."

Shaw chuckled. "Looks like you'll have to head across the street for that coffee."

I decided that I needed the break anyway. "Yeah, thanks."

As I walked out of the building and across the street to the café, I couldn't stop replaying the conversation in my head. Shaw's attitude wasn't just dismissive. He knew something I didn't. But if that were the case, why wasn't he sharing it?

As I carried my coffee back to the office, the bitter taste helped me focus. But Shaw's words kept gnawing at me.

As soon as I stepped inside, I saw my desk—where I'd spread out some of the files from my mother's case—was clear.

My pulse quickened. I'd left them right here. Right on top of the desk.

Frantically, I opened the drawers, thinking maybe I'd shoved them inside before I left for coffee. But no. They were gone. Every file related to my mother's investigation was missing.

Storming down the hallway, my heart racing, I headed straight for Shaw's office. The door was closed, but when I yanked it open, I found the office empty.

He was gone.

My head spun as I stood there in his doorway, the files gone, Shaw gone, and the unsettling realization sinking in—someone knew what I was digging into.

And they didn't want me to find it. My thoughts raced, scrambling for answers, but I was coming up empty.

Footsteps echoed down the hall. I quickly stepped back from Shaw's office and pretended to be looking at a nearby bulletin board when Lisa appeared around the corner. The smile on her face quickly faded when she noticed my expression.

"Alex? Are you okay?" she asked, her voice tinged with concern. "You look flustered."

I straightened, forcing a casual smile. I couldn't tell her about the files. I wasn't ready to involve anyone else in this. Not yet. "Yeah, I'm fine. Just a long morning. What are you doing here?"

Lisa gave me a curious look, but didn't push. "Prepping for a prelim on Monday," she said, holding up a file folder. "Figured I'd get some work done while it's quiet around here."

"Prelim, huh?" I asked, grateful for the distraction. "What's the case?"

"A group arrested for manufacturing fake IDs," Lisa said, leaning against the doorframe. "Pretty straightforward, but I want to make sure I've got everything ready. It's a decent-sized operation."

"Fake IDs?" I raised an eyebrow, slipping into mentor mode despite my frayed nerves. "Any prior convictions on the defendants?"

"Just some minor stuff—disorderly conduct, a few misdemeanor thefts." Lisa flipped through the pages, landing on one. "But this one feels a little more serious. The operation was pretty organized."

"Sounds like you've got it under control," I said, nodding. "Just make sure you emphasize the coordination and the scale of the operation during the prelim. Judges don't care as much about the minor stuff, but if you can show it's an organized scheme, you'll be in a good spot."

Lisa smiled, tucking the file back under her arm. "Thanks, Alex."

"You'll do fine," I said, unable to stop thinking about those missing files. "Just stick to the facts."

Lisa seemed satisfied and turned to head back down the hall, but before she left, she glanced back at me, a slight frown on her face. "You sure you're okay, though?"

I gave her another forced smile. "I'm fine, really. Just got a lot on my plate. Good luck with the prelim."

She gave me a nod, but I could tell she wasn't convinced as she headed off to her office. I let out a breath, my nerves still buzzing.

When I returned to my office, I closed the door behind me, leaning against it for a moment, trying to steady myself. Whoever had taken those files—whether it was Shaw or someone else—knew I was digging into something I wasn't supposed to. And that meant I had to be more careful from here on out.

I was about to sit down when my phone rang, causing me to jump away from the doorframe. I grabbed the phone, my heart racing as I checked the caller ID.

Unknown number.

For a moment, I hesitated, my thumb hovering over the answer button. I knew who it was. The anonymous caller. The voice that had been haunting me since this whole thing started.

I answered.

"Hello?" I said, trying to keep my voice steady.

There was a brief pause, then the same distorted voice crackled through the line. "You're getting closer," the caller said, their words slow and deliberate. "But you're not there yet."

A chill ran down my spine. "Who are you?" I demanded, my voice sharper than I intended. "What do you know about my mother?"

The caller didn't answer the question directly. Instead, they said something that sent a fresh wave of panic through me.

"She may still be alive."

The ground shifted beneath me and I stumbled back against the door. "What? What do you mean she's alive?"

Another long pause. "Keep digging, Alex. The answers are at the DA's office. But be careful. Not everyone is who they seem."

Before I could ask anything else, the line went dead.

CHAPTER TWELVE

MOST OF MY Sunday I spent holed up in the kitchen. A mess of scribbled notes were scattered across the table.

The phone buzzed on the counter, the screen lighting up with a text from Erin: *Hey, just checking in. How are you holding up?*

I stared at it for a moment, my brain too fried to come up with a response. *I'll answer later*, I told myself, setting the phone back down. I didn't have the energy to get into it right now. Not when my thoughts were already stretched so thin.

The files were still fresh in my mind, and I'd written down everything I could remember from them. But it felt pointless. Nothing was adding up in a way that made sense. And I still couldn't shake off my suspicions about who might've taken them.

It had to be Shaw, right? Or maybe someone else who'd been around the office, but Shaw was the only one who'd seemed suspiciously interested in what I was doing. It couldn't have been Lisa—at least, I didn't think so. I'd suspected her once before, back when I'd been in full-on paranoia mode during the Martin trial, and I didn't have the energy to go down that road again. She'd only just shown up after I'd noticed the files were gone.

I leaned back in my chair. My eyes hurt. The notes blurred in front of me. I didn't even know what I was looking for. I was just convinced that it—whatever it was—was out there. The truth about my mother, about Pierce—somehow, they were connected. I just needed to find out how.

The sound of the back door swinging open pulled me out of my thoughts. I looked up to see my father walking in, wiping dirt off his hands onto his jeans. He was covered in it—mud streaked across his shirt and smeared on his face. He'd been out in the yard, throwing himself back into one of his keep-busy projects.

"Hey, Alex," he said, raising an eyebrow as he took in the mess of papers on the table. "Looks like you're working yourself into a corner here. You seem more stressed than usual."

"More stressed than usual?" I echoed, giving him a half-hearted smile. "Guess that's my new normal, huh?"

He didn't laugh. Instead, he studied me with that familiar, scrutinizing look. "Seriously, Alex, you sure going back to work was the right choice? Seems like it's really spinning you up."

Looking down at my notes, I sighed. Tempted to brush off his concern and tell him everything was fine, his gaze made me pause. I knew he wouldn't just let this go. He knew me too well.

I hesitated, tapping my pen against the table. But I didn't want to keep secrets from him. Not anymore. Not after everything we'd been through. The shadow of guilt that followed me had only grown since he'd come home, since I'd seen what prison had done to him. I'd spent so many years doubting him, and even longer putting off visiting him in prison, convincing myself it was too hard to face. Yet, he'd always told me he didn't harbor grudges.

Wishing I could be as forgiving as he was, he didn't know how close I'd come to moving on, to never looking back. He had forgiven me, but I hadn't forgiven myself. That rift between us—the rift I'd put there—seemed insurmountable some days.

Watching him now, I could see the lines etched deeper into his face, and I couldn't ignore them. He'd gone through hell while I'd built my career, hardly glancing in his direction, convincing myself he'd somehow make it through, or that I wouldn't care if he didn't.

He cleared his throat, his expression softening. "Alex, you know I'm here. Whatever it is, I'm here to listen."

A lump formed in my throat. This was what I'd wanted back then, someone who understood without judgment. But I hadn't reached out when I should have. I was too proud, too angry at a system that had taken him away. Too angry at him for what I thought he'd done. Now, with all the walls broken down, there was no reason to keep anything from him.

Clearing my throat, I met my father's gaze. "Dad, I … found something. A file for a case Mom was working on when she disappeared."

I traced a finger over a small scratch on the edge of the table, a detail I'd never noticed until now.

At first, he didn't react, just stood there, hands still covered in dirt, absorbing my words. "A file?" he repeated slowly.

"Yeah. It was in the DA's storage. A trafficking investigation. And I think the ring she was investigating back then might be connected to the Pierce case. Maybe even her disappearance."

He let out a sigh and sank into the chair across from me. "So … that's what's got you worked up."

I nodded, moving my fingers to fidget with the edge of a notebook, considering whether to tell him about the anonymous calls. But I held back. Wanting to believe that those calls weren't real and were just some twisted figments of my imagination. Telling anyone about them would only cement them in reality. And the last thing I needed was for him to start worrying about my sanity.

"Do you know anything about it?" I sidestepped, my voice quieter now. "About the case?"

His expression turned distant as he looked out the window. "I only knew what your mother told me," he said, as if the words were being pulled from a place he hadn't visited in a long time. "She was frustrated. Kept saying they weren't looking close enough, that they didn't have the right guy."

As he shook his head, sadness softened his eyes. "She was so determined. Kept pushing even when they told her to back off. I didn't realize how deep she was in until …" He trailed off, and I could see the full weight of her loss settling over him like an invisible burden.

I leaned forward, pressing him gently. "Do you remember any names? Anything that might help me?"

"One name's stuck with me over the years." He frowned and

sighed as he dug through his memory, rubbing his hands together as the dirt streaked across his palms. "Mark Blakely. He was the detective she worked with on that case. They worked close on it."

"Mark Blakely," I repeated, mentally filing the name away. "I thought Mom worked mostly on her own?"

"She did … mostly. But Blakely, well, they were close—maybe too close, in my opinion. He was a senior detective. Usually trusted his gut and wasn't afraid to push limits. Sometimes she'd talk about him. About how he was the only one who believed her about the case. I knew him a little, from my own time on the force. Solid guy, but a little rough around the edges." He looked at me thoughtfully. "He'd remember. You should try to talk to him."

"Do you know where he is now?"

"The last I heard, he was in a retirement home—The Gardens, I think it's called. Over on the north side of town."

I nodded, feeling the significance of this lead settle in. "Thanks, Dad."

He placed a hand on my shoulder. "I just wish I had more to tell you, kiddo. I really do."

I gave him a small smile. "It's more than I had before."

Looking at the scattered papers on the table and then back at me, his face softened. "You really should think about putting all of this down. Taking a break. You're young—you should enjoy it. Go on a date or something. What was that one guy's name?"

"Ryan Chen," I offered up.

"Oh yeah. What happened to him?"

"He transferred to another office," I said with a shrug.

He sighed, shaking his head. "Too bad. You know, lawyers need love, too."

"No love for lawyers, Dad. But I appreciate the sentiment."

He shook his head again, muttering something under his breath about "stubborn as her mother."

CHAPTER
THIRTEEN

THE GARDENS LIVED up to its name. A quiet retirement home on the edge of the city that boasted well-manicured landscaping. As I arrived, the setting sun cast a golden glow over the grounds, making the place feel slightly less sad. Inside, the smell of antiseptic mixed with faint traces of lavender from an air freshener.

At the front desk, a young clerk glanced up as I approached. "Hi," she said, hastily flipping her nametag into place. "Can I help you?"

"Yes, I'm here to see Mark Blakely."

She looked a bit surprised. "Mark Blakely? Really?"

"Really," I said, trying not to look as puzzled as I felt. "I'm a … friend."

Glancing down at her visitor log, her pen hesitating over the paper. "He doesn't usually have visitors. I think the last time someone stopped by was—well it's been a while."

I tried to keep my expression neutral, but her statement made me sad. Blakely had once been a public servant, dedicated to his work and to his community. And now, here he was. Alone, tucked away from the world he'd put his life on the line to protect.

"Can I get a visitor pass?" I asked, trying to hide the tug of sympathy in my voice.

"Oh, sure." She handed me a pass with a little sticky label that said

"Visitor," in big, cheerful letters. "Here you go. Room 214. Just take the elevator up and head left down the hallway."

"Thank you," I said with a polite nod.

Walking down the quiet hallway, I found myself wondering what had happened to him. Why didn't he have visitors? Had his years in law enforcement really left him so isolated? It was hard to reconcile that with the image I had of him in my head—a sharp, dedicated detective who'd go to any length to find the truth.

And now, I realized, I was here to ask him to do it all over again.

In front of his door, I gathered myself before I knocked.

"Come in," came a voice from inside. It was a bit gruffer than I'd expected.

I stepped inside, and there he was. Sitting by the window in an old leather armchair. His frame was slightly slouched, but he still gave off that unmistakable air of a man who had spent his life reading people. Hair mostly gray now, thin on top, and his wire-rimmed glasses perched low on his nose as he peered up at me.

"Can I help you with something?" he asked, looking me over with a quick, assessing glance. "The nurses sent you to check on me, huh?"

Managing a small smile, I shook my head as I took a step closer. "Not quite. I'm actually here to visit. I'm Katherine Hayes' daughter."

His expression changed instantly, the edges of his mouth falling as he set his book down, folding his hands over it. "Katherine's daughter?" Again, he looked me over, slower this time, the lines around his eyes softening. "Alex, right?"

"Yes. Alex Hayes." I slowly took the seat across from him, unsure whether he'd be happy or wary of the visit. "Thank you for seeing me, Mr. Blakely."

A warmth creeped into his voice. "Mark. None of that formal stuff." He gave me a small, approving nod. "I heard about that Martin trial. Quite a case. And you handled it well. Your mother would be proud, you know. Standing up for the truth. It's in your blood."

"Thank you," I said, a bit taken aback. I hadn't expected him to know about the case, let alone have followed it. But hearing that he thought my mother would be proud meant more than I'd anticipated.

Chuckling, softer this time, the lines around his eyes crinkled.

"Didn't expect to see anyone from the DA's office, though, especially not Katherine's daughter."

His approval felt like an opening. Maybe he would be willing to share what he remembered of her.

For a moment, he just studied me. It was as if he were looking for traces of my mother in my face.

I twisted my fingers nervously in my lap. "I appreciate it. I... I actually wanted to talk to you about my mother. And the case she was working on before"—I cleared the emotion welling up in my throat—"before she disappeared."

Blakely nodded slowly, his gaze turning somber. "Katherine. She was one of the best. Stubborn as hell, but that's what made her good. She never could leave well enough alone when she knew something didn't sit right."

"That's what I heard. I found a case file she was working on. It was part of an investigation into a trafficking ring. I thought maybe you could tell me more."

He let out a long breath, his gaze drifting out the window. "I know exactly the case you're talking about. I wasn't assigned to that one, but Katherine would come to me anyway. She'd sit in my office, late at night, stacks of papers under her arm, looking for guidance. She knew it wasn't a simple matter. Knew it went higher than anyone wanted to admit."

"Why didn't she pull back?" I asked, almost pleading. "Why didn't you tell her to let it go?"

Blakely looked down, a shadow passing over his face. "I tried, Alex. I told her more than once that it was dangerous. That people like the ones she was investigating don't play by the rules she and I were bound to. But Katherine wasn't one to back down. She thought she could handle it. Thought she could get to the truth without them noticing."

He sighed, rubbing a hand over his face. "I blame myself, you know. For not pushing harder, for not doing more to keep her safe. Should've made her see that it wasn't worth the risk."

The regret in his voice was raw. I shifted in my seat, glancing down at the notes I'd hastily scribbled in my notebook before coming. "Do you remember anything specific about the case she was working on? People she might've mentioned?"

Blakely was quiet for a moment, as if weighing how much to say. "There was a man named Shaw. Robert Shaw. He was another assistant DA, working with her on the case, or at least, he was assigned to it around the same time. She didn't trust him completely, though. I could tell."

A chill ran down my spine. Shaw. I'd known he'd been involved but hearing it from Blakely made it feel more real, more ominous.

"Why didn't she trust him?" I asked, trying to keep my voice steady.

Blakely shrugged, his gaze heavy. "He had connections. Friends in high places. Katherine worried that if the case got too close to something they didn't want exposed, he'd be pressured to look the other way. Didn't say it outright, but I could tell it was on her mind."

I nodded, my mind racing. Shaw's dismissive attitude, his reluctance to consider any leads beyond Pierce—all of it fit too well. I was beginning to understand why my mother might have been wary of him.

Blakely must've noticed the look on my face, because he leaned forward, his eyes narrowing. "Alex, listen to me. It's easy to jump to conclusions when you're desperate for answers. Shaw was frustrated, too. And after Katherine disappeared, he blamed himself. Felt he should've done more to protect her. I don't know if he's guilty of anything other than guilt itself."

I bit my lip, struggling to contain the conflicting emotions roiling inside me. "It's hard not to be suspicious when people keep secrets."

"Everyone has secrets," Blakely said softly, almost to himself. "But not everyone's a villain." He shifted in his chair, looking back out the window, as if the memory of my mother haunted the edges of his vision. "There was one place. An old warehouse. Katherine mentioned it once. She thought it might be one of the main sites for this operation, but she couldn't prove it. She was so close, Alex. So damn close."

"A warehouse? Do you know where it was?"

"Down by the industrial park, off Harris Road. It's probably long abandoned by now, but it's where she thought some of the bigger players met, where deals went down. She tried to get a warrant to search it, but the higher-ups wouldn't allow it. Said there wasn't enough probable cause based on just her speculation."

I scribbled the address in my notebook. "Thank you, Mark. This could be what I need."

Blakely gave me a sad smile, his eyes softening. "Be careful, Alex. Katherine thought she could handle it, too. She thought she could bring them down and look where it got her." He paused, then added, "The same people she was after—they don't just disappear, you know. They're still out there, watching. Waiting."

I swallowed hard, the weight of his words settling over me. "I understand. But I can't just let it go."

He nodded. Twice. A hint of pride mingled with the sadness in his gaze. "You're your mother's daughter. Just be smarter than we were. Sometimes knowing when to walk away is just as important as knowing when to fight."

I nodded, though I knew deep down that walking away wasn't a possibility. "Thank you, Mark. For everything."

"Just promise me one thing, Alex. Whatever you find, whatever answers you dig up, don't lose yourself in the process."

I stood, feeling the full weight of his words, and managed a small smile. "I'll try. But you know how stubborn we Hayes women are."

Blakely chuckled, a sound that was both weary and fond. "That I do. Good luck, Alex."

CHAPTER
FOURTEEN

THE MONDAY MORNING bustle was already in full swing as I walked into the DA's office, but my mind was still stuck on everything that had unfolded over the weekend. The meeting with Blakely lingered in my head, heavy as a stone.

Shaw. I couldn't stop thinking about him. His connection to my mother, the files that had mysteriously disappeared, and the guarded looks he'd given me every time I'd tried to press him about Pierce.

I pushed through the lobby, weaving past colleagues who offered quick nods or mumbled "good mornings." But my mind was spinning. Every instinct I had told me Shaw was hiding something, something he didn't want me to find. The missing files were the first clue, and now, with Blakely's hints about my mother's investigation, it felt more obvious than ever.

I was lost in thought when I spotted Lisa by the elevators. She glanced over, her brows knitting as she caught sight of me. "Hey, Alex. You look … like you spent the weekend in a wrestling match."

"Close enough," I muttered, stepping beside her as we waited for the elevator. "It was an interesting weekend."

The doors dinged open, and we stepped inside. Lisa turned to me, her eyebrows raised expectantly. "Anything you care to share?"

I forced a half-smile, but was sure it didn't reach my eyes. "It's

Shaw. I've learned some information—stuff that could really help us with Pierce—and I think he took a file from me." Pausing, I watched her reaction as I added, "I don't think he wants me to know everything about this case."

Lisa's brows shot up, surprise flickering in her eyes. "Shaw? Are you serious? He's been with the DA's office for what—two, three decades? He's basically part of the foundation." She shook her head. "Why would he be hiding files? What could he gain from keeping you in the dark?"

I shrugged, the frustration knotting in my stomach. "I can't explain it, but it's this sense I keep getting. Like he's deliberately keeping me away from something important. Every time I bring something up, he shuts it down. He's got the seniority, yeah, but the way he's handling this just doesn't sit right with me."

"Alex, that's a big accusation. I mean, Shaw's old-school. You can't just go in there guns blazing and accuse him of hiding evidence."

The frustration I'd been holding back bubbled over. "Then how am I supposed to get that file back, Lisa? He's probably buried it somewhere. I can't just ask him outright without raising every red flag possible, and I don't exactly have the luxury of waiting for him to hand it over."

Lisa's expression softened. "I get it, believe me. But Shaw's been at this a long time. He knows every loophole and regulation, every way to work a case. He'll have a dozen ways to counter you. Not to mention, if you're wrong—"

"Wrong?" I asked, incredulous. "I'm telling you, I know he's hiding something. This isn't a coincidence. Not after all the resistance he's put up. And now I find out he was working with my mother on the exact same case?"

Lisa's eyes widened, clearly taken aback. "He was working with your mother? On a murder case?"

I nodded. "Trafficking. From what I've been able to piece together, she didn't trust him back then, either. It's like history repeating itself and I can't just stand by and let it happen."

"Look, I'll admit, it sounds suspicious." Lisa bit her lip, clearly torn.

"But if you go after him directly, you might as well hang a flashing sign over your head. You need another approach. Maybe a subtler one."

Raising an eyebrow, a glimmer of hope sparked in my frustration. "Subtle? What did you have in mind?"

Lisa's eyes lit up as an idea seemed to form. She gave me a mischievous smile. "Janice."

It took a beat before I understood, but then a grin spread across my face as the thought took root.

"We get her on board," Lisa said, clearly warming to the idea. "She's probably seen every file that's gone in and out of his office. If he's got something hidden in there, Janice would be the one to know— or at least to get access to it."

I let out a sigh, a new surge of determination flooding in. "All right. Janice it is."

"We'll need fuel. Want to grab a little 'thank you' kit for our favorite assistant?"

I couldn't help but smirk. "I've taught you well, grasshopper. Frappuccinos and croissants it is."

"Hey, you're the one who showed me how effective Janice's sweet tooth could be. I'm just following protocol here."

As the elevator doors slid open to our floor, we exchanged a glance, then silently agreed to ride it back down. A coffee shop run felt like a better move. We crossed the street and ducked into the café, quickly gathering up an iced caramel frappuccino, a gingerbread latte, and a bag of fresh croissants. I balanced the bag while Lisa carried the drinks.

As we walked back, Lisa nudged me with her elbow. "You know, this whole bribery thing is probably a little gray on the ethics spectrum."

"A little?" I snorted. "I'm a public servant, not a saint. And Janice isn't exactly known for following protocol herself."

Lisa gave a mock sigh, her eyes glinting with humor. "I have to say that I'm a little proud myself. A year ago, I didn't have the guts to pull off something this sneaky. Now I'm bribing people with pastries."

"Ah, my work here is complete."

The Monday morning crowd had settled, and Janice was stationed behind her desk, scrolling through her emails. Her eyes lit up as she saw the treats in our hands.

"Oh ladies, what a surprise," she said, clasping her hands together as we set down the goods. "To what do I owe this little burst of generosity?"

I gave her a warm smile, pushing the bag toward her. "Just a little something to say thank you. You always go above and beyond for the office, and we really appreciate it."

Lisa slid the frappuccino over to her. "Especially today. We're in a bit of a bind."

Janice's eyes twinkled with interest as she took a sip of her drink. "What kind of bind? And more importantly, what do you need from little old me?"

I exchanged a quick glance with Lisa. I leaned in, lowering my voice. "We need a file box. From Shaw's office. A box, actually. An old one. You'll know it when you see it."

I could tell she was trying not to look surprised as she set her drink down. "Now, you two know that Mr. Shaw isn't exactly the kind of guy who leaves things lying around."

"We know, but this is important." Lisa gave her a sympathetic look. "Think of it as a little favor."

Janice tilted her head, considering us. "And what do I get in return for this little favor?"

I grinned, nudging the croissant bag toward her. "More treats, any time you want. We're at your service."

Janice looked at the bag, then back at us. "You drive a hard bargain, Alex." She picked up a croissant and took a bite. "All right, I'll see what I can do."

She sauntered down the hallway, leaving Lisa and me standing there, trying not to look too eager.

We waited, glancing at each other as the minutes stretched on. Finally, we heard footsteps approaching, but the look on Janice's face made my heart sink.

She shook her head slowly, her expression both amused and a little anxious. "Sorry, ladies. Shaw's here. And he doesn't look happy."

Before we could even process her words, a familiar voice echoed from down the hall, cold and unmistakably irritated. "Ms. Hayes. My office. Now."

CHAPTER
FIFTEEN

SHAW CLOSED his office door with a heavy, foreboding thud. He crossed his arms, standing behind his desk with a face as hard as granite. I could tell he was simmering, but his voice was low, clipped, controlled.

"Would you like to tell me why you were trying to get Janice to snoop around my office?"

I shrugged and met his gaze with as much defiance as I could muster. "I don't know, Shaw. Maybe you'd like to explain why I had to go looking for files that went missing from *my* office."

His eyes narrowed as he shook his head. "What are you even talking about? You're crossing a line here, Alex. You do realize I could get you in a lot of trouble for trying to go behind my back like that, right?"

"Funny, because I was about to say the same thing to you. Stealing files from my office isn't exactly a shining example of professional conduct either."

His eyebrows raised in what I wasn't sure was feigned or real surprise, and then he gave a dismissive shake of his head as he reached for a stack of files on his desk. "I didn't take anything from your office, Alex. And I have no idea what you're accusing me of here."

He shuffled through the papers on his desk with an air of irritation, halfheartedly organizing them, like he couldn't be bothered to even look at me directly. He flipped through a few pages, treating this entire conversation as some minor inconvenience interrupting his real work, then closed one of the files with a loud snap before meeting my gaze.

"Don't you?" I clenched my fists, barely able to keep my composure. "You're acting like this is no big deal, but those files vanished right after our last conversation. I know I didn't misplace them, and you and I were the only ones in the office."

He sighed and rubbed a hand over his face, visibly frustrated. "You're starting to sound paranoid, Hayes. I didn't take anything from your desk. Do you think I don't have enough on my plate without rummaging through your files? Why don't you take another look? For all you know, they're sitting exactly where you left them."

"An entire file box doesn't just disappear from my desk and magically reappear." I bit the inside of my cheek, fury simmering just under my skin. "I'm not losing files by accident, and you know it. If you're trying to keep me from seeing something, it's not going to work."

Shaw let out a heavy sigh. He clasped his hands behind his back and began pacing slowly, as if he were trying to decide what to say. "Alex, you need to focus on what's in front of you. This case—it's about Pierce. Not some shadowy conspiracy. You're letting your suspicions cloud your judgment."

"Cloud my judgment? Shaw, I'm not the one refusing to consider the whole picture. If there's even a chance Pierce is part of something bigger, we should be looking into it. That's what this office is supposed to be about—finding the truth."

Turning to face me, his gaze hardened. "This office is about prosecuting the cases in front of us. Not chasing ghosts." He paused, his voice lowering as if choosing his words carefully. "Some things are better left where they are. The sooner you focus on what's in front of you, the better you'll do here."

"Is that why you're shutting down every lead that doesn't fit with Pierce being our man?" I shot back, trying and failing to hide the bitterness in my tone. "You're so eager to wrap this up that you're ignoring the evidence, or lack thereof, right in front of *you*."

Something flickered across Shaw's face before he masked it, the tone of his next words patronizing. "Alex, I've been in this job a long time. I know what I'm doing. Pierce is guilty. The grand jury will convene Friday, and we're positive we'll get the indictment we need. That's all there is to it."

My patience snapped. I moved toward him. "Is that really all there is to it? Or is there something you're not telling me? Something that's stopping you from looking at Pierce the way we should be?"

Shaw's expression shifted, the impatience gone, replaced by a steely finality. "Yes, that's all there is. And if you're smart, you'll drop whatever it is you think you're doing. You're a good attorney. Don't waste your time chasing the past."

The tone was dismissive. The message clear: *Back off.*

I straightened, keeping my voice as steady as I could manage. "Fine. Then I'll just go over this with Tom. Just to make sure we're all on the same page about how this case is being handled."

Shaw's lips curved in a tight, almost mocking smile. "Don't bother, Alex. Tom is fully on board with moving forward on Pierce. He knows where I stand, and he can't afford to go down rabbit holes." His hands rested on the desk in a way that made it clear he considered the conversation over. "Trust me. There's no need to waste his time on this."

A surge of frustration moved through me, but I held his gaze, letting him see that I wasn't convinced, wasn't ready to drop anything. Without another word, I turned and left, barely holding back the urge to slam his door shut behind me.

The trip back to my office felt longer than usual, the frustration boiling inside me with every step. Shaw was dismissive, evasive, and yet utterly certain about Pierce. But why? Why was he so determined to shut down any possibility of other leads?

When I reached my office, I stopped in my tracks. Sitting on my desk, as if it had never left, was the file box. The same one that had gone missing.

I crossed the room, my heart pounding as I looked it over. Everything seemed in place, untouched, but I knew better than to trust appearances. Shaw's words echoed in my head: *For all you know, they're sitting right where you left them.*

With a sigh, I sank into my chair, staring at the files with renewed resolve. Whatever Shaw was hiding, whatever this case with Pierce really was, I wasn't backing down. If there was more to this story—more to my mother's case—I was going to find out.

And Shaw wouldn't be able to stop me.

CHAPTER SIXTEEN

THE GRAND JURY hearing was over in the blink of an eye. A closed-door hearing meant to determine if there's enough evidence to indict, and Tom and Shaw got what they wanted. Forty-four counts of first-degree murder. The indictment was swift and severe, but as I watched Shaw field questions at the impromptu press conference on the courthouse steps, I couldn't shake the unease in my gut. He was in his element, every line delivered with a practiced confidence, as if the whole case were an open-and-shut miracle of investigative work.

One reporter shot a question, barely waiting for Shaw to recognize him. "Mr. Shaw, are you confident that Pierce is the only killer in so many cases?"

Shaw nodded, clasping his hands in front of him as if he were delivering a sermon. "Absolutely. The evidence we've presented to the grand jury speaks for itself. Randall Pierce has been connected to the victims through numerous leads, and the grand jury agrees. This is the beginning of justice for these women and their families."

Another reporter leaned forward, microphone extended. "But Mr. Shaw, given the lack of direct forensic evidence tying Pierce to any one of the victims, how can you be so sure?"

Shaw smiled, a polished, reassuring grin that didn't quite reach his eyes. "We are not relying solely on physical evidence here. This is a

case built on pattern, opportunity, and connection, and those connections point directly to Pierce."

I bit the inside of my cheek, fighting the urge to roll my eyes.
Circumstantial evidence only got you so far in cases this massive, and
Shaw knew that. He was skating over the holes, and the reporters
weren't even buying it. But he was skilled enough to dodge anything
he couldn't address directly.

A third reporter, closer to me, fired off another question. "Do you
expect Pierce to go to trial, or are you anticipating a plea deal?"

Shaw's eyes gleamed. "We're preparing for trial. Mr. Pierce
deserves his day in court, and we're ready to present a case that will
leave no room for doubt. We owe it to the victims, to the families, and
to this community."

Standing just behind him, I forced myself to keep my expression
neutral, professional, as if I, too, was completely satisfied with the
grand jury's decision. But inside, I was churning. Shaw was spinning
the story with every answer, presenting Pierce's guilt as an ironclad
fact, a foregone conclusion. Watching him made my skin crawl. There
were still so many open questions, so much that just didn't add up. We
were charging toward the finish line with our shoelaces tied together.

As Shaw wrapped up his final answer, he gestured to the crowd
with his polished, reassuring smile. "Thank you, everyone, for being
here today. We will continue to work tirelessly to bring closure to these
families and ensure that justice is served."

With a firm nod, he turned to leave, catching my eye for just a
moment. His expression was calm, but I could see something steely
underneath, a silent warning daring me to push further. He walked
past me without a word, the reporters parting to let him through. I
stood still, forcing myself to keep my expression neutral and professional, even as irritation simmered under the surface.

As the reporters dispersed, I finally let out a slow breath. The past
few days had been intense, and the reappearance of that missing file
box only complicated things further. I'd combed through its contents,
spending hours piecing together fragments of my mother's old notes.
Names, dates, addresses, scrawled on pages with a sense of urgency
that made my heart ache from the adrenaline rush. But something was

still missing. If Shaw had put the box back, or if someone else had, it could have been tampered with.

At least I had a few names to check out. And then there was that warehouse address Blakely had given me. I couldn't ignore it; if my mother had been suspicious about that location, there was no way I was going to let it slide.

Lost in thought, I almost missed the woman standing off to the side, partially hidden by the shadow of a nearby column. She was bundled in heavy clothing, a thick scarf wrapped around her head, excessive in spite of the chilly weather.

My pulse quickened as our eyes met. Her face was partially obscured by the scarf, but her gaze was intense, focused. I blinked, trying to shake the feeling she was staring at me. When I glanced back, she had turned, quickly disappearing into the small crowd lingering near the courthouse entrance.

I took a step forward, an inexplicable urge to follow her welling up inside me. But just as quickly, I stopped. What was I doing? For all I knew, she was just another onlooker, maybe even someone who'd lost someone close in a case Pierce was connected to.

Instead of heading home like most of the team, I returned to the office, eager to dig further. My desk still bore the traces of the case files from this week, stacks of papers threatening to spill over onto the floor. But I cleared a small space to hop on my computer, pulling up the address Blakely had given me.

A quick search brought up an unexpected result: the warehouse was tied up in a pending case for a squatter, an open file handled by another ADA—Evan Thompson, a junior prosecutor I vaguely remembered meeting in the hallways once or twice. The case was small, probably not even worth a second glance, but my gut told me it wasn't a coincidence.

I grabbed my notebook and made my way down to Evan's office. I found him staring blankly at his computer screen, his desk littered with a mix of coffee cups and case files.

"Hey," I said, leaning against the doorframe.

Evan jumped and looked up from his trance, momentarily startled. He was hunched over a mountain of paperwork, glasses slipping down his nose, with a pencil tucked behind one ear and an untouched coffee going cold beside him. He looked every bit the overworked junior ADA: slight, with a mess of dark hair and an earnest expression that made him seem younger than he probably was.

"Oh, hey, Alex," he said. "How can I help you?"

"I saw you're handling a case for the warehouse over on Harris Road," I said. "Mind if I ask what you've got on it?"

"The squatter case?" He blinked as he processed my question. "It's … well, it's not much, to be honest." He rubbed the back of his neck, glancing at the file on his desk. "Probably just going to plead out. Just some guy living in an abandoned warehouse, minimal damage. Typical squatter stuff."

I nodded. "Mind if I take it over?"

He looked a little taken aback, his eyes narrowing as he processed the request. "Take it over? Uh, it's pretty low-level, to be honest. Are you sure you want it?"

I kept my tone casual. "Yeah, I'd like to take a look. Sometimes these cases have a way of connecting to other things. And besides," I added, giving him a faint smile, "seniority has its privileges."

He shifted in his seat but nodded, probably reluctant to argue with a more senior ADA. "All right. I'll, uh, let Tom know. And here, you can have the case box." He handed it over with a slight shrug, obviously confused but resigned.

"Thanks," I said, lifting the box and giving him a nod before heading back to my office.

Back at my desk, I set the box down and flipped the lid open to reveal the haphazard stack of paperwork and photos inside. I began sorting through them, noting each item, the routine police reports, evidence logs, minor property damage reports. But as I flipped through the documents, certain details began to stand out.

First, there was an evidence log mentioning a couple of smartphones found on the premises—strange, since squatters rarely left anything valuable behind. Then, another log indicated several receipts for large sums of money from cash-only businesses. There were even remnants of documents that had been burned—half-legible scraps that hinted at larger transactions, possibly overseas. A prickle of suspicion ran up my spine.

And then I saw it. A single page of an old, water-stained ledger. At the bottom of the page was a name I knew too well.

Pierce.

My pulse quickened, trying to process the implications. If Pierce's name was showing up here, then this warehouse wasn't just some random location. There had to be a reason he was linked to this place —a reason that might have tied back to my mother's original investigation.

I looked over the rest of the contents, but there was nothing more directly connecting Pierce, at least not in this box. Still, it was enough to set off alarm bells. There was something larger here, threads pulling together in a way that felt almost too convenient. This wasn't just about Pierce, or even the victims he'd allegedly murdered. This was about a network that operated under the surface, hidden in plain sight.

I sat back in my chair and tapped my pen against the desk, the questions tumbling over each other in my mind. Why was this place, the same warehouse my mother had been investigating, cropping up now? And how did Pierce fit into the bigger picture? I could almost see the connections, but not quite. This case was far from over. If anything, it felt like it was just beginning.

Just as I let out a heavy sigh, my phone buzzed on the desk, making me jump. I glanced at the screen. *Unknown Number.*

My heart skipped a beat. Another call from the anonymous tipster? I hesitated, but curiosity won over caution. I picked up, keeping my voice steady. "This is Alex."

There was a brief pause on the other end, just enough to make my skin prickle. Then, the same distorted, almost mechanical voice came through, low and chilling.

"You're looking in the right place," the voice said, each word deliberate. "But you're not the only one interested in the past."

A cold shiver ran down my spine. "Who are you?" I demanded, trying to keep the frustration and suspicion out of my voice.

"Someone who knows what's at stake," the voice replied. "And someone who knows that the closer you get, the more dangerous this becomes."

I gritted my teeth. "If you really want to help, then stop speaking in riddles. Why are you telling me this? And what does Pierce have to do with it?"

The voice was silent for a moment, then added, "Pierce was just a pawn. But pawns can be replaced."

The line went dead.

I lowered the phone slowly, staring at it as if it might provide answers. But there was only the empty silence of my office and the echo of those words.

Pawns can be replaced.

CHAPTER
SEVENTEEN

THE PHONE WAS STILL in my hand when the line went dead. The caller's words echoing in my mind. *Pierce was just a pawn. But pawns can be replaced.*

I was still shaken and trying to gather my thoughts, when the phone rang again, the sudden sound making me jump to my feet.

I half-expected to see *Unknown Number* flash again. Instead, it was the courthouse clerk. Letting out a shaking breath, I cleared my throat to steady my vocal cords.

"This is Alex."

"Ms. Hayes," the clerk said, his tone all business. "We've just completed the in-camera review for the Maria Alvarez testimony. It's ready for you to come down and view at your convenience."

"Thank you," I replied, clearing my throat again. "I'll be down shortly."

The line disconnected, and I took a steadying breath before heading out of my office to find Lisa.

I spotted her down the hall, poring over some files at her desk. "Hey, Lisa," I said, catching her attention. She looked up, eyebrows raised.

"Got a minute?" I asked, my tone making it clear this wasn't casual. "I know it's getting late but, the in-camera review of Maria Alvarez's testimony is ready at the courthouse. Thought you might want to come with me."

Lisa's expression shifted to one of intrigue. "Absolutely. Let me grab my things."

We walked side by side out of the DA's office into the brisk air, crossing the square toward the courthouse. Mind spinning, pulse refusing to settle after that call, I tried to focus on the steps in front of me and the sounds of the city. The distant hum of traffic, the occasional blare of a car horn, and the rhythmic clatter of shoes on pavement—anything to quiet the questions that kept popping up in my head.

Lisa seemed to pick up on my tension. She nudged my shoulder gently. "Are you okay?" she asked, shooting me a concerned look.

I forced a small smile, brushing off the concern. "Just thinking about what Alvarez might say in this testimony," I replied, hoping it sounded convincing.

Lisa nodded, though a flicker of confusion crossed her face. "How are you going to handle this, anyway? I mean, wouldn't a normal statement or deposition be enough?"

As we walked, the winter breeze tugged at my coat, and I pulled it a little tighter around me.

"This is something pretty rare," I explained, stepping over a cracked patch of pavement. "In sensitive cases, a court can sometimes grant an *in-camera* review—basically a private screening—for a witness's testimony." I watched Lisa absorb this, her gaze flicking briefly to the courthouse looming up ahead. "Maria claims her information could put her in danger," I said, "so the court's treating it with extra caution. We get to watch it first, before deciding what to do with it."

Lisa's pace slowed a little as she considered this. A faint frown appeared as she adjusted her bag over her shoulder. "If it's that sensitive, it must be important," she said, sounding both curious and apprehensive. "What's your move, then? Are you actually going to strike a deal with her?"

I shrugged, my hands slipping into my coat pockets, fingers brushing the cold metal of my keys. "Depends on what she says. If Maria's information is as critical as she claims, then we'll have to make some concessions." I glanced down, watching my footsteps as they echoed on the stone steps of the courthouse steps. "Honestly, though, I've never dealt with anything quite like this before. I'm walking into this as much in the dark as you are."

We paused outside the courthouse doors and Lisa's gaze searched mine. Her expression was a mix of intrigue and concern. She exhaled, her breath fogging in the cool air. "Let's hope it's worth the wait," she said, giving me an encouraging smile as she fell back into step beside me.

We headed through security and down a winding hallway lined with portraits of past judges. The courthouse clerk, a young man with a brisk manner, met us just outside the records room. He nodded his greeting and led us down a quieter corridor to a small, windowless witness room tucked away at the back of the courthouse. A single screen was set up in the room, waiting for us.

"The video's cued and ready," he said, nodding at the setup. "You'll have the room to yourselves. Just let me know if you need anything."

"Thanks," I replied, taking a seat at the small metal table, and Lisa settled in beside me. The clerk closed the door as he left, leaving us alone in the dim room.

I pressed *Play*, and the video screen flickered to life, the face of Maria Alvarez appearing on the monitor. She looked exhausted, as though every word she was about to say would remove all the energy she had.

"State your name for the record," a voice off-camera instructed.

"Maria Alvarez," she replied, her voice barely audible.

"And you're here to offer testimony in exchange for leniency on your pending charges?"

She nodded. "Yes." Her eyes darted around the room as if she was afraid someone else might be watching. "I want to help. I want a chance to get out of this life."

There was a slight hesitation before the off-camera voice continued. "Ms. Alvarez, please describe the information you have and why you believe it would be of value to the DA's office."

Maria licked her lips as her eyes continued to dart around

nervously. Glancing down for a moment, she then looked back up at the camera. Her voice wavered slightly when she finally spoke.

"It started with a lead from a guy I used to work with. Said he knew people who could help me get new clients—big clients, the kind that would pay top dollar. At first, I thought it was just, you know, business connections. Seemed harmless. A referral here, an introduction there. I figured I was just expanding my network, getting a foot in the door with the right crowd."

She hesitated, swallowing hard before she continued. "But it wasn't just that. They weren't just a group. They were organized." Her face twisted, the words catching in her throat. "And they made it clear that I wasn't supposed to be out there looking for clients on my own anymore. I was only supposed to work with the ones they brought to me. They controlled everything. I didn't even know who these men really were—never even met most of them face-to-face."

Lisa and I exchanged a glance as we both tried to process the weight of what we were hearing. Maria took a shaky breath and went on, a bitter edge creeping into her voice.

"I told myself it was just good business. They were bringing in the clients, sure, but they were cutting me out of my own money—taking their 'share,' they called it. At first, it was just a few bucks here and there, but it didn't take long before they were keeping most of it. I barely had enough left over to scrape by."

Maria looked down again, the anger and fear on her face telling their own story. "When I tried to stop, when I told them I didn't want to be part of this anymore, that I'd go back to finding my own clients, they made it clear that wasn't an option. I got a call, and the guy on the other end didn't even bother hiding the threat. He told me they knew where I lived, and where my family was. He said if I ever thought about walking away, they'd make me disappear. Just like that."

A shiver ran through me, and Lisa tensed up beside me, her lips pressed into a thin line. Maria was trembling now, but her words poured out with a kind of resigned desperation.

"That's when I realized they weren't just trying to control my work —they were a part of something bigger. Something dangerous. They made it clear they could do whatever they wanted, that people like me didn't matter. I was nothing to them."

Pausing, her hands clenched into fists in her lap. "I know some names—I didn't meet the real players, but I can tell you who I was supposed to listen to. The ones who made the threats, who set up the clients, who collected the money."

The off-camera voice prompted, "And you're willing to share these names?"

"Yes," Maria replied, nodding. "But only if I get time served and a chance at rehabilitation."

The video ended with Maria looking down, defeated and visibly shaken. I stared at the screen for a long moment, processing everything she'd said. The weight of what we'd just heard settled between Lisa and me, the silence thick and oppressive.

Lisa finally broke it. "So she's connected to a larger organization." She shook her head. "I didn't think it would go that deep."

"Neither did I." The implications dawned on me. Maria's testimony wasn't just about her survival—it was leading us to something far darker and more dangerous than we'd anticipated.

"What are you going to do?" Lisa asked. Voice low and almost reverent, as if she were afraid to disturb the stillness around us.

Taking a deep breath, I felt the weight of the decision settle in my chest. "Not much choice. If Maria really has the names of people tied to a trafficking ring, we need to get them. I'll have to make a deal for those names."

Lisa nodded, but her eyes still held doubt. "Do you think this could have anything to do with Pierce?"

There was no way it couldn't be connected, not with the way all the threads seemed to be winding together—the trafficking ring, Pierce, the anonymous tips, and even my mother's case all those years ago. The implications were too big, too layered with dark possibilities. But I didn't want to go there, didn't want to let the full weight of those connections settle on me just yet.

"Maybe," I said, keeping my tone neutral, but my mind was racing. I looked away, hoping Lisa couldn't see the flicker of apprehension in my eyes.

She exhaled slowly, folding her arms. "If it's all connected, this could be bigger than we thought."

"Yeah," I replied, staring at the blank screen where Maria's image had just been. "It could be a lot bigger."

CHAPTER
EIGHTEEN

JANICE'S DESK outside Tom's office was empty. Normally, she was stationed there, glancing up with that knowing smile, a silent reminder that she was already two steps ahead. But today, her chair was vacant, her coffee half-finished on the desk.

I pushed the thought aside and knocked once on Tom's door. I stepped inside to find him hunched over a stack of papers. His glasses were perched on the tip of his nose, and he barely looked up when I entered.

"Tom." I waited a moment and took a seat across from him. He still didn't look up at me. "I wanted to talk to you about a plea deal for Maria Alvarez. We had an in-camera review of her testimony and—"

He held up a hand, finally lifting his gaze to meet mine. "No deal, Alex."

I blinked, certain I'd misheard. "What? She has information that could lead us to a bigger trafficking ring, Tom. We could finally start connecting dots, maybe even link it to Pierce. She's offering names."

He sat back, his expression unreadable. "We've given Alvarez too many breaks already. She's a repeat offender, and frankly, we don't need whatever scraps she's dangling in front of us."

His dismissive tone hit me like a slap. "Tom, I've seen the video. This isn't some vague claim—she's offering three names. People she took orders from. That's a direct link to a bigger network."

He shook his head, unyielding. "And I'm telling you, no deal. We're not risking credibility for her. We have enough on our plate, and honestly, Alex, we don't need her information. We're building a case against Pierce without chasing down leads from someone with her record."

My temper started rising as indicated by my hands clenching in my lap. "This could be our big break. You're not even willing to consider it?"

Tom sighed and pinched the bridge of his nose. "Alex, we don't have the resources to investigate every tip from people like Alvarez. We need to focus on Pierce, not go off on tangents that could lead to nowhere."

I swallowed the lump of frustration in my throat. Tom wasn't being straightforward about this. Now both he and Shaw have shown this bizarre resistance to pursuing any lead that might stretch beyond Pierce. Almost as if they didn't want to know what was out there.

I forced myself to nod, trying to keep my expression neutral. "Alright," I said, standing up. "I understand."

As soon as I was out of Tom's office, I pulled my phone out, gripping it like a vise. Tom's refusal was a wall, but I was done taking orders that didn't make sense. If he wouldn't back me up on this, I'd do it myself.

I dialed Donovan's number, pacing the hallway as it rang. He picked up on the second ring.

"Hayes," he answered, that familiar mix of irritation and curiosity in his tone.

"Get to the courthouse," I said, not bothering with pleasantries. "Now. We're signing a deal. I want those names."

Donovan chuckled, sounding surprised. "What changed?"

I gritted my teeth. "Nothing you need to worry about. Just be there in thirty. And bring everything."

I hung up, not waiting for his reply. If Tom and Shaw thought I was going to sit on my hands and let this case slip through the cracks, they had another think coming.

Back in my office, I sat down at my desk and quickly pulled up a blank plea agreement template, my fingers flying over the keys. My pulse pounded as I typed, knowing full well this was against protocol —hell, it was borderline reckless. Technically, I needed Tom's approval to make this kind of deal, but he wasn't going to give it, and I was tired of playing by his made-up rules.

Once this agreement was in place, it'd be career suicide for Tom to try to back out. No DA could risk the public fallout of reneging on a deal that promised to expose a major trafficking ring.

I skimmed over the document to make sure everything was in order. Nodding, I hit print, and the quiet hum of the printer filled the silence of my office. Yanking the pages from the tray, I folded them, and shoved them into my bag. Without a second thought, I headed down the hallway and out the door, ignoring the curious glances of a few late-working colleagues as I passed.

I made it to the courthouse in record time, my hands in a death grip around my bag as I spotted Donovan lingering just inside the entrance. He was leaning casually against the wall as though he had all the time in the world. Straightening when he saw me, his usual smug smile tugged at the corners of his mouth. It was all an act.

"You're in a hurry," he remarked, looking me over with that usual glint of amusement.

I didn't respond, already pushing through the courthouse doors and heading toward security. The guard at the checkpoint nodded in recognition. "Ms. Hayes, Mr. Donovan."

I gave a quick nod, barely slowing down, and grabbed my things as soon as they cleared the scanner.

We navigated through the courthouse hallways, our footsteps echoing in the otherwise quiet space. Donovan opened the door to the first witness room available, gesturing for me to go in first. The room was small, its walls a dreary beige, with a round table in the center and a few uncomfortable chairs scattered around it.

Donovan looked around. "So, a witness room in the courthouse. Why aren't we handling this in the DA's office, again?"

I ignored the question, pulling the documents out of my bag and laying them on the table. "Here's the deal," I said curtly, sliding them toward him. "I assume you're capable of reading it."

Donovan took the document, his eyes scanning the fine print. After a few seconds, he glanced back up at me, noting the conspicuously missing signature on the line designated for Tom's approval. He raised an eyebrow, holding up the paper. "No Tom's John Hancock on this one?"

I stepped in close, plucking the pen from his jacket pocket without so much as a request, and signed my name to the line with one swift, firm stroke. I met his gaze, my expression as unyielding as my tone. "You know what this means, Donovan. If you're as smart as you think you are, you'll get me those names. Now."

A look of understanding dawned in his eyes as he nodded slowly, his expression losing some of its usual sarcasm. He carefully folded the document and tucked it into his own briefcase. "I'll get you the names and Maria's signature."

He paused, studying my face as if searching for something. "Why go to such lengths for this, Alex? You're sticking your neck out. This could blow back on you."

I looked past him, at the courthouse hallway stretching out behind us, lined with portraits of men and women who probably never made a risky decision in their lives. "I only hope it's as big and worth it as I think it might be."

Donovan nodded, a glimmer of something like respect in his eyes. "Let's hope it's as big as we think," he said, his voice softer. Without another word, he turned and headed down the hallway.

CHAPTER NINETEEN

SITTING IN MY OFFICE, I stared at the three names scrawled on the notepad in front of me. I tapped my pen against the desk. These were the names Maria Alvarez had given through Donovan. Three names I had bargained my career for, and yet, all I felt was frustration.

Of the two names—Sam Whitaker and Slim—only one appeared on my mother's list. That alone was unsettling enough. The other one, however, was just a nickname: Scorpion. I rubbed my temples, trying to tamp down the building headache. Had I known I'd be staking my entire career on two names I already had and a random alias, would I still have gone through with it? Probably not—but it was done now. No use dwelling on it.

Whitaker. It was just an ordinary name, common enough to be vague. Sam Whitaker could have been any number of men in Texas— or across the country, for that matter. But the fact that Maria had mentioned him, and it matched someone my mother had been track- ing, meant something. Now I just needed to figure out what.

I leaned back, massaging my temples. Maybe Maria could help me put the pieces together. Under Donovan's bluster, she'd been more willing to share scraps of information. She'd probably had countless clients like him—quick to negotiate, but rarely interested in her as a person. That made her slightly easier to crack, if I approached her carefully.

But how to get her talking? She'd already put out the name in the protective review, and the promise of a plea deal wasn't leverage anymore. I'd need a stronger hook if I wanted real answers. Maybe I could get her to remember something useful about Whitaker—an odd habit he had, a strange comment he'd made, or even something about his associations. Anything that might make him less of a ghost and more of a real target.

The trouble was, even if she did remember more, I wasn't sure it would be enough. Sam Whitaker was a needle in a haystack of countless names and shady figures involved in trafficking.

If my mother had noted him down, he must've been connected to the people she was investigating. I just had to connect him to Pierce and to the bodies now piling up in the morgue.

The sound of raised voices down the hallway shook me from my thoughts. I looked up just in time to see Tom storming into my office, his face a mask of barely contained rage. I'd expected this. I'd actually been waiting for it.

He barged into my office, not bothering to knock. "Hayes!" He slammed the door shut behind him. "What the hell were you thinking, signing a plea deal for Maria Alvarez without my approval?"

I leaned back in my chair, folding my arms. "I was thinking it was the right thing to do."

Tom narrowed his eyes, his voice tight with barely contained fury. "*The right thing to do*? You don't get to decide that. Especially not after I explicitly refused to sign off on this!" He crossed his arms, his posture stiff. "You don't seem to grasp the concept of chain of command, or maybe you just don't respect it. Either way, you are not just being reckless. You're being insubordinate."

Shaking his head, the frustration showed in every tense line on his face. "In case you've forgotten, the DA's office isn't your personal playground for crusades. You can't just bulldoze ahead with whatever deal you think is 'right' without considering the ramifications on the whole office, on the case, or on your career. Do you understand that? There are protocols, checks, and balances in place for a reason."

"Tom—" I started to say, but he didn't stop his rampage to listen.

"You've got every rookie ADA and intern talking about how you're acting like a loose cannon on this case. You're making *me* look like I don't have a handle on my team, like I've let this office become a circus. And for what? So you could follow your gut, ignoring everything we've built here? Alex, you've stepped way over the line here."

I stood, forcing him to meet my gaze. "With all due respect, Tom, it seems to me that you don't even *want* to approach the line these days. You, Shaw, Turner … none of you are interested in doing a proper investigation into this trafficking ring that Pierce is obviously connected to!"

Tom's face went red, and he let out an exasperated sigh. "Alex, you're seeing shadows again, just like you did with the Martin trial. Every time you can't see the path clearly, you jump to conspiracies."

I clenched my fists, anger surging within me. "And I was right about the Martin trial, wasn't I?" I shot back, my voice sharp. The words hung between us like a challenge, and for a moment, the office was silent. Tom's jaw clenched, and his eyes shifted, unwilling to acknowledge the truth of my statement.

He took a deep breath, clearly trying to rein in his frustration. "Maybe," he said slowly, "you need to take some time away from the office before this trial starts. Clear your head."

I pushed myself back from my desk, glaring at him. "How dare you even suggest that? If you try to take me off this trial, you'll have to answer for it publicly."

He crossed his arms, his tone icy. "That's a serious threat, Alex."

I lifted my chin. I wasn't going to back down. "I'm not threatening you, Tom. I'm telling you exactly how I'll take it."

For a long moment, we stared each other down. The tension was so thick it pressed against my skin. Finally, with a frustrated shake of his head, he turned and stormed out of my office. The door slammed behind him, rattling my office walls. I felt my own hands shake slightly as I exhaled, trying to release the anger coiled tight inside me.

I looked over at the file box sitting in the corner of my office—the one containing the warehouse case that was supposedly nothing more than a squatter's dispute. I grabbed it, deciding I couldn't stand to stay in this office another minute.

If Tom was going to play politics and undermine my work, fine. But I'd find my own way to get to the truth.

CHAPTER
TWENTY

AS I MADE my way down to the holding room where Victor Lane was waiting, I could already feel my blood pressure rising. I'd been poring over files from the warehouse case for hours, and everything in those documents screamed that Lane wasn't just some random squatter down on his luck. The man had connections—likely the kind that could lead me to the people running this trafficking ring. Whether he wanted to cooperate, I was going to find out.

The room was sterile and uninviting. Harsh fluorescent lighting, scuffed-up metal chairs, and a bolted-down table in the center. Lane was already seated, his legs stretched out in front of him, looking far too relaxed for a man in his position. He had a smirk plastered on his face, his eyes lazily tracking me as I entered.

I shut the door behind me, trying not to roll my eyes at the show he was putting on. "You seem pretty comfortable, Victor," I said, settling into the chair across from him. "A little too comfortable for someone squatting in an abandoned warehouse."

When he shrugged, his smirk widened. "What can I say? Some people just know how to make the best of a situation."

I raised an eyebrow, flipping open my file. "Funny. I usually see people in your situation looking more desperate. Down on their luck, you know? But here you are, acting like you own the place."

Lane leaned back, folding his arms behind his head like he was settling in for a nice chat. "Maybe I just don't scare easy."

I wasn't about to play his game. I flipped through a few pages of my notes, pausing at the inventory list of what had been found at the warehouse: ledgers, documents written in code, and various IDs. "You know, for a squatter, you've got some interesting taste in décor. Those ledgers, the coded notes, the ID cards we found there... not exactly what I'd expect from someone just trying to get by."

"Hey, a man's gotta keep himself entertained, right? Maybe I'm into puzzles."

"Because nothing says 'hobbyist' quite like keeping ledgers full of numbers and codes, IDs that don't belong to you, and," I flipped to the photograph of the evidence bag, "a little stash of fake passports. Care to explain that?"

Lane's smirk didn't falter. He leaned forward, resting his elbows on the table, and said, "Look, lady, I don't know what kind of conspiracy theories you're working on, but I don't know anything about any of that. I was just there to stay out of the cold."

"Oh, really?" I said, fighting to keep my tone neutral, but my patience was thinning. "So, it's just a big coincidence that you're found squatting in a warehouse filled with documents that point to some kind of trafficking operation? Just your average unlucky day, huh?"

Lane shrugged again, that infuriating grin never leaving his face. "I'm just a guy who needed a place to crash. I don't know about any of that other stuff. Whatever you found there—it's got nothing to do with me."

I leaned in, narrowing my gaze. "Do you really expect me to believe that?"

"Believe what you want, lady. I don't have to explain myself to you."

"Here's the thing, Victor," I said, leaning back in my chair and crossing my arms. "I could go for the maximum sentencing recommendation on this case. We're talking about a lengthy sentence for squatting, trespassing, and tampering with property connected to potential criminal activity. But if you cooperate—if you give me something real —maybe I could be persuaded to change my mind."

He scoffed, a derisive laugh escaping his lips. "Are you seriously trying to scare me with a squatting charge? Come on. No one's buying that."

"Are you sure about that?" I shot back, holding his gaze. "Because I don't think we're just talking about squatting here. I don't think you just stumbled into that warehouse looking for a roof over your head. In fact, I don't think you've been forthcoming about any of this."

His smirk wavered just a bit, but he quickly recovered, shaking his head. "You've got nothing. You're fishing."

"Fishing?" I leaned forward again, pressing my palms flat against the cold metal table between us. "You're sitting in the middle of a mess you can't explain, surrounded by items that suggest you're involved in something way bigger than a squatting charge."

For the first time, I saw a flicker of something in his eyes—uncertainty, maybe even a hint of fear. But then he forced a lazy grin back onto his face, shrugging it off. "I don't know what you're talking about," he said, voice a little less steady than before. "And I'm done talking. I want my lawyer."

I held his gaze for a long beat, the tension thick between us. Then I straightened, pushing my chair back and gathering my files. "Fine. Have it your way. But understand this. We're just getting started. And I don't think you'll like where this is headed."

Without another word, I turned on my heel and strode out of the interrogation room, barely resisting the urge to slam the door behind me. The fluorescent-lit halls of Harris Joint Processing Center felt stifling, and I wanted nothing more than to get back to the office, clear my head, and figure out my next steps.

———

Back at the DA's office, I stepped out of the elevator and let out a long, controlled breath, trying to shake off the frustration. Just as I started down the hall, I spotted Lisa heading in my direction, her arms full of folders, looking like she'd been holed up in courtrooms all morning.

Her eyebrows rose as she saw me approach. "Rough interrogation?"

"You could say that," I muttered, my irritation still simmering. "Lane just fed me the story of a lifetime. Apparently, he's an innocent squatter who just happened to stumble into a warehouse full of fake IDs, passports, and coded ledgers."

Lisa let out a low whistle. "Bold move. Does he think you're new to this?"

"Seems like it. And he asked for a lawyer the second I hinted at pressing for more details."

"Fake IDs, huh?" She shook her head, glancing at the folders in her arms. "I was just coming from a prelim for that fake ID case."

I blinked. "Wait. The case with those kids handing out IDs at clubs?"

"You think there could be a connection?"

I nodded, already working through the possibilities. "Victor's little warehouse was full of them. Different names, different photos, all fake. It wouldn't surprise me. He didn't seem like the type to be scrambling for a place to stay. I'm thinking he's tied to something bigger. And fake IDs would definitely be useful in trafficking circles."

Lisa bit her lip, glancing down at the folders in her hands. "My case isn't much—just a handful of arrests from a sting at a club. They were handing out IDs to underage kids, and a few of them were caught with IDs that didn't match up to any databases. But the names ... they're random, just aliases."

I ran a hand through my hair, thinking it over. "That's exactly the kind of low-level connection we might be missing. The warehouse IDs weren't matching up to any real people either. If someone's mass-producing these, it could be for more than just underage drinking."

"You think it's tied to a larger operation?"

"Maybe. And if it's connected to Pierce ..."

Lisa's eyes widened. "You really think this could be part of the same network?"

I looked down the hall, my mind racing. "It's possible. Pierce, the IDs, Lane's attitude ... It's all circling something bigger. Something organized."

Lisa chewed her lip. "So what's the next step?"

Straightening, I clutched the folder of notes tighter. "I'll need to dig deeper into those names Maria gave us. Maybe I should take a look at your fake ID case, too. See if any of the names match up."

Lisa nodded. "Let me know how I can help. I'll dig through my case notes too, see if anything stands out."

I placed a hand on her shoulder, grateful for the solidarity. "Thanks, Lisa. At least someone is willing to look further than the first guy they find. You'd think with forty-four bodies turning up, people might actually want to investigate all angles instead of just handing Pierce the whole case on a platter."

She smiled. "If there's a bottom, we'll get to it."

CHAPTER TWENTY-ONE

THE WAREHOUSE DISTRICT was even more desolate during the day. Its emptiness during the daytime wasn't as haunting as it was at night. Instead, the vacancy was harsh, glaring in the sunlight. Every detail stood out: the peeling paint on the corrugated metal walls; the discarded fast-food wrappers and cigarette butts littering the cracked concrete. There was no mystery here in the daylight, no shadows to hide the truth. Just stark reality.

I parked my car and waited for Turner. It wasn't lost on me that I'd practically dragged him here against his better judgment. I rubbed my shoulder absentmindedly as I got out of the car and a gust of wind blew against me. The winter air always had a way of making it ache a little bit more. My phone buzzed, and Turner's name flashed on the screen. I swiped to answer.

"You seriously think this is a good use of time?" Turner asked, his tone exasperated, before I could even say hello.

"What I think is, it's the only thing we haven't done," I countered, scanning the building's exterior. "I want to look for myself. This was only investigated as a low-level squatter's case, and I think there's more to it. I want to see if there's anything they missed."

Turner sighed, long and loud. "We've had forensics comb through every square inch. You think you're going to find something they didn't?"

"I don't know, Turner. But sitting on my hands waiting for trial doesn't feel right either."

There was a pause, followed by a long sigh. "Fine. I'm two minutes out. Don't touch anything."

Hanging up, I shoved the phone into my pocket as I paced the lot. The warehouse stood in front of me, its battered exterior almost mocking in its simplicity. I was already starting to hate this place. Something just didn't feel *right* about it. Like it had a history it was trying to cover up.

Turner's car pulled in, his SUV kicking up dust as it rolled to a stop beside mine. He stepped out, looking every bit as irritated as he'd sounded on the phone. His tie was loosened, his jacket slung over one shoulder, and his expression said, *I'd rather be anywhere but here.*

He slammed his car door shut. "Let's make this quick."

I led the way to the side entrance. The metal door creaked as I pushed it open, the sound grating in the stillness. Inside, the air was stale, carrying that faint metallic tang of rust and something more indefinable—an almost sweet decay that made my stomach turn.

The vast, empty space swallowed us as we stepped inside. Turner flicked on a flashlight despite the daylight filtering in through broken windows high above. The beams created harsh, angular shadows that flickered across the walls.

"I'm telling you," Turner said, his voice echoing within the space. "There's nothing here. This place has been swept clean."

"Then humor me," I shot back, moving toward the far corner where the office was.

The floor was scuffed, but not in a way that suggested anything recent. Pallets were stacked haphazardly, but they were empty and covered in dust. Crouching down, I ran my fingers over the concrete, feeling the grit stick to my skin.

Turner leaned against one of the pallets, watching me like I was wasting both our time. "What are you hoping to find, Alex?"

"Anything," I muttered, brushing my hands off on my jeans. "Anything that connects this place to Pierce. To someone."

"You think Pierce's DNA is just lying around waiting for you to find it in a random warehouse? And how are you going to find it anyway? By rubbing your own fingerprints in dust?"

I stood, narrowing my eyes at him. "I don't know, Turner. But if he didn't do this, then someone else did, and this place was part of it."

Turner sighed again, shaking his head. "You're spinning your wheels. This isn't how we win the case."

"We're not exactly winning it the way we're going, either."

He followed me toward the office, his footsteps heavy on the concrete. "You really think Pierce is innocent?" he asked, his voice quieter now but still carrying an edge.

I stopped at the office door, my hand on the handle, and looked over my shoulder at him. "I just know we don't have enough. Not for forty-four murder convictions."

Turner crossed his arms, leaning against the doorframe as I stepped inside. The office was just as grimy and barren as the warehouse floor —an overturned chair, a desk with one broken leg, a few scattered papers that turned out to be useless receipts for industrial supplies.

"You can't keep second-guessing the case," Turner said, his voice firmer now. "It doesn't help anyone."

"And you can't keep brushing off the gaps," I shot back. "We're not supposed to get convictions based on what feels convenient."

"We have a job to do. You can't let your personal feelings about Pierce—or anyone, for that matter—cloud your judgment."

"That's rich," I said, my voice rising. "Coming from the guy who doesn't even seem to care if we have the right man on trial."

His eyes narrowed. "Watch it, Hayes."

I stepped closer, my anger bubbling to the surface. "I'm tired of being dismissed, Turner. You and Shaw act like I'm some rookie who doesn't know what I'm doing. But I've been through hell for this job, and I'll be damned if I let someone like you tell me how to do it."

His expression softened for a moment, but he recovered quickly, his posture stiffening. "This isn't about you," he said quietly. "It's about justice. And sometimes, justice means working with what you've got."

"Or maybe," I said, my voice shaking, "it means not settling for half-truths and hoping no one notices."

Without giving him a chance to respond, I Turned on my heel, brushed past him and headed for the exit. My footsteps echoed through the warehouse, each one a sharp reminder of how much work lay ahead—and how little faith I had in the people around me to do it.

Outside, the sunlight felt harsh and unrelenting. I took a deep breath, trying to steady my pounding heart. Turner emerged a moment later, but he didn't say anything. He just stood there, watching as I got into my car.

I didn't look back as I drove away. The warehouse disappeared in my rearview mirror, but the weight of it—the emptiness, the futility, the nagging feeling that we were missing something—stayed with me.

CHAPTER TWENTY-TWO

I KNOCKED LIGHTLY on Shaw's office door, fully aware he'd probably been expecting me. He looked up, barely disguising the irritation on his face.

"Ah, Alex," he said, his voice clipped. "Something I can help you with?"

I took a steadying breath, leaning against the doorframe. "Just checking in on the Pierce trial status. Wanted to see where we stand with scheduling."

He didn't look up from the file he was marking up. "Everything's lined up. I already had a scheduling conference with the judge and defense. Trial's set to begin in sixty days."

I blinked, stunned. "Sixty days? Why are we rushing things?"

Shaw's eyes finally met mine, his expression impassive. "Defense agreed. They want this done with quickly."

Of course they would. But that wasn't the only issue. "You held a scheduling conference without me?" My voice was barely controlled, my irritation clear. He'd done this deliberately, sidestepping me once again.

"Not at all," Shaw replied smoothly, a faint smirk tugging at his lips. "I went and looked for you, but apparently you were off at some warehouse. I couldn't keep the judge waiting."

I bit back the retort on the tip of my tongue. I knew Shaw well enough by now to understand that he was testing boundaries, trying to box me out. But I wasn't about to let that slide.

"Fine," I said tightly, crossing my arms. "Have there been any updates from Turner on forensics? Any additional evidence that actually ties Pierce to the murders beyond just proximity?"

Shaw waved a dismissive hand. "Nothing new has come up. But it's not a concern. We have what we need to move forward."

Clenching my jaw so hard it hurt, I wanted to confront him then and there about his connection to my mother. But I knew better. Now wasn't the time. Shaw was already watching me closely, waiting for any sign of pushback. And besides, I had another case to take care of.

"Fine," I replied, my tone resigned, though I felt anything but. "Let me know if anything else comes up."

I left his office without another word, making my way toward the parking lot to head back to JPC. The drive was quiet, my mind spinning with Shaw's dismissive attitude and the unanswered questions piling up faster than I could deal with them. I was becoming more convinced by the day that Shaw and Turner were trying to keep me in the dark about the full extent of Pierce's connections. Maybe even Tom was in on it.

At JPC, I checked in and made my way down the drab corridor to the assigned meeting room. Rachel Saunders was already seated on the other side of the table, dressed in an orange jumpsuit, her arms crossed defensively. In her late twenties, slim, with pale skin that looked as if she hadn't seen sunlight in months. Her brown hair was pulled back in a messy bun, and her eyes darted to the door when I entered, full of suspicion.

I noted Rachel's guarded expression. Her shoulders were tense, and she kept glancing toward the door as if planning her escape route.

Seated next to her was her attorney, a wiry man in his forties with glasses perched low on his nose. He looked up as I stepped in, giving me a polite nod.

"Ms. Hayes," he greeted. "We've been waiting."

I nodded back, pulling a chair out across from them and setting down my case file. "Ms. Saunders, Mr ...?"

"Franklin," the attorney replied, extending a hand. His grip was firm but quick, businesslike.

"Mr. Franklin," I acknowledged, then turned to Rachel. "Rachel, I'm here to discuss the charges against you."

She looked away, chewing on her lip, clearly nervous. I took that as my cue to continue.

"You're facing charges of embezzlement and attempted flight from justice," I began, glancing down at the file. "You allegedly stole a substantial sum from your employer and tried to flee the country. Care to explain?"

Rachel's gaze snapped back to me, a flash of defiance lighting up her eyes. "I was tricked into doing it."

Her attorney shifted beside her. "Rachel, maybe it's best if you—"

"No," she interrupted, shaking her head. "I want her to know. I wouldn't do something like this of my own accord."

I arched a brow, watching her carefully. "You'll have to explain that."

She pressed her lips together, glancing sideways at Franklin as if seeking permission. He gave her a resigned nod, clearly sensing that she wasn't going to keep quiet.

"I applied for a job online," she started. "It was supposed to be remote, just admin work, you know? Seemed harmless. No interviews or anything—they just sent me instructions and checks. At first, it seemed too good to be true, I guess. But I needed the money."

She looked down, her hands trembling. "Then things changed. The tasks they gave me got more suspicious. Like, I was asked to transfer money to different accounts, go to specific banks, meet specific people. But no one ever used names."

"Go on," I said, leaning in slightly.

"It all happened so fast," she continued, her voice wavering. "One day, I got a notification that there was a warrant out for me. I panicked. I tried to reach out to whoever it was, these people I'd been working for. They just told me to keep quiet and that they'd take care of things. The next thing I knew, they gave me a plane ticket and told me to get out of the country."

Opening the file, I scanned the details. My eyes landed on the destination for the ticket: Venezuela. The same destination on Pierce's plane ticket. Coincidence was starting to feel like an absurd notion in this case.

"This plane ticket," I said, holding up the document from her file. "Do you know why they wanted you to go to Venezuela?"

Rachel shook her head quickly. "No. I didn't ask any questions. I was terrified. They'd gotten me into so much trouble already. And I thought if I didn't do what they said—I thought they'd hurt me."

I leaned forward, my gaze fixed on her. "What made you think they'd hurt you?"

Rachel's eyes darted to her attorney, who gave her a small, reassuring nod. She swallowed hard and barely met my eyes, her voice dropping to a whisper. "There were … other girls. Sometimes, I'd be told to meet them and do a handoff—exchange money, packages, things like that. They were like me, I think. Pulled into this without really knowing what they were doing."

She looked down, her hands twisting in her lap. "But after a while, they'd just disappear. I'd ask the guys what happened, where they went, and they'd just shrug it off. Told me to mind my business and focus on my own work." Her hands gripped the edge of the table. "One girl, Jenny—she was scared all the time, just like me. She'd talk about getting out, leaving it all behind. And then, one day, she was just gone. Poof. Like she'd never existed. I didn't ask about her after that."

Nodding, I let the silence hang between us for a moment. "So, you're telling me these girls just vanished? And no one would tell you why?"

Rachel's voice trembled. "No one would say anything. It was like—I don't know, like they'd been erased. That's when I realized I was in too deep. It wasn't just money. It was something bigger, and if I didn't play along, I was afraid I'd be next."

I leaned back, processing this. "Rachel, I need you to think carefully. Can you describe any of the people you worked with? Anyone who stands out?"

She looked down, seeming to search her memory. "They were all ordinary-looking, honestly. Except for one guy. He had a scorpion tattoo on his neck. He ... he was different. Gave orders, didn't say much, but when he did, everyone listened."

Scorpion. The same name I'd gotten from Maria.

Franklin cleared his throat, shifting in his seat. "Ms. Hayes, in light of what Rachel has shared, I'd like to ask if the DA's office would consider a plea deal. Rachel's involvement here was coerced, and she's clearly willing to cooperate."

I kept my gaze steady on him. "If Rachel continues to be honest with us and is willing to help identify those she worked for, then yes, a plea deal is on the table. But I'm going to need every detail she can remember, and we'll need to compile everything on the people she worked for."

Franklin nodded, visibly relieved. Rachel's face relaxed slightly as well, though she still looked on edge.

"Alright," I said, standing up. "Mr. Franklin, work with Rachel to gather everything you can. I'll need you to help me corroborate as much as possible—records, communications, anything that could help establish a pattern. We'll review her bank statements and try to piece together her transactions."

Franklin gave me a sharp nod. "Understood. I'll make sure you get everything."

I cast one last look at Rachel, who seemed a little more grounded now that she knew there was a way out. "Thank you for telling me all this. Just remember, every detail matters."

Rachel nodded, her voice quiet. "I will. I don't want to be a part of this anymore."

With that, I gathered my files and left the room. As I got in my car to drive back to the office, my phone buzzed. Lisa's name lit up on the screen.

When I answered, her voice came through, tense and urgent. "Alex, I think I found something."

CHAPTER
TWENTY-THREE

I LEANED over the edge of Lisa's cubicle, making her jump as she juggled a stack of files. "What've you got for me?"

Looking up, a little startled, her eyes sparkled with that look she got when she'd cracked something big. "I think you're going to want to sit down for this one."

I raised an eyebrow. "I think we're beyond surprising each other at this point, don't you?"

She laughed, but there was a tension there, too. "Trust me, this one might do it. Let's go to your office so we don't have any accidental eavesdroppers."

My interest piqued, I nodded, motioning toward my office. She gathered a thick bundle of files plus her laptop and followed me, managing to keep pace despite the weight of what she was carrying. Once inside, I shut the door, and Lisa immediately spread the files across my desk, sorting through them until she found the folder she wanted.

Lisa leaned in, her eyes practically gleaming with excitement. "Okay, so here's what happened. Originally I was just trying to sort out some of the bank statements from my fake ID case. But there was this one account that kept coming up with weird deposits and withdrawals, all tied to a business name that felt a little too generic. I decided to cross-check it with the Pierce evidence folder to see if there were any ties, figuring it'd be a long shot."

I nodded, urging her to continue, already feeling a prickle of anticipation.

"Then I hit a pattern," Lisa continued, clearly enjoying the reveal. "That same business name was also on one of the financial documents they'd found at the warehouse. It wasn't much, just a few transfers and one or two phone records, but it was enough for me to dig deeper." Flipping open a file, she pointed to a few highlighted lines. "I followed it back, searching through all these shell companies and subsidiary businesses. And boom. Every single one of them linked back to a company called Lighthouse Ventures, LLC."

I leaned forward, the name already imprinting itself on my mind. "So, Lighthouse Ventures is behind all of it?"

Lisa nodded, beaming. "I was so excited when I found it! But then I kept going, just to make sure. When I ran a background check on Lighthouse Ventures, I found something even better." She pulled another paper from the stack, handing it to me. "Check this out. Back in the early days, they had one annual report signed by an actual owner before they switched everything to registered agents."

I skimmed the document she handed me, and my eyes stopped cold on a single name. "Sam Whitaker," I said aloud, my mind racing.

"Exactly! I recognized it from Maria Alvarez's tape. He's listed as the original owner, which means he was involved from the very start. And he's not just any Sam Whitaker, either. This guy's got connections. He's a criminal defense attorney, mainly working in another circuit, but he's also a state legislator. He's one of those low-profile, high-influence types who work in the background, pulling strings. He's donated to multiple political campaigns over the years."

A chill ran down my spine as she went on. "In fact, he's backed some people we know pretty well—Tom's last re-election campaign, for one. And even our good old former mayor."

I took a slow, steadying breath, tightening my fingers around the edge of my desk as I processed the connections Lisa had uncovered. My mind ran through the implications, a web of potential leads stretching out before me. But one thought pulsed above the rest: If

Whitaker was in any way tied to Pierce or the trafficking network, this might explain Tom's reluctance to dig deeper.

Lisa looked at me, her eyes still alight with excitement. "I mean, what are the odds, right? Whitaker's name doesn't just pop up on a shell company tied to Pierce, the fake IDs, and your warehouse case by coincidence. And it could explain why we keep hitting resistance every time we try to open this investigation. If Whitaker's got his fingers in everything, this could be way bigger than just Pierce."

Swallowing hard, I tried to keep my face neutral even as my thoughts spun. I didn't want to consider that Tom might be involved—his loyalty and dedication had always seemed unwavering. But Whitaker's ties to him, that was hard to ignore.

I cleared my throat. "Good work, Lisa. This might be our first solid lead into something bigger. We can't let this go."

"I can keep looking into Whitaker's campaign contributions, any other holdings he's got, and even his cases. But I have a feeling we're going to need more than just us on this."

"You're right," I said, my mind landing on the one person who could help us dig deeper. "Actually, I know someone who can get us even further with Whitaker's financials."

Without another word, I dialed Cheryl Moultrie's number. She picked up on the second ring, her tone all business as usual. Cheryl was a sharp, no-nonsense attorney from the transactional side of the office, known for her uncanny ability to find patterns in financial chaos. She'd traded a high-paying career as an actuary for the steadier pace of government work, and her precision with numbers made her an invaluable ally when cases involved complex financial evidence.

"Cheryl, it's Alex. Lisa and I need your expertise on a certain individual's finances and holdings," I said, a faint smirk tugging at my lips. "How soon can we meet?"

"For you? I've got an opening in five," she replied, her voice sharp and curious. "Bring me something interesting, Alex."

"On our way," I replied, hanging up.

Lisa raised an eyebrow as I grabbed my notes and motioned for her to follow me out. "Guess we're about to get an expert opinion," she said with a grin.

"Cheryl's the best," I said, as we made our way to the elevator. "If there's a money trail, she'll find it."

————

We made our way to Cheryl's office, pausing before knocking. Inside, a mix of incense and faint perfume hung in the air, courtesy of the two incense sticks burning on her desk. Cheryl looked up, her expression both focused and welcoming. She was in her mid-fifties, her hair flecked with gray, and she had a steady gaze that hinted at years of experience mixed with a wry humor.

Her office had only grown more distinct since I'd last seen it—a cozy clutter of personality layered over the official paperwork of her job. A large coffee mug with "I'd rather be cross-examining" printed in bold letters held an assortment of pens next to a small potted plant that looked suspiciously like a succulent she'd rescued from neglect. A few new frames adorned the walls, displaying feline-themed cross-stitches that made me smile despite myself. "I practice claw and order," one read, alongside a simpler one with "Judge Cats, Not Meow."

Cheryl looked up as we entered, her sharp eyes narrowing with curiosity as she spotted the unfamiliar face beside me. "Well, well," she said, setting her mug aside. "Alex Hayes, bringing fresh faces to my office?"

I gestured to Lisa, who stepped forward. "Cheryl Moultrie, this is Lisa Cooper, one of the ADAs working with me. Lisa, meet Cheryl, our in-house expert on all things buried and bureaucratic."

Cheryl extended her hand, her expression warming. "Nice to meet you, Lisa. I'm the one who digs up what's left after everyone else is done shredding."

Lisa shook her hand with a smile. "I've heard great things about your work, Cheryl. And I'm a fan of the décor."

Cheryl chuckled, leaning back in her chair. "Well, now that the pleasantries are out of the way, what's got you two traipsing into my den?"

I handed over the top document with Whitaker's name highlighted.

"We need to know everything about this man's finances. Campaign contributions, shell companies, bank accounts. If he's so much as put a dollar down on anything shady, we need to know about it."

She took the file, her gaze flicking over the name and the details Lisa had found. "Sam Whitaker … rings a bell. Isn't he in the state legislature?"

I nodded. "He's also been involved with some questionable business practices, to say the least. We're connecting him to Lighthouse Ventures, LLC, which has come up in three separate cases."

Cheryl's eyebrows shot up as she leafed through the pages. "So, he's covering up illegal activities through this shell company?"

"That's what we're trying to figure out," Lisa chimed in. "We think he's tied to a trafficking ring—maybe not directly— but we're starting to see his name pop up in too many places to ignore."

Cheryl glanced between us, a shrewd smile tugging at the corner of her lips. "This sounds like my kind of challenge. Give me a few hours, and I'll see what I can pull together."

"Thanks, Cheryl," I said, feeling a surge of relief. "This could be exactly what we need to start unraveling his connections."

Cheryl nodded, already absorbed in the documents, her pen moving as she made notes in the margins. "I assume you want this kept quiet?"

Lisa and I exchanged glances. "Very quiet," I said, keeping my tone low. "As far as anyone knows, we're looking into some corporate irregularities for a standard review."

"Got it," Cheryl said with a nod, her eyes gleaming. "I'll have something for you soon."

As Lisa and I headed back to the elevator, she glanced at me, her expression thoughtful. "If Cheryl does find something big … what's our next move?"

I let out a breath, mentally bracing myself for the direction this was heading. "We take it to Tom. He won't have a choice but to look into it if it's right in front of him. But let's cross that bridge when we get there."

The elevator doors slid open, and we stepped inside, both lost in our own thoughts as we rode back up to our floor. Lisa finally broke the silence, her voice tentative.

"Do you think maybe Tom knows more about Whitaker than he's letting on? Like, is there any chance he's actively trying to bury this?"

I didn't answer right away, the thought hitting a little too close to the suspicions I'd been fighting off since this whole thing started. "I don't know, Lisa. But if he is, we're about to find out."

CHAPTER
TWENTY-FOUR

IT WAS FRIDAY AFTERNOON, and I'd spent the morning at my desk, getting caught up on much needed low-level items. Lisa sat across from me, working on a few of her own cases. I couldn't blame her for wanting to sit in my office rather than out in her cubicle. It was definitely a quieter environment as far as getting work done was concerned.

As soon as my phone buzzed, I picked it up to hear Rachel Saunders' attorney on the other end. I shot Lisa a quick look, signaling her to hang tight, and leaned back in my chair.

"This is Alex Hayes."

"Ms. Hayes, this is Phil Franklin, Rachel Saunders' attorney. She's been more cooperative, and I think I've got something that might help."

I straightened in my seat, pen in hand. "Alright, go ahead."

"Rachel finally described the man who recruited her for the job," he said. "Middle-aged guy, maybe late thirties. Clean-cut, always dressed business casual. And there's a younger guy she worked with, bald with tattoos. And as you know, the one with a scorpion tattoo on his neck."

I raised an eyebrow, jotting it down. "Anything else?"

Franklin hesitated before he continued. "She said she was approached by a staffing agency, supposedly. But here's where it gets odd. Rachel noticed they never hired anyone openly. The name of the agency kept changing, like they'd register under a different name for each assignment."

Interesting. I'd already suspected the agency was a front for something more, and this fit the pattern we'd seen. "Did she ever meet the owner or know who was behind the agency?"

"No," he replied. "They were careful about that, always referring to someone just called 'the office.' And from what she said, they used drop points around town for money pickups. These 'safe houses' were always located in the same handful of spots."

"Houston locations?"

"Yeah, mostly around downtown. You might want to check with the more reputable businesses in that area—Rachel said these locations were hidden in plain sight."

"Can you get this typed up and sent over to me?"

"I think I can arrange that. How are we on a plea deal?"

"I'll have it to you in the next few days," I said, internally wincing at the idea of going to Tom about another deal.

"I'll be waiting for it."

I thanked him and ended the call, still processing what he'd shared when Lisa leaned in, raising an eyebrow.

"So, are you going to take this to Tom? See if he'll approve a plea deal?"

I exhaled. "I'll have to. Franklin and Rachel are giving us something real here. Tom can't ignore this."

Lisa nodded, looking satisfied. Just then, my phone buzzed again. Cheryl.

"Hey, Alex," Cheryl greeted me. "I've got some updates on Whitaker's financials that might interest you. Can you and Lisa come up here?"

"We're on our way," I replied, and with a quick nod to Lisa, we headed for the elevator.

When we reached Cheryl's office, she waved us inside, her usual organized chaos scattered across her desk. She'd already pulled up documents on her computer and cleared a spot for the mess of printouts and notes she'd prepared for us.

"Alright," she started, motioning us into chairs. "I've been digging around in Whitaker's financials. He's meticulous, I'll give him that. Lots of shell companies and 'consulting' expenses that don't seem to add up. But here's what I found."

She turned her monitor toward us, displaying a flowchart linking Whitaker's business connections to various names and companies. "He's got a stake in three shell companies, all of which are connected to Lighthouse Ventures, LLC."

I leaned in to look.

"Lighthouse Ventures, according to public filings, is in the business of 'logistics and workforce solutions,' but when I dug deeper, they have no verifiable employees."

"Suspicious," Lisa muttered, crossing her arms as she studied the screen.

Cheryl tapped a few keys and pulled up another screen. "Now, here's the kicker. Whitaker's been doing more than just shady legal work. Turns out, he's been cozy with several figures connected to our former mayor.

"Whitaker not only represented some of his associates, but even funneled campaign funds to support him. He's got his hand in a lot of dirty pockets."

Lisa's jaw dropped. "It's like every rock we turn over, he's under it."

I nodded, turning to Cheryl. "Have you looked at his legislative record?"

"I pulled that, too," she said, handing Lisa a thick stack of papers. "He's voted down every bill related to workplace protections. Like he's actively working to keep these loopholes open."

Lisa thumbed through the pages, shaking her head in disbelief. "He's helping to keep these operations running. I'll go through this in more detail, see if there's any pattern or ties that might signal he's doing favors for his friends."

The weight of it all settled on me. Whitaker was connected to Pierce, to Lighthouse Ventures, and now to this network Rachel had stumbled into. And if Whitaker had been involved with my mother's case … I didn't want to finish that thought, not here, and not with Lisa and Cheryl watching.

"Thanks, Cheryl. This is more than I expected. It's … it's big."

Cheryl just shrugged, but there was pride in her eyes. "I don't trust half the people he's been tied to, but I'm glad to help you nail him."

Lisa tapped the stack of documents on her lap. "So, what's next?"

I took a breath. "We need to dig into Whitaker's campaign contributions, his investments, everything he's touched in recent years. If he's tied this closely to Pierce's operation, we need to bring it to light."

Cheryl nodded, and Lisa gave a determined nod of her own. We thanked Cheryl and left her office, both of us walking back to our floor in silence, each processing the implications of what we'd just learned.

After dropping Lisa at her cubicle, I returned to my office, locking the door behind me. Grabbing a legal pad from the drawer, I quickly wrote down a transcript of the anonymous calls. The voice and its words were so ingrained in my head, it wasn't like I could forget what they said. I traced my finger over each line, rereading them as if they might suddenly reveal some hidden meaning.

Your mother's disappearance was not an accident.

Be careful. Not everyone is who they seem.

Pierce was just a pawn, and pawns can be replaced.

She may still be alive.

The connection to my mother's case felt like a vise tightening around me. The idea that she could still be alive wasn't something I could even fully think about or process at the moment.

And then there was Whitaker. He was more than just a name—he was a link to Pierce, to the warehouse, and possibly to my mother's disappearance. The more I uncovered, the more certain I became that this case went far deeper than I'd ever imagined. Far deeper than Turner, Shaw, or even Matthews seemed to want to dig.

I debated telling Lisa about the calls, about how Whitaker's name had come up before. She'd be able to help me piece it together. Having someone else to weigh in might finally bring some clarity to these shadows I'd been chasing. But I wasn't ready to share it all, not yet. I tore off the piece of a paper and shredded it before tossing the pieces in my trash.

CHAPTER
TWENTY-FIVE

A MONTH FROM NOW, Randall Pierce would be standing trial. The case preparation was in full swing, or at least it was supposed to be. I'd been poring over evidence files, names, bank accounts, and campaign contributions for weeks alongside Lisa and Cheryl. Together, we'd combed through Sam Whitaker's legislative record and financial dealings, hoping to find something concrete that connected him to Pierce or the trafficking ring.

The connections were there, but frustratingly thin—a messy network of campaign donations and strategic voting records that painted a troubling picture but offered no solid evidence. Just a trail of whispers that Whitaker was involved in more than just passing state laws. Every day, our suspicions were ignored. Shaw and Turner had dismissed nearly everything we'd brought forward, waving away any leads beyond Pierce himself.

It left a bad taste in my mouth. After weeks of feeling like I was running circles, my interactions with Shaw had dwindled down to terse emails and silent meetings. But my suspicions of him and Turner had only grown.

A knock on my door barely registered through the clutter of paperwork I'd been drowning in for the past hour. I looked up to see Lisa leaning against the doorframe, a slight smirk on her face. She held a folder in her hand, tapping it against her thigh.

"Got something interesting," she announced.

I set my pen down. "Please tell me it's a lead worth following. I'm about ready to throw half these files out the window and call it a day."

Lisa slipped into my office, easing into the chair across from my desk. "Just got word of a case in Galveston County. Marcus Ellis is defending a guy charged with domestic violence against his girlfriend."

I straightened, eyeing her with interest. "Ellis? He usually only takes big-ticket cases. Why would he take a run-of-the-mill domestic assault in a neighboring jurisdiction?"

"Exactly what I thought," she replied, crossing one leg over the other. "It doesn't add up. The guy Ellis is defending—there's nothing remarkable about him on the surface. It's not like he's some wealthy businessman or politician. Makes you wonder what's special about him, doesn't it?"

Tapping my fingers against the desk, I felt a familiar itch of curiosity start to build. "Got time for a road trip?"

She grinned. "Always."

———

The drive to Galveston County took about an hour, but it felt like we'd stepped into another world. The quiet, palm tree-lined streets and slower pace of the coastal town felt surreal compared to the relentless pulse of Houston. As we pulled up in front of the Galveston County District Attorney's office, I glanced at the building—smaller, less imposing than what we were used to. The beige, almost sun-bleached walls and clean, manicured front steps made it feel strangely approachable.

We walked up the front steps, passing a few palm trees that swayed lazily in the breeze. It was odd to be handling anything serious in a place that looked so tranquil. But I reminded myself that appearances could be deceiving. I'd learned that lesson enough times to know better.

Inside, I approached the receptionist, a young woman who looked like she'd just graduated college. "Hi," I said, putting on my best professional smile. "I'm here to see ADA Collins."

She nodded, motioning for us to take a seat before picking up the phone. "Ms. Collins will be out in a minute," she said, placing the receiver down.

Silence prevailed as we waited for a few minutes, my heart beating faster in the sterile white walls and hum of the fluorescent lights. Lisa, in contrast, practically buzzed with anticipation beside me.

Finally, a woman in her late thirties with shoulder-length brown hair and a warm, but no-nonsense look about her appeared. "Alex Hayes, right?" she said, extending a hand. "I'm Rachel Collins."

I shook her hand, noting her firm grip. "Thanks for taking the time to meet with us, Ms. Collins. This is my colleague, Lisa Cooper."

As soon as we entered her office, Collins offered a polite smile, but I could see the curiosity flicker in her eyes. She gestured for us to sit and settled into her chair. "So, what can I do for you?"

I leaned forward, glancing at Lisa before speaking. "We're here to discuss the Emily Wells case. We're hoping you can fill us in on some details."

Collins raised an eyebrow. "Emily Wells? I wasn't expecting anyone from Harris County to take an interest in that one. What's brought it to your attention?"

"Word got to us that Marcus Ellis is handling the defense. For someone like Ellis to pick up a routine domestic violence case is unusual, to say the least. That alone raised red flags. He's defense on another case, and I want to see if they could be related."

Collins nodded, thumbing through a stack of files on her desk before finding the right one and pushing a thin folder toward me. "You're right. It didn't sit right with us either. Emily Wells is young. Just twenty-two. The defendant, Jack Hendricks, is in his forties. The whole situation feels off."

I flipped open the file and studied the mug shot of Jack Hendricks. Gruff-looking, with narrow eyes and a faint scar along his jawline, he had that cocky, defiant look I'd seen a hundred times before—a face that seemed to dare anyone to question him. I handed the file over to Lisa, who glanced at the photo, her brow furrowing.

"He could be a match for 'Slim,'" she murmured, almost to herself. "Maria mentioned that scar and the lean build. It lines up, doesn't it?"

I nodded. "Has Hendricks been cooperative?"

Collins let out a humorless laugh. "If by 'cooperative' you mean stonewalling us every step of the way, then yes. Ellis has been working overtime to make sure we don't get anything from him."

I leaned back, trying to make sense of it all. "And what about Emily? Has she been willing to talk?"

Collins sighed, a hint of frustration in her eyes. "It's been hit or miss. You know how it goes with domestic violence victims. They start to talk, then they backpedal. The cycle of abuse is brutal to break."

A familiar weight settled in my chest. I'd seen it so many times before. The way some men manipulated, controlled, and isolated women until they felt they had nowhere to turn. And even if they managed to escape, the psychological scars were deep enough to make them question their own reality. "Yeah," I said quietly. "It's heartbreaking. And infuriating."

Collins nodded. "Emily started to open up a bit, though. At first, it sounded like just another tragic case. She mentioned how he'd slap her around if she didn't listen, but then she hinted at something more."

I sat up straighter. "What do you mean?"

"She told us that the night of the last incident, they'd come home from a party. And apparently, he was furious because she didn't 'follow orders.'" Collins's mouth twisted with distaste. "She didn't explain much, but from the little she shared, it sounds like these 'parties' were more than just social gatherings."

Lisa and I exchanged a glance. I could feel the tension in the air between us. "Did she describe these parties?" I pressed.

Collins hesitated, her gaze shifting. "Not in detail. But she mentioned that they were gatherings with lots of young women, most of them barely of legal age, and older men. She said the women were 'passed around' and expected to ... follow instructions."

My stomach twisted. "And Hendricks? Did she say what he did at these parties?"

"Not much, but it was clear he had a role in controlling the women, and he wasn't working alone." Collins's voice softened. "Emily stopped talking after that. She's scared. I can't blame her."

"Is there any chance she'd be willing to talk to us?" I asked, my voice careful. "Even just for a few minutes?"

Collins sighed, looking uncertain. "I can't make any promises. She's been through a lot. But I can give you her address. Just go easy on her, alright?"

"Of course," I said, nodding. "Thank you, Rachel."

As we left, Lisa looked as grim as I felt. We climbed into the car, the weight of what we'd just learned pressing down on us. This wasn't just a routine domestic violence case. There was something bigger going on here, and Hendricks seemed to be right in the middle of it. And if he was, then so was Ellis, whether he knew it or not.

CHAPTER
TWENTY-SIX

AS WE PULLED AWAY from the courthouse, my mind wandered back to the days when I'd done these types of field visits with Andrews. He'd been gruff and mostly unbearable, but I'd learned from him. More than that, we'd had a real partnership, the kind where you could see where the other was going without saying a word.

Turner, on the other hand, was a different story. If I could even call it a "partnership," it felt forced, shallow. And Shaw? I couldn't figure him out either. Both were disinterested in pushing this investigation any further.

I glanced over at Lisa, who was scrolling through something on her phone as I drove. She caught my eye and raised an eyebrow. "What?"

"Shaw, Turner, and Matthews," I began, weighing my words. "Why are they all so quick to shut down any lead that could connect Pierce to something bigger?"

Lisa pursed her lips, her fingers stopping mid-scroll. "Maybe they just don't want to complicate things. High-profile cases attract scrutiny, and if there's nothing solid, maybe they just don't see the point in following thin threads."

"That's the thing, though," I said, tightening my grip on the wheel. "There's this whole web tangled around Pierce, but they don't want to look past him. It's almost as if they don't want to see what's there."

"Maybe it's just the pressure, Alex. High-profile cases can make people play it safe. Could be they're just trying to avoid any wild-goose chases." She was quiet for a beat. "But I get what you're saying."

I thought about telling her more, about the anonymous calls that kept nudging me in different directions, about how they hinted at things just beyond my reach. But I held back, letting that impulse fade as we turned onto the street leading to the address Rachel had given me.

The neighborhood was quiet, lined with neatly pruned hedges and broad, stately trees. The house itself came into view, larger than I'd expected, with a sprawling lawn and a modern, well-kept exterior. Not exactly the kind of place I'd pictured for a twenty-two-year-old without a high school diploma who'd been mixed up in shady circles.

Lisa looked at me, her expression mirroring my own confusion. "Emily's place, huh?"

"Apparently," I said, pulling up to the curb.

We climbed out and approached the door. The silence was thick, only broken by the occasional bird or the soft rustle of leaves in the slight breeze. I knocked on the door, exchanging a glance with Lisa as we waited.

The door swung open, revealing a man who could've been a bouncer in some upscale nightclub. Tall, broad-shouldered, and a face that practically screamed trouble. He had a tattoo peeking out from just below his left ear, partially obscured by his short hair—small, easily missed unless you were looking for it. But it was there. A scorpion.

My pulse quickened as I straightened. "I'm Assistant District Attorney Alex Hayes," I said, flipping open my badge. "We're here to speak with Emily Wells. Is she home?"

The man's face shifted, his posture turning defensive. "She's not talking to anyone. And neither am I."

"Wait," I said before he could shut the door, my mind racing. "We spoke to Slim. He told us to give you a message, Scorpion."

That made him pause. He stared at me, clearly surprised, but trying to hide it. That pause was all I needed to confirm what I suspected: Hendricks was Slim. And this man, with his stony silence and wary eyes, was Scorpion.

He didn't move. Just stood there, watching me, waiting, as if expecting me to recite some secret code. That hesitation—that single second where he waited for me to deliver something specific—was enough to make me think he'd had his share of dealings with people on the inside. Was it possible he'd paid off other ADAs to look the other way? My mind ran through the possibilities as I quickly cobbled together a message in my head.

"Whitaker and Pierce are moving things around again," I said, keeping my tone low and cryptic. "Thought you'd want to know."

The man's jaw tightened just slightly, a flicker of something in his eyes that I couldn't quite place—surprise, irritation, or maybe just suspicion. Whatever it was, he didn't give me much more before his expression hardened, and he shook his head.

"We're done here," he said, slamming the door shut.

Lisa and I exchanged a look, the weight of what had just happened settling between us as we turned and walked back to the car.

"That went well," she muttered, slipping into the passenger seat.

I slid in behind the wheel and started the car, pulling away from the curb.

"What do you think?" Lisa asked, studying me as I kept my eyes on the road.

My mind was racing with implications. "I think this was bigger than just some intimidation tactic," I replied. "The fact that he paused at all tells me that there's a lot more going on here. He knew exactly who Slim was. He knew about Whitaker and Pierce."

Lisa nodded, clearly considering it. "But the trial starts in a month. We're on a clock here, and there's only so much we can do before they really start shutting things down on us."

I gritted my teeth, the tension simmering beneath my skin. "Believe me, I'm aware. We're cutting it close, but that just means we need to work twice as hard. We can't afford to miss anything."

Lisa was silent for a while as I drove, the weight of our shared thoughts filling the space between us. She knew as well as I did that we were up against the clock—and people actively trying to keep us from uncovering the truth.

CHAPTER
TWENTY-SEVEN

THE CLOCK on my desk clicked over to 8:37 a.m., a taunting reminder of how little progress I'd made and how quickly time was slipping by. Papers and files lay scattered across my desk in a chaotic mess—notes from every lead Lisa and I had pursued over the last month, each one promising to be the breakthrough, and each one fizzling into nothing. The frustration sat heavy in my chest, an ache I couldn't shake.

The Pierce trial was set to start in one week, and I had nothing left to offer. Nothing substantial to link the trafficking ring to Pierce. Nothing to solidify the knowledge that he was just a pawn, a cog in a much larger and more sinister machine. And certainly nothing that would help me make sense of the scorpion-tattooed man or the mysterious names like Whitaker, Slim, and Scorpion that seemed to float just out of reach, teasing me with their connection to it all.

A sharp knock at my door snapped me out of my spiral. I looked up, and there was Shaw, standing in the doorway, his expression unreadable as always. We hadn't exchanged more than a handful of words in weeks, and the tension between us had grown thick enough to cut with a knife.

I gestured vaguely toward the chair across from my desk, resisting the urge to roll my eyes. "Come in."

He closed the door behind him but didn't sit right away. Instead, he stood there, staring at me as if assessing my mood. "I wanted to talk strategy for the trial."

I leaned back in my chair, crossing my arms. "I figured you'd be handling everything. That's how we left it, right?"

Shaw finally sat, but his posture was stiff. He wasn't the relaxed, cocky senior ADA who usually sauntered through the office like he owned the place. Today, he looked wary. "I want you to handle opening statements."

I blinked at him, trying to gauge whether he was serious. "You think I should do opening?"

He nodded, his expression unreadable. "You'll resonate better with the jury. You've got the conviction and the presence for it. I want you on the opening and direct, to set the tone from the start. I'll handle cross and closing. And I'll need you there for jury selection."

I narrowed my eyes at him, suspicion prickling at the back of my mind. "Interesting. You didn't seem to have much faith in me for the past month. What changed?"

"This isn't about faith. It's about strategy."

"Fine. But if I'm opening, I need to be honest with you, Shaw." I let out a slow breath, trying to keep my frustration in check. "I'm not convinced Pierce is our guy."

His brow furrowed. "What do you mean?"

I leaned forward, resting my elbows on the desk. "I mean, what if he's just a lackey? The guy who manages the logistics? What if he's not the one responsible for those bodies? We still don't even have direct evidence tying him to the murders."

Shaw's jaw tightened, and his voice took on an edge. "You need to get it out of your head that there's some larger conspiracy here. There's no evidence of that. Pierce owned the land. The bodies were found there. He's guilty."

"But what if you're wrong?" I shot back, my voice rising. "What if he's just a scapegoat? Conveniently left holding the bag while the real players get away scot-free?"

Shaw's lips pressed into a thin line, his gaze hardening. "This isn't about conspiracy theories, Alex. This is about facts. The facts point to Pierce."

"What facts, Shaw? The fact that the bodies were on his land? That he's conveniently the only suspect because we haven't bothered to look any further? What about the fact that we have names, names that keep cropping up in everything I've dug into?"

Shaw rolled his eyes, the dismissiveness in the gesture stoking the fire in my chest. "You're stringing together circumstantial evidence and rumors. Slim and Scorpion? They're nicknames. They could be anyone. And Whitaker? He's a state legislator with nothing remotely linking him to these crimes. You sound like a conspiracy theorist."

"Do I? Because Slim is tied to Maria Alvarez's testimony. Scorpion was identified by Rachel Saunders, and Whitaker is the common thread in all of this. Even his shell company, Lighthouse Ventures, connects to the warehouse case. And let's not forget the campaign donations and legislative record that paint a very interesting picture."

Shaw threw his hands in the air, his voice tight with exasperation. "You're grasping at straws! You've got nothing concrete. Meanwhile, we've got a grand jury indictment, a trial date, and forty-four bodies on a man's property. I'd say that's enough to argue that he's guilty beyond a reasonable doubt."

"Barely enough!" I countered, standing now, my chair screeching against the floor. "You're rushing this trial, shutting down every avenue of investigation that doesn't fit your neat little narrative. Why, Shaw? Why are you so eager to pin everything on Pierce and ignore what's right in front of you?"

"Because this is about facts, Alex," he snapped. "Not wild theories about trafficking rings or mysterious nicknames. The jury isn't going to care about your hunches or your gut feelings. They care about evidence. Hard evidence. And Pierce is the only one we have tied to those bodies."

I yelled back, my voice shaking, "You don't *have* hard evidence! You have proximity, that's it. And if you'd open your eyes for one second, you'd see that there's more going on here. This isn't just about Pierce, it never was."

Shaw leaned across my desk, his face inches from mine, his tone cutting. "You're chasing ghosts, Alex. And if you keep this up, you're going to sink this entire case."

"I'd rather chase ghosts than close my eyes to the truth. What are you so afraid of, Shaw? That I'll uncover something you don't want me to find?"

His expression darkened, his voice dropping to a dangerous calm. "Watch what you're implying."

The room fell into a tense silence, my heartbeat pounding in my ears. And then the words slipped out, sharper than I intended. "Right. Let's stick to the facts. Like the ones you helped my mother with before she disappeared?"

The room went still. Shaw's face didn't change, but I saw the flicker of something in his eyes—something he quickly tried to bury. "Your mother's disappearance was hard on all of us."

"Hard on all of us?" I repeated, my voice trembling with anger. "You mean to say it was harder on you than a little girl who lost her mother, her entire world, because she was uncovering something bigger than you imagined?"

Shaw flinched, just barely. For the first time, I saw something like regret on his face. "Your mother …" he started, but then stopped, shaking his head. "This isn't the time to dredge up the past."

"No, of course not," I said, my voice dripping with sarcasm. "Because every time I try to push for answers, you shut me down. Just like you shut down any attempt to look deeper into Pierce or Whitaker or anything that might actually explain what's going on here."

Shaw stood abruptly, his chair scraping against the floor. "I want your draft of the opening statement by the end of the day tomorrow. Jury selection starts Wednesday. We'll coordinate on strategy, then."

I stared at him, my hands curling into fists under the desk. "That's it? That's all you have to say?"

"That's all that needs to be said," he replied, his voice cold. He turned and walked to the door, pausing only briefly before opening it. "Get out of your own head, Alex. Focus on the trial."

And then he was gone, leaving the door ajar and the tension in the room suffocating. I sat there for a long moment, staring at the empty doorway, my anger simmering just below the surface.

Finally, I stood, pacing the small confines of my office. Shaw's words replayed in my head, over and over, like a broken record. Focus on the trial. As if that were easy when every instinct screamed that there was more to this case than anyone wanted to admit.

I walked over to the window, looking out at the Houston skyline. The trial was a week away, and I was no closer to the truth than I had been a month ago.

CHAPTER
TWENTY-EIGHT

THE COURTROOM BUZZED with low chatter as the morning sun filtered through the high windows, casting slanted beams of light onto the polished wooden benches. It was a familiar setting, the kind of place I'd spent countless hours, but the weight of this case made everything feel heavier. The Texas flag hung in one corner, its edges slightly frayed, and the seal of Harris County loomed above the judge's bench, an imposing reminder of the gravity of what we were here to do.

I sat at the counsel table, adjusting my notes and glancing at the juror profiles we'd prepped the night before. Shaw sat to my left, flipping through his own stack of papers, his expression set in a mask of professional indifference. Lisa, ever diligent, had taken a seat just behind us in the audience section, her legal pad at the ready.

The jury box stood empty for now, its twelve padded chairs waiting to be filled. A dull ache settled in my stomach as I thought about the day ahead. Jury selection was as much an art as a science, and with evidence as thin as ours, the jurors we chose could make or break this case.

We'd spent hours coordinating our strategy. On the surface, we'd agreed to prioritize women and people with a deep respect for government institutions. But in the back of my mind, I knew we also needed jurors who wouldn't question the holes in our evidence too closely.

Shaw didn't say it outright, but he knew it too. We needed people who trusted authority—or at least weren't overly skeptical.

The courtroom door creaked open, drawing my attention. Turner slipped in, his sharp suit crisp and unwrinkled despite the humidity outside. He made his way to the audience section and took a seat next to Lisa, leaning over to murmur something. Lisa glanced at me, a brief flicker of concern crossing her face before she turned her focus back to the proceedings.

I barely had time to process Turner's arrival before my gaze shifted to the back of the room—and froze. There she was. The woman I'd seen during the press conference outside the courthouse. Her heavy scarf and layered clothing were even more out of place in the heated courtroom than they had been in the mild Houston winter.

She sat motionless, her eyes locked onto me, an unsettling intensity radiating from her stare. My stomach tightened as recognition flared. Why was she here? Was it coincidence, or had she deliberately followed me?

"Alex." Shaw's voice cut through my thoughts like a scalpel. I snapped my head back around, realizing I'd been staring.

"What?" I asked, trying to mask the unease in my voice.

"Focus," he said again, this time with more irritation. "We're up."

I bristled, but didn't respond, straightening in my seat as the first group of potential jurors was called. They filed in, looking anywhere but at us, each of their expressions a mixture of curiosity and unease. Shaw stood to address them, launching into the standard questions about biases, occupations, and willingness to serve impartially.

I tried to pay attention, jotting notes in the margins of my legal pad, but I couldn't shake the feeling of being watched. It wasn't unusual for people in the gallery to observe the attorneys, but this woman's gaze felt different—unrelenting, almost probing.

Every so often, I risked a glance over my shoulder. She hadn't moved. Her hands were folded neatly in her lap, but her eyes never wavered. Once, when I turned back, I caught Lisa looking at me with a raised brow, as if to ask what was going on. I shook my head slightly and refocused, but my unease lingered.

"Alex," Shaw hissed, leaning closer. "Are you even listening?"

"Yes," I snapped, though it wasn't entirely true. I forced myself to sit straighter, ignoring the burn of his glare.

As jury selection progressed, I found myself nodding along to Shaw's choices, making occasional notes but contributing little. My attention kept drifting to the back of the room. The woman's presence gnawed at me, a distraction I couldn't afford but couldn't shake.

"Juror number eight," Shaw said, his tone clipped. "Any objections, Ms. Hayes?"

I blinked, realizing I hadn't even heard juror eight's responses. "No," I said quickly, hoping it was the right answer.

Shaw's jaw tightened, but he didn't press further. He turned back to the judge, addressing the court with his usual confidence, while I berated myself silently. Whatever game this woman was playing—or whatever paranoia I was feeding—was starting to affect my focus.

Finally, after what felt like an eternity, jury selection came to a close. The twelve chosen jurors filed out, their expressions a mixture of relief and trepidation. Marcus Ellis, as usual, left without a word, his long strides taking him out of the courtroom before I could so much as glance in his direction.

I stood, gathering my papers and shoving them into my bag with more force than necessary. Lisa approached the counsel table, her face a mix of curiosity and concern, but before I could say anything, Shaw rounded on me.

"What the hell was that?" he demanded, keeping his voice low enough that only I could hear.

I frowned, feigning ignorance. "What was what?"

"You were completely unfocused," he hissed, his tone sharp. "This is one of the most important parts of the trial, and you were staring off into space half the time."

"I wasn't staring into space," I said defensively, although I didn't bother elaborating.

Shaw scoffed, shaking his head. "You need to pull it together. We don't have time for distractions."

I bit back the urge to snap back at him. Instead, I glanced toward the gallery, hoping to catch one last glimpse of the woman, but she was already gone.

Lisa touched my arm, grounding me for a moment. "Are you okay?" she asked softly.

"Fine," I lied, slinging my bag over my shoulder. "Let's go."

Lisa followed me out of the courthouse, her heels clicking against the pavement as we made our way back toward the DA's office. We walked in silence for a few blocks, but I could feel her eyes on me, waiting for me to speak.

I veered toward the coffee shop on the corner. "Need caffeine," I muttered, not bothering to ask if she wanted anything. Lisa, of course, trailed after me.

The familiar hum of the coffee shop was a welcome reprieve from the chaos of the courthouse. The scent of roasted beans and baked goods filled the air, and for a moment, I could breathe again. I ordered an iced coffee, hoping it might cool my temper, Lisa a chai latte, and we found a small table near the window.

Lisa stirred her drink, watching me carefully. Finally, she broke the silence. "Are you going to tell me why you kept looking over your shoulder in there? Because Shaw looked like he was about ready to commit his own murder."

I took a sip of my coffee, the cold bitterness grounding me for a moment. "You noticed that, huh?"

She raised an eyebrow. "Alex, a blind juror could've noticed. What's going on?"

Sighing, I leaned back in my chair. There was no point in dodging the question. Not anymore. "There was someone in the audience," I admitted. "A woman. I saw her at the press conference outside the courthouse a while back."

Lisa frowned, leaning forward slightly. "And?"

"And she was staring at me the whole time," I said. "I don't know who she is, but ... there's something about her. Something unsettling."

Lisa's lips pressed into a thin line. "Do you think she's connected to Pierce? Or Whitaker?"

"I don't know. But it feels like more than a coincidence that she showed up to court today."

Lisa nodded slowly, her brow furrowed. "You think she's following you?"

"Maybe," I said, shrugging. "Or maybe I'm just being paranoid. I don't know. But it's weird."

Lisa took a long sip of her latte, her gaze distant. "You should've said something sooner," she said finally. "We could've tried to figure out who she is."

"I know," I said, my voice quieter now. "There's a lot I haven't said."

Her eyes snapped back to me, sharp with curiosity. "Like what?"

I hesitated, my fingers tightening around my cold glass. The anonymous calls. The cryptic messages. The constant feeling that I was being watched, manipulated. I'd been carrying it all alone, and it was starting to weigh on me more than I could handle. Lisa deserved to know. If anyone could help me make sense of this mess, it was her.

"I need to tell you something," I said, my voice steady despite the storm brewing inside me. "But not here."

Lisa tilted her head, concern flickering in her eyes. "Okay," she said carefully. "When you're ready."

I nodded, the resolve solidifying in my chest. The time for secrets was over.

As we stepped out into the bright Houston sun, the air felt heavier than it should have. The trial was just a week away, and for all the planning and preparation, I felt like we were on the edge of a precipice. We were missing something, something critical, and I couldn't shake the feeling that the woman in the courtroom was somehow connected to all of it.

CHAPTER
TWENTY-NINE

THE RIDE to my house was quiet. Lisa sat beside me, hands folded in her lap, eyes occasionally flicking over to me as if she wanted to say something but couldn't figure out how to start. Keeping my grip on the wheel tight, the tension in my shoulders practically hummed. I couldn't have this conversation at the office. I didn't know who might be listening, and didn't trust anyone except Lisa.

As we pulled up to the house, my dad was out front, raking leaves into a neat pile near the curb. The late afternoon sun stretched our silhouettes over the yard, and the rhythmic scrape of the rake was oddly grounding. Lisa and I got out of the car, and my dad looked up, his face brightening when he saw us.

"Hey there," he called out, leaning on the rake. "You two hard at work?"

"Something like that," I replied, forcing a smile. "We're going to do some trial prep inside."

Lisa nodded politely. "Nice to see you again, Mr. Hayes."

"You too, Lisa. Don't let her overwork you," he joked, shooting me a mock stern look.

I rolled my eyes. "We'll be fine. Dinner later?"

"Already taken care of," he said with a grin. "I'll leave you two to it."

We stepped inside. The house smelled faintly of coffee and pine cleaner—my dad's attempt to keep things orderly. I led Lisa down the hallway to my room, my mind racing. The knot in my chest tightened with each step. I hadn't told anyone about the calls, not even my dad.

But it was time.

I couldn't make sense of them on my own, and the clock was ticking. If sharing them with Lisa meant we had a better chance at cracking this case—or even understanding why someone was trying to reach out to me—it was worth the risk.

Closing the door behind us, I gestured for Lisa to sit on the edge of the bed while I crouched by my dresser. I pulled out my journal and held it for a moment, my fingers brushing the worn leather cover. I turned to her, extending it.

Lisa looked at me, puzzled. "What's this?"

I sat beside her, running a hand through my hair, the tension in my chest finally breaking into words. "It's everything I've written down about these calls I've been getting. Anonymous calls." I met her eyes, watching as they widened in surprise.

Lisa frowned, leaning forward. "Wait—what calls? What do you mean?"

I sighed, the weight of it all pressing down on me as I tried to organize the tangled mess in my head. "The first one came when I was picking my dad up the day he was released. I'd just parked outside the prison, and my phone rang. It was a number I didn't recognize, but I answered it anyway. The voice on the other end was distorted, like they were using one of those voice changers. They told me—" I paused, swallowing hard. "They told me my mother's disappearance wasn't an accident."

Lisa's eyes widened further. "Why didn't you tell me about this before?"

"Because I couldn't make sense of it. And honestly, I didn't know if I could trust it. But that call stayed with me. It was the reason I decided to come back to work. To see if maybe, somehow, I could find more information about her."

Lisa stared at me, her expression unreadable. I pressed on, the words tumbling out now.

"Since then, they've come at random times. I can't figure out any pattern—sometimes it's on my drive home, sometimes it's when I'm sitting at my desk. It's always the same distorted voice. They keep telling me I'm on the right track or to keep digging. Or that Pierce is just a pawn."

Lisa blinked, shaking her head as if trying to process. "And you've written everything down? Every word?"

"Every single word." I nodded toward the notebook in her hands. "I didn't know what else to do. It's like they know exactly what I'm looking into and when. But I can't figure out why they're reaching out to me or even if they're helping or trying to lead me off course."

Lisa flipped through the pages again, her brow furrowed in concentration.

"I've been trying to piece it together on my own, but I can't. And now ..." I hesitated, unsure if I wanted to voice what had been nagging at me.

She opened the journal and started flipping through the pages, her brow furrowing as she read. I didn't need to look at the entries; I had them memorized.

Your mother's disappearance was not an accident.

You're getting closer, but you're not there yet.

She may still be alive.

Keep digging, Alex. The answers are at the DA's office. But be careful. Not everyone is who they seem.

You're looking in the right place, but you're not the only one interested in the past.

The closer you get, the more dangerous this becomes.

Pierce was just a pawn. But pawns can be replaced.

Lisa looked up at me, her expression a mix of concern and curiosity. "Do you have any idea who it could be?"

" No. The voice is altered every time. It could be anyone—or even multiple people." I hesitated, glancing at the journal in her hands. "But the woman at jury selection—the one I saw at the press conference—I can't shake the feeling she's connected."

Lisa leaned forward. "What makes you think that?"

"I don't know. It's just a feeling." I chewed on my thumbnail, the nervous habit breaking through despite my efforts to stop. "When I saw her in that courtroom, it was like she was watching me—specifically me. It was distracting. Unsettling."

Lisa frowned, flipping back to the entry about Pierce being a pawn. "Do you think she could be the one who called in the tip about the pit of bodies?"

The question caught me off guard. My mind raced back to the initial stages of the case—the anonymous 911 call, the officers stumbling onto the dump site. I blinked, staring at her. "I hadn't thought about that. But it's possible. Maybe we should go back and listen to the 911 recording."

Lisa nodded. "If she shows up again, we can try talking to her. See what we can figure out." She paused, her gaze sharpening as she studied me. "But Alex … what if these calls are meant to throw you off? To lead you away from something—or someone?"

I sighed, leaning back against the headboard. "I've thought about that," I admitted. "I've thought about everything else, too, though. And none of it makes sense. But if this is someone on the inside, trying to mislead me, then we're walking into something even bigger than I imagined."

Lisa's expression turned grim, and for a moment, neither of us spoke. The weight of the situation pressed down on me, heavy and suffocating.

A knock on the door broke the silence, and both of us turned to see my dad standing in the doorway, a slight smile on his face. "Dinner's here. Thought you two might be hungry."

"Thanks," I said, mustering a smile. "We'll be out in a minute."

He nodded, glancing between us before disappearing down the hall. Lisa closed the journal and handed it back to me. I tucked it away, locking it back in the drawer before following her into the kitchen.

My dad was unpacking takeout containers on the counter—burgers and fries from a local diner. He looked up as we joined him, his expression warm. "How's the trial prep going?"

"Busy," Lisa said, grabbing plates from the cabinet. "Alex has been working hard."

My dad chuckled, shaking his head. "You both have, I'm sure. Any new leads?"

I hesitated, then sighed. "A lot of close calls, but nothing solid. It's frustrating. We can't seem to tie everything together."

"It only takes one string to pull everything together." My dad placed a hand on my shoulder, his grip firm but comforting. "If that's what you're looking for, it'll show up eventually."

CHAPTER THIRTY

THE HIGHWAY STRETCHED AHEAD, the dark asphalt illuminated by the faint glow of streetlights. Lisa sat in the passenger seat, arms folded as she stared out the window. We were heading back to the office so she could grab her car. The air in the car was heavy, weighed down by everything I'd shared with her earlier.

Lisa broke the silence, her voice cautious. "This whole thing about the calls … they mentioned something about answers being at the DA's office?"

I tightened my grip on the steering wheel, keeping my eyes on the road. "Yeah, they did. That's part of why I've been so wrapped up in this."

"And your mom?" Lisa pressed, her tone softer now, a mixture of curiosity and concern. "Do you think this all ties back to her?"

I hesitated, gripping the steering wheel a little tighter. It wasn't like I hadn't thought about it—hell, I'd been consumed by it. Ever since I'd started connecting the dots, it was all I could think about.

My voice was quiet when I replied, "I found out she was working on a case involving a trafficking ring before she disappeared."

Lisa turned fully to face me, her eyebrows knitting together. "She was?"

I nodded, my throat tightening. "Yeah. She'd just become an ADA when she took on this case. Apparently, it was intense. She'd come home frustrated, angry even, saying that the people in charge weren't looking deep enough. She didn't think they had the right guy—or at least not the only guy. She thought it was bigger."

Lisa's gaze didn't waver, her attention sharp. "And the box? The one you mentioned before?"

I exhaled slowly, letting the words spill out. "When I found that file box in the DA's storage unit, it was hers. It had her handwriting in it. Notes. Names. And one of those names was Whitaker."

Lisa blinked. "Whitaker, as in the same guy who's all over Pierce's case and everything else we've been looking into?"

"Exactly." I glanced at her briefly before returning my focus to the road. "And then the box went missing. Just disappeared from my office one day. I thought for sure Shaw had taken it."

"Why Shaw?" Lisa asked, leaning slightly toward me.

"Because he worked with her on that case," I said, the frustration simmering in my chest all over again. "Shaw was the last person I know of who worked with her before she went missing. And yet, he hasn't said a damn thing about it. Not to me, not to anyone. And then, after I confronted him, that box just shows up again. Back on my desk like it had never disappeared."

Lisa frowned, her forehead creasing. "Do you think he was the one who brought it back?"

"I don't know," I admitted, my voice strained. "But whoever took it, there's no way they didn't go through it first. And if they did, who knows what they took out—or what they put in."

Lisa rubbed her temples. "Okay, I know I'm usually the one trying to play devil's advocate, but that's a lot to explain away. Even for me."

I gave a humorless laugh. "Tell me about it. I don't want to sound like some conspiracy theorist, like Shaw's been accusing me of. But then again …" I trailed off, unsure of how to put my suspicions into words without sounding unhinged.

"But then again, what?"

"I know my time working with Andrews probably made me more jaded than I should be."

The memory of Andrews cut through me like a dull blade—his steady guidance, his camaraderie, the way he'd seemed like the one person I could rely on in the chaos of the DA's office. Only for it all to crumble when he betrayed not just me, but my entire family. That wound hadn't healed, and maybe it never would.

"But Tom, Shaw, Turner … I can't shake the feeling they're all hiding something."

Lisa was quiet for a moment, watching the lights blur past outside her window. "Do you think they know about the calls?"

"Maybe. If someone's on the inside, it would make sense. But the calls feel different. Like someone who's trying to help. Or maybe manipulating me into thinking they are, like you said. Hell, I don't know anymore."

The silence settled again as we neared the office. The downtown skyline glimmered in the distance, its sharp lines cutting into the inky sky.

When I pulled up next to Lisa's car in the parking lot, she unbuckled her seatbelt but didn't open the door right away. She turned to me, her expression thoughtful. "If your gut is telling you something this strongly, maybe you should listen to it."

I raised an eyebrow.

"Seriously. You were right last time. Being jaded doesn't make you wrong. And let's face it, your instincts are usually pretty damn good."

I managed a small smile. "Thanks, Lisa. I appreciate that."

She opened her door, stepping out but leaning down to look at me once more. "I'll see you tomorrow, bright and early. You ready for this trial to start?"

"No," I admitted with a laugh. "But what else is new?"

Lisa smirked and shut the door, waving as she walked to her car.

My drive back home was quiet, the usual cacophony of Houston traffic somehow muted. My thoughts churned as I replayed everything I'd just shared with Lisa. The calls, my mom's case, Whitaker's name cropping up—it all felt connected, but the pieces refused to fall into place.

Shaw's dismissal echoed in my head.

Get it out of your head that there's a larger conspiracy.

But how could I, when everything kept pointing to exactly that?

One man doesn't just murder and cut up forty-four people and bury them in an empty lot.

The houses blurred by as I drove down the street before pulling into my driveway. My dad's truck was still parked in the same spot, and I could see the faint glow of the porch light through the trees. He always left it on for me, no matter how late I was.

I grabbed my bag and headed inside, the familiar scent of coffee and pine cleaner hitting me as I walked through the door. My dad wasn't in the kitchen or the living room; he'd probably gone to bed.

I climbed the stairs to my room, the knot in my chest tightening with every step. Tomorrow, the trial would begin, and I still felt like I was walking into an ambush.

I dropped my bag on the floor and sat on the edge of my bed, running a hand through my hair. Lisa was right—my gut was screaming at me. But was it leading me toward the truth or straight into a trap?

I grabbed my notebook from the dresser and flipped through the pages, scanning the words I'd written over and over. The calls, the cryptic warnings, the lingering doubts about everyone around me— they were all here. But none of it made sense.

Not yet.

I closed the notebook with a sharp snap, tossing it onto the bed. Tomorrow would bring answers. Or at least, I hoped it would.

CHAPTER THIRTY-ONE

I PULLED into the courthouse parking lot just as the sky shifted from dark gray to the pale blue of early morning. Trial days always made me feel tense, but today the weight felt heavier.

This was it. The trial of Randall Pierce. A man accused of murdering and dismembering forty-four people. And yet, we were about to go into court with barely enough evidence to tie him directly to the crimes.

I parked my car and sat for a moment, staring at the looming courthouse. Stomach churning, nerves and caffeine battling for dominance, I grabbed my bag, slung it over my shoulder, and stepped out, taking in a deep breath of the cool morning air. It did little to calm me.

As I walked toward the courthouse, I spotted three figures standing near the far end of the parking lot. Marcus Ellis, Pierce's defense attorney, was the first I recognized, his sharp suit cutting a confident silhouette. Next to him was Tom Matthews, my boss, whose stiff posture betrayed his usual calm demeanor. And then, standing a little to the side, was Sam Whitaker.

My steps slowed. What the hell was Whitaker doing here?

Ellis was gesturing, speaking animatedly, while Tom nodded along. Whitaker, dressed in a casual blazer, stood with his hands in his pockets, watching the exchange. I couldn't hear what they were saying, but their body language screamed that this was no casual conversation.

Before I could second-guess myself, I altered my course and headed straight for them. Their conversation ceased as I approached, all three of them turning to face me.

"Good morning," I said, trying to keep my tone neutral but firm. My gaze flicked between them, landing on Whitaker. "I didn't realize you'd be attending today's trial, Mr. Whitaker."

"It's a big case, darlin'," he said, his thick Texas accent curling around the words like oil in water. "Naturally, it's drawn some interest."

I clenched my jaw, feeling the sting of the condescension. *Darlin'*. The word rolled off his tongue with the kind of casual arrogance that set my teeth on edge. He might as well have patted me on the head and told me to run along.

"And your interest?" I pressed, forcing a polite smile that didn't touch my eyes. "What specifically brings you here?"

"I'm a criminal defense attorney, and this is a high-profile trial." He smiled, an easy expression that didn't reach his eyes. "It's not unusual for someone in my line of work to observe these kinds of proceedings."

"That doesn't explain why you're here before the courthouse has even opened for the day," I countered, glancing pointedly at Tom and Ellis. "Especially in the company of the defense counsel and the district attorney."

Tom stepped in, his tone clipped. "Alex, this isn't the time for baseless suspicions. We're all professionals here."

"Professionals discussing what, exactly?"

Ellis smirked; the kind of smirk that made me want to smack it off his face. "Just sharing thoughts on the trial ahead. Nothing you need to worry about, counselor."

Before I could respond, Whitaker added, "I'd hate to distract you from your responsibilities, Ms. Hayes. I'm sure you have a busy day ahead."

"Right," I said, keeping my tone tight. "Well, I hope you enjoy the show." I turned on my heel and marched toward the courthouse, my frustration mounting with each step.

Inside, the courthouse was still quiet, the usual bustle of trial days not yet in full swing. I took a seat near the entrance, my mind racing. What the hell could they have been discussing? And I didn't believe Whitaker was here just to observe, not for a second.

When Lisa walked in, holding her ever-present travel mug of coffee, I jumped up and grabbed her arm. "Come with me," I said urgently, leading her toward one of the empty witness rooms.

"Good morning to you, too," she said, her brow furrowed as I pulled her along.

Once inside, I closed the door and turned to her. "Whitaker was in the parking lot with Tom and Ellis. They were talking, and when I approached them, they completely brushed me off. Wouldn't tell me why Whitaker's here or what they were discussing."

Lisa's eyes widened. "Whitaker? As in *Sam Whitaker*?"

I nodded. "Yes. And it just doesn't make any sense. Why would he be here? Why would he be talking to them?"

Lawyers rarely observe trials outside of their own. That was more of a law student thing.

Lisa bit her lip, clearly trying to piece it together. "Okay, that's odd. But you need to focus. You've got opening statements to deliver."

"I know," I said, running a hand through my hair. "But Whitaker can't be here just by coincidence."

She sighed, then gave me a look. "If you're that concerned, I can sit in the audience and keep an eye on him. But you need to keep your head in the game. This trial is too important."

Reluctantly, I nodded. "You're right. But watch him. Watch *all* of them."

As we left the witness room, Shaw was walking down the hallway toward us. His sharp gaze landed on me. "Hayes," he said, motioning for me to step aside.

I exchanged a glance with Lisa before following him a few steps away. His expression was unreadable, but the tension in his jaw put me on edge.

"Are you ready for this?" he asked, his tone clipped.

"Yes," I said, meeting his gaze evenly.

He studied me for a moment, then frowned. "You sure? Because you've seemed distracted."

I bristled at his insinuation. "I'm ready, Shaw. This trial has been all I've thought about."

"Good," he said, though his tone was clipped, as if he didn't entirely believe it.

I hesitated, then said, "I saw Tom talking with Ellis earlier."

Shaw's eyes narrowed slightly. "What of it?"

I folded my arms. "If there are last-minute plea negotiations happening, don't you think we should be privy to that?"

Shaw leaned back slightly, giving me a look that was both dismissive and irritated. "I doubt that's what it was about."

"Then why else would Tom have a reason to speak with defense counsel?" I pressed, my voice sharper now. "On the starting day of the trial. That's not normal."

He sighed, running a hand down his face as if he were done humoring me. "It doesn't matter, Hayes. Whatever it was about, it doesn't change what we need to do."

I stared at him, incredulous. "It doesn't matter? We're walking into trial, and our own boss might be having closed-door talks with the other side?"

"It. Doesn't. Change. What. We. Need. To. Do," he said. "Opening is today. Get your head in the game and focus."

Opening my mouth to argue, I stopped myself. Shaw wasn't going to budge, and as much as I hated to admit it, he was right about one thing: opening was today. I had to focus, no matter how many red flags were waving in my face.

He turned and walked away, leaving me fuming. I clenched my fists, my nails digging into my palms as I tried to rein in my frustration. Lisa touched my arm lightly, grounding me.

"Let's go," she said softly.

The courtroom was beginning to fill by the time we entered. The jury box sat empty for now, but soon it would be filled with twelve individuals who would eventually decide Randall Pierce's fate.

Then the door at the back of the courtroom opened, and Randall Pierce was led in by two deputies. The room seemed to collectively hold its breath as the deputies escorted him to the defense table. He was dressed in a suit, but it didn't do much to soften his presence. His face was calm, almost as if he were entirely unaffected by the fact that he was on trial for forty-four counts of murder.

I studied him as he sat down. There was no hint of anxiety, no sign of the desperation I'd seen in most other defendants. His demeanor was wrong. It wasn't the composure of a man who believed in his innocence, but the detachment of a man who didn't care.

Ellis leaned over and whispered something to him. Pierce nodded; his expression unchanged. Irritation flickered in my chest. Whatever slimy tricks Ellis had up his sleeve, he was undoubtedly going to pull them all.

The judge entered the courtroom promptly at 9:00, the quiet rustle of robes and the bailiff's booming, "All rise," snapping me out of my thoughts. We all stood as Judge Elaine Carter took her seat, her sharp eyes scanning the room like she could sense every lie and half-truth lurking within it. Thank God she was presiding over the actual trial instead of Morley, who'd handled the bail hearing. She'd presided over her fair share of high-profile cases, and her reputation for being no-nonsense preceded her.

"Please be seated," she instructed, her voice steady and commanding. The courtroom obeyed in unison, the creak of benches echoing through the air.

The jury filed in shortly after, twelve faces that we'd painstakingly selected. I scanned them as they settled into the box. A mix of men and women, most of them middle-aged, with expressions ranging from apprehensive to outright disinterested. These were the people who would determine Randall Pierce's fate, and I couldn't help but feel a twinge of doubt. Had we picked the right ones? Would they see the gaping holes in our evidence? Or would Shaw's confidence in their susceptibility to the narrative carry us through?

Judge Carter began with her instructions, carefully outlining the jury's role and responsibilities. "You are tasked with determining the facts based on the evidence presented. Not speculation. Not conjecture. *Evidence.*"

The word lingered in the air, and I fought the urge to glance at

Shaw. Evidence—or lack thereof—was our Achilles' heel. The thought twisted in my stomach, a knot tightening with every passing second.

As Judge Carter continued with her instructions, I noticed Lisa sitting just behind me in the audience, her presence a small but welcome anchor. Turner had taken a seat next to her, and the two were whispering quietly, although Lisa occasionally shot me a reassuring look.

The sound of the gavel brought me back to the moment. "Opening statements will now commence," Judge Carter announced, her tone brisk. She glanced at me. "Prosecution, you may proceed."

CHAPTER
THIRTY-TWO

THE COURTROOM WAS UNUSUALLY quiet as I stood, the creak of my chair echoing in the stillness. I smoothed the front of my blazer with trembling hands, a nervous habit I couldn't seem to shake. The jury box was filled, each face a blank slate, waiting for me to shape their impressions of the man sitting across from me. The weight of their collective gaze pressed down on me, but it was nothing compared to the cold, impassive presence of Randall Pierce.

I turned, glancing at him briefly before stepping to the podium. His expression was unreadable, his eyes fixed straight ahead like he was studying the grain of the table instead of the weighty accusations hanging over him. For a moment, I caught his eye—dark, unwavering, as if daring me to see something in them. I froze, gripping the edge of the podium tighter than I intended.

What if Shaw, Turner, and Matthews were right? What if I'd over-analyzed everything, chasing ghosts and threads that didn't exist? What if Pierce was nothing more than a psychotic killer, completely devoid of remorse, playing this courtroom like his stage? His stillness unnerved me, and for a brief second, I doubted everything. Maybe my paranoia, the specter of what had happened in the Martin trial, had clouded my judgment. Maybe all these connections I'd been chasing weren't connections at all, but desperate attempts to avoid another loss —another personal failure.

I forced myself to look away from him, to focus on the jurors. They didn't know my doubts. They couldn't know. My job was to convince them beyond a reasonable doubt that the man sitting at the defense table had butchered forty-four innocent people. No matter what I thought—no matter my fears—I had a job to do.

Taking, a long, deep breath, I began.

"Ladies and gentlemen of the jury, thank you for being here today. The case you are about to hear is one of unthinkable brutality. Over the course of this trial, you will see evidence that Randall Pierce is responsible for the deaths of forty-three women and one man, whose bodies were left to rot in what can only be described as a mass grave site."

The words came more easily than I'd expected, flowing as if I'd rehearsed them a dozen times. My voice was steady, my tone firm. Years of courtroom experience kicked in like muscle memory, the weight of this moment propelling me forward. Despite the rushed preparation, I didn't even glance at the notes I'd hastily scrawled in my legal pad that morning, tucked inside the folder on the podium. I didn't need them. The facts—the details that mattered—were etched into my mind after weeks of living and breathing this case.

I scanned the faces of the jurors, noting how some leaned slightly forward in their seats, their attention fixed on me. Others were more reserved, their hands folded, but their eyes tracked my every movement. The room shifted as I spoke, the energy drawing tighter. They were listening. That was only half the battle.

"You'll hear from forensic experts who will testify about the tools used to dismember the bodies. You'll see photographic evidence of the pit discovered on Mr. Pierce's property—gruesome, horrifying evidence that no one should have to see. And you'll hear from law enforcement officers who will explain how Mr. Pierce's actions led them to his doorstep. By the end of this trial, you will have no doubt in your minds that this man"—I gestured toward Pierce without looking at him—"is responsible for these murders."

This was the moment I had to sell the story, to make them feel the weight of those forty-four bodies, the horror of the pit on Randall Pierce's property. It was working—or at least, I hoped it was. Whatever doubt I'd carried with me walking into the courtroom faded, replaced by the drive to win this trial.

My confidence grew stronger with every word I spoke. I stepped away from the podium slightly, making eye contact with several jurors, gauging their reactions. They were all engaged. This was what I needed to focus on—the evidence, the story, the victims.

I opened my mouth to continue. And then, out of the corner of my eye, I saw her.

The woman from before. The headscarf tucked neatly around her head, the same darting, elusive air. She slipped quietly into the back of the courtroom, moving like a shadow as her gaze swept the room. My stomach knotted, my focus splintering. Who was she? What did she want? Why here, why now?

I stumbled over my next word, an awkward pause stretching before I covered it with an apologetic, "um." The polished rhythm I'd been building shattered. I cleared my throat, forcing my voice to steady, gripping the edges of the podium as if it were an anchor.

"The evidence will speak for itself," I said, though the sharp conviction I'd begun with was gone. My voice wavered, and I could feel the shift in the room—the jurors leaning back slightly, the air growing heavier with skepticism. "The story it tells is one of cold calculation, of someone who believed he could commit murder—over and over again—and escape justice."

I tried to push forward, but my words had lost their momentum, and the finishing note of my statement felt more like a question than a conclusion. I glanced back toward the audience, but the woman's face was obscured by her scarf as she looked down at her hands. A calculated move, or just my paranoia?

As I stepped away from the podium, the silence in the room was deafening. I could feel Shaw's eyes on me as I sat down. His expression was schooled, perfectly neutral for the jury's sake, but the tightness in his jaw and the subtle tap of his pen against the table spoke volumes. He wasn't happy.

I ignored him, turning to look at Lisa. She had noticed the woman too. Her gaze flicked between me and the back of the courtroom, a silent question in her eyes. I tilted my head toward the woman, and Lisa nodded, slipping quietly out of her seat.

The woman must have sensed our attention. As soon as Lisa began to move, she stood and made her way toward the exit. Lisa quickened her pace, following her out of the room. I wanted to chase after them, to find out who this woman was and what she was doing here, but I couldn't. Not right now.

Shaw leaned toward me as Marcus Ellis pushed his chair back and rose to his full height, buttoning his jacket with deliberate precision. Shaw's voice was low but firm, cutting through my spiraling thoughts. "Stay focused."

Nodding stiffly, I forced my eyes back to the front of the room as Ellis adjusted his cuffs and approached the jury with the slow confidence of a seasoned performer. The man could command a room with his presence alone, and he knew it. His smile was faint but deliberate, a calculated attempt to appear approachable, relatable—even to a jury tasked with deciding the fate of a man accused of unspeakable crimes.

Judge Campbell cleared her throat, bringing the room to attention. "Mr. Ellis, you may proceed."

"Thank you, Your Honor," Ellis said smoothly, inclining his head toward the bench.

He turned to the jury, his expression softening as if he were about to share a personal anecdote instead of addressing a trial involving forty-four gruesome murders.

I shifted in my seat, trying to steel myself against the unease building in my chest. Ellis was about to weave his narrative, to plant doubt in the minds of those twelve jurors, and I could feel Shaw watching me out of the corner of his eye, as if daring me to slip up again.

Whatever happened next, I had to push everything else—Lisa, the woman, the phone calls—out of my mind. For now, all I could do was watch and wait, bracing for the defense's opening volley.

CHAPTER
THIRTY-THREE

ELLIS WRAPPED up his opening statement with a confident flourish, his words lingering in the charged courtroom air. My jaw tightened as I watched him return to the defense table, his smug expression barely concealing the satisfaction of a well-delivered performance. The judge announced a fifteen-minute recess, and the jury filed out of the room.

I forced myself to look at each of the jurors, my stomach twisting with unease. I studied their faces, searching for any indication of how Marcus Ellis's words might have landed.

Juror number three—a woman in her late forties with sharp features and neatly pinned-back hair—kept her eyes trained on the defense table. Her lips were pressed tightly together, as if mulling over something serious. Not a great sign.

Beside her, juror number five—a young man who couldn't have been older than twenty-five—shifted in his seat before standing. He avoided looking at anyone, his gaze fixed on the floor as he followed the others out. Indecision radiated off him like heat waves.

Juror number seven—a middle-aged man with graying hair and a meticulously pressed suit—paused at the door, glancing back at Pierce. His expression was neutral, unreadable, but the fact that he lingered sent a ripple of doubt through me.

Then there was juror number nine—a petite woman with a colorful scarf wrapped around her neck—who gave a slight nod as she passed the defense table. I couldn't tell if it was subconscious or deliberate, but it set my nerves on edge.

As they exited, I let out a slow breath, trying to tamp down the rising sense of dread. The jury wasn't lost yet, but Ellis had clearly planted seeds of doubt in some of them. If I didn't find a way to counter his narrative, those seeds would take root. And once they did, it would be nearly impossible to uproot them.

Shaw stood, nodding toward the door. "Let's go."

Lisa and I followed him through the bustling hallway into our assigned counsel room. The fluorescent lights buzzed faintly, and the air was thick with the smell of stale coffee and legal briefs. Shaw shut the door behind us, spinning on his heel to face me.

"What the hell was that?" he snapped, his voice low but cutting. "You lost focus out there."

I set my bag on the table, forcing myself to meet his gaze. "I didn't lose focus."

"Oh, really?" he challenged, crossing his arms. "You faltered. The jury saw it, Alex. You handed Ellis an opening."

"I didn't lose focus," I repeated, my voice firm and my knuckles curling into fists. "And even if I did, maybe you should consider that you're being unreasonably harsh on me."

Shaw narrowed his eyes before shaking his head and walking to the coffee machine. He grabbed the coffee pot, his hand tightening around the handle as he poured a cup with slow, deliberate movements. "Unreasonably harsh? Alex, this isn't a debate club. This is a murder trial with over forty victims. You need to be on your game."

"I am on my game," I snapped, leaning forward. "But I can't figure out why you're coming down on me like this. Maybe you should take a second to ask yourself why I'm distracted."

His brow furrowed, his expression hardening, still not looking at me. "And what, exactly, is that supposed to mean?"

"It means I've had enough of you and Turner brushing off every legitimate lead we've had in this case. And don't think I didn't notice you not caring at all when I mentioned Tom talking to Ellis this morning."

"What are you insinuating?" His voice dropped, cold and sharp, as if daring me to continue.

"I'm saying it's not just me who's distracted here. Ellis talking to Tom in the parking lot? That doesn't raise any red flags for you? You keep looking the other way when it's glaringly obvious something isn't right, and I'm starting to wonder why."

Shaw slammed the coffee pot back into place, the sound echoing in the small room. He turned to face me, his face a mask of restrained fury. "You're accusing me of what? Negligence? Complicity?"

"I'm just saying it's suspicious." I crossed my arms and narrowed my eyes. "Your refusal to consider anything outside the neat little box you've built around this case. It's like you don't care to dig any deeper."

Shaw's nostrils flared as he took a step back, his fish clenching around the coffee cup so hard I worried the Styrofoam cup might crumple. For a moment, I thought he might yell, but instead, he drew in a sharp breath, forcing himself to stay composed.

"I need a minute," he muttered, his voice tight. Without another word, he turned on his heel and strode out of the room, the door swinging shut behind him.

I exhaled slowly, but it did nothing to relieve the tightness in my chest, nor the mix of anger and confusion within it. Shaw's reaction wasn't just defensive—it was charged, almost volatile, like I'd struck a nerve he was desperate to protect. Lisa shifted beside me, her expression caught between concern and curiosity.

Sinking into one of the chairs, my fingers tapped restlessly against the table, the tension building in my chest.

"Alex," Lisa said, her tone measured but firm. "I think you're a little over the line here."

I looked at her, my brows furrowed. "What's that supposed to mean?"

"I mean ..." She hesitated, as if weighing her words. "I get being suspicious, I do. But you're basically accusing Shaw of being a criminal. You weren't just doubting him—you're throwing him into the same pile as Pierce and Whitaker."

Stiffening, the heat rising in my face, I snapped, "You can't deny that something is off. Shaw's behavior, the way he shuts everything down, brushes things aside—it doesn't add up."

Lisa sighed, her hand still on my arm. "I get it, Alex. But there's a difference between being thorough and letting paranoia take over. If you keep going at him like this, you're not going to get answers. You're just going to push him further away."

After staring at the table for a moment, the weight of her words sank in. She wasn't wrong. I had let my frustrations with Shaw, Turner, and Tom build into something sharper, more accusatory. But wasn't I justified? Hadn't their actions—or lack thereof—warranted this level of scrutiny?

Lisa softened her tone and leaned in closer. "Maybe you should talk to Shaw. About your mom, about all of it. He clearly knows more than he's letting on."

I scoffed. "I've tried. He'll just dismiss me like he always does."

"Maybe," Lisa admitted, nodding. "But, I think it's worth trying again. He worked with your mom. He might have insights on this that you don't. It's worth one more push, in my humble opinion."

I exhaled sharply, rubbing my temples. "Yeah," I said, my voice quieter now. "Maybe you're right. But that doesn't mean I trust him."

"You don't have to trust him. But you'll need him if you're going to figure this out."

Before I could respond, the door opened, and Shaw walked back in, coffee cup still in hand. He glanced between us, his expression unreadable.

"Ready to strategize?" he asked, his tone clipped.

I exchanged a look with Lisa, then nodded. "Fine. Let's talk direct."

We spent the next few minutes outlining our approach for the witnesses, but my mind kept drifting. Randall Pierce's demeanor in court had been unnerving, to say the least. While the rest of us were battling nerves and tension, he'd sat there like a statue—calm, detached, as if the trial were someone else's problem.

"Anything on Pierce's behavior we can use?" I asked Shaw, interrupting his train of thought.

He glanced at me, then shook his head. "Nothing unusual. He's playing the part of the wrongly accused."

"It's more than that," I said, my voice tinged with frustration. "He's too calm. It's like he doesn't care. Does that not bother anyone else?"

Lisa glanced at Shaw, then back at me. "It's odd. But maybe that's his defense strategy—to look as harmless as possible."

"Or"—I leaned forward—"he knows something we don't."

Shaw sighed, checking his watch. "Save the speculation for later. Recess is almost over. Let's get back in there."

I followed him out of the room, Lisa close behind. My thoughts were spinning as we made our way back to the courtroom. I couldn't shake the feeling that we were missing a crucial piece of the puzzle.

The room buzzed quietly, the audience settling into their seats. Lisa slipped into the front of the audience section as I placed my notes on the table, glancing briefly toward the defense. Pierce was already seated, his face as expressionless as ever, and Marcus Ellis was organizing his files with an air of unshakable confidence.

I adjusted my chair, scanning the room and trying to refocus. Before I could dwell too much on Pierce's unnerving composure, the judge and jury were announced. Everyone stood as the they took their places.

I took my seat again beside Shaw, but my thoughts weren't on Pierce anymore—or even the jury. They were on Lisa and the empty seat where the strange woman had sat before.

I realized I hadn't asked her about it during recess. Shaw hadn't allowed me the opportunity. But she hadn't started the conversation either. Had she managed to catch up to her before the recess? Did she speak with her? Get any kind of lead?

The flurry of tension with Shaw had consumed my focus, but now the questions crept in. I needed to know. If this woman had something to do with the calls, then she could be the key to cracking this wide open. Or at least in understanding what the hell was going on.

Shaw's earlier words echoed in my mind: *Focus on the trial.* As much as I hated to admit it, he was right. Whatever the woman represented, whatever connection she might have to the case, or my mother's disappearance, it would have to wait.

CHAPTER
THIRTY-FOUR

THE OFFICE WAS NEARLY SILENT, save for the occasional hum of the heating system and the faint tapping of Lisa's fingers on her keyboard. The only ones left on our floor, after the grueling first day of trial, I felt like I had been put through a wringer—twice.

I couldn't stop thinking about the mysterious woman from the courtroom. Lisa told me the woman had slipped away before she could even get close when she'd followed her out before recess. I nodded and muttered something about focusing on the trial, but the truth was, it hit me harder than I wanted to admit.

This woman had been around for every critical moment—outside the press conference, during jury selection, and now today's hearing. Her presence lingered like a shadow I couldn't shake. What did she know? Was she connected to all of this, or was I chasing ghosts? I couldn't decide what was worse: the thought that she might have answers and wasn't sharing them, or the possibility that I'd built her up in my mind into something more important than she actually was. Both scenarios left me grasping at straws.

Lisa swiveled her chair to glance at me, her expression weary but expectant. "You've been staring at that wall for five minutes straight, Alex."

I shook my head, rubbing my temples. "I'm just replaying today over and over again. Officer Briggs was supposed to be our strongest witness to set the tone, and Ellis dismantled him like it was nothing."

Lisa nodded, her expression grim. "I thought Briggs would hold up better on cross."

Briggs, the first officer to respond to the scene, had been called to give a detailed account of what he saw: the scattered remains in the pit, the overwhelming stench of decay, the bloodied clothes partially buried among the dirt. His testimony was supposed to paint the horrors of the crime for the jury, to make them feel the weight of the forty-four lives lost.

Then Ellis had stepped up, all charm and precision. His questions were scalpel-sharp, picking apart every detail of the officer's testimony. He'd latched onto inconsistencies in the initial report, hammering away at small discrepancies like the exact time Briggs arrived on the scene or the specific condition of one piece of evidence.

By the time Briggs left the stand, his credibility had been so thoroughly shredded that the impact of his testimony was almost negligible. Instead of walking out as a reliable, composed witness, he'd seemed defensive, flustered, and unsure.

"It's like he's got a sixth sense for sniffing out every weak point," I muttered. "I was sitting there, watching it happen, and there was nothing I could do to stop it."

Lisa pushed her chair back and crossed her arms. "Ellis knows how to spin things, but you still have the jury's attention. You just need a strong follow-up tomorrow. The trial isn't lost."

"I hope you're right," I said, though I wasn't convinced. I leaned back in my chair, letting the exhaustion sink in. "What are you working on?"

"Just poking around the archives," she said, tilting her screen slightly so I could see. "Trying to find anything useful to piece this whole mess together."

I got up and walked over to her desk, glancing at the grainy scanned documents on her screen. "The archives?"

"Yeah. When they started digitizing the old files, they uploaded a bunch of scanned memos and correspondence. It's a lot to sift through, but I thought maybe I'd find something relevant."

When she clicked on one document, my breath caught. It was an old memo dated over a decade ago. The header indicated it came from some obscure task force within the DA's office. The content was even more jarring—a list of connections between known associates, naming both Randall Pierce and Sam Whitaker. The Lighthouse Group was mentioned in several places, too.

"Look here," Lisa said, pointing to the bottom of the memo. "Recognize that name?"

I leaned closer, my stomach twisting as I saw it. "Robert Shaw."

Lisa leaned back in her chair, folding her arms, her expression thoughtful. "I think it's time you talked to him, Alex. About your mom, about all of this. He's clearly involved somehow. But it might be different than what you think."

I shook my head, exhaling sharply. "And say what, exactly? 'Hey Shaw, I think you might be covering up something about my mother's disappearance. Care to clarify?' That'll go over well."

Lisa gave a small, dry laugh but didn't let up. "Look, I get it. You have every reason to be skeptical. It's probably what makes you a good prosecutor. But maybe you're letting your paranoia get the better of you this time."

I shot her a look. "Paranoia?"

"Think about it," she pressed, her tone calm but firm. "You've been trying to connect dots that might not actually connect. Shaw working on a case with your mom doesn't mean he's involved in her disappearance. Maybe he feels guilty, sure, but that's not the same as being complicit."

"Or maybe guilt is the exact reason he's so dismissive of everything I bring up about Pierce and Whitaker," I countered. "Because he knows where it leads."

Lisa leaned forward, her gaze steady. "And maybe you're right. But the only way to find out is to have a *calm* conversation and settle it once and for all. Either way, this cloud hanging over you—it's not helping. What you need is clarity."

I rubbed the back of my neck, her words sinking in. She wasn't wrong. My skepticism had served me well in the past, kept me from being blindsided more times than I could count. But Lisa was right about something else, too. I couldn't keep chasing shadows and assuming they were monsters. Either Shaw was hiding something, or I was letting my doubts consume me. Either way, I needed to confront him.

I sighed, meeting her eyes. "You think I'm letting this get the better of me?"

"I think," she said carefully, "that you're carrying a lot right now. Your mom's case, this trial, these anonymous calls. It's a lot for anyone to handle. But you're one of the sharpest people I know. If your gut is telling you something, trust it. Just make sure you're looking for answers at this point, not more questions."

I swallowed hard, staring at Shaw's name on the screen. "You're right," I said, my voice quieter than I intended. "I'll do it tomorrow."

"Tomorrow works." Lisa shut down her computer, stretching as she stood. "Now let's get out of here. I'm exhausted."

We walked toward the elevators together, the weight of the day still heavy on my shoulders. As we passed Shaw's office, I stopped. His light was on, spilling out from beneath the door.

Lisa noticed my hesitation and glanced toward the door. "Looks like he came back."

I nodded, feeling my pulse quicken. "Maybe I should just do it now."

Lisa gave me a cautious look. "Are you sure?"

"I'm sure," I said, though my nerves were buzzing. "It's better to get it over with."

She placed a hand on my arm. "Good luck. I'll see you tomorrow."

As Lisa headed for the elevator, I took a deep breath and knocked on Shaw's door. His gruff voice called out, "Come in."

CHAPTER
THIRTY-FIVE

I PUSHED the door open and stepped inside. Shaw sat at his desk, his tie loosened, and a number of files spread before him. He looked exhausted, the dim light from the desk lamp casting sharp lines across his face. When he looked up and saw me, his eyebrows lifted slightly.

"Hayes," he said, leaning back in his chair. "Still burning the midnight oil?"

Closing the door behind me, I hesitated for a moment before sitting across from him. The air in the room was charged with the weight of what I was about to say.

"We need to talk," I said, my voice firm.

He studied me for a moment, his expression unreadable. "Alright. What about?"

I gripped the arms of the chair, steadying myself. "I know you worked with my mother on the trafficking investigation before she disappeared."

His body stilled, the slight tension in his jaw the only indication he'd registered my words. For a moment, I thought he might deny it. But then he sighed deeply, rubbing a hand over his face.

"I figured you'd find out sooner or later," he said, his voice resigned.

"Why didn't you tell me? All this time, Shaw, and you said nothing, borderline denied it. Why?"

His eyes met mine, a mix of weariness and regret. "Because it's not something I'm proud of, Alex."

His honesty caught me off guard. I'd expected defensiveness, maybe anger. Instead, his tone was low and raw, as if the words had been sitting in his throat for years, waiting to be released.

"Your mother—" He paused as if searching for the right words. "Your mother was one of the most determined people I've ever worked with. Once she got her teeth into something, she wouldn't let go. And when it came to the trafficking case, she was like a dog with a bone."

I let his words settle, and they only raised more questions. "But you worked with her. You were part of the investigation. Why didn't you warn her? Or anyone else?"

Shaw leaned forward, resting his elbows on the desk. "I did try to warn her, Alex. She didn't listen. I told her to back off when the threats started coming in, but she just doubled down." He sighed. "It's not that she was reckless. I think she just had more faith that the system would protect her."

"What kind of threats?" I asked, my voice quieter now but no less intense.

His gaze dropped for a moment before meeting mine again. "The kind that come from people who operate above the law. They weren't just threats to her—they were aimed at you, at your father."

My chest tightened, the words hitting harder than I'd expected. "So, you just let her keep going?" My voice cracked, anger and something close to grief slipping through. "You didn't do anything?"

"I tried." His jaw clenched, and for the first time, I saw something I hadn't expected—guilt. A deep, unrelenting guilt was heavy in his eyes. "I tried to steer her away, to protect her. But your mother was your mother, Alex. She wouldn't listen. I thought if I stayed close, I could shield her somehow. I was wrong."

The weight of his words settled over the room, thick and suffocating. For years, I'd carried anger and frustration over the mystery of my mother's disappearance. Now, seeing the pain etched into Shaw's face, I felt something I hadn't expected: understanding.

My eyes dropped to the floor. "She always said the truth was worth fighting for."

Shaw nodded, his expression somber. "And she was right. But the fight she was taking on was bigger than anything I could control."

"Is that why you didn't push to go further than Pierce?"

"Taking on the entire ring—it could've cost more than we could afford to lose. Lives, careers, the entire case falling apart if we missed even one step."

"And Matthews?"

"He saw it the same way. It wasn't just the risk of failure; it was the risk to his bid for re-election. I convinced him it wasn't worth it. That stopping at Pierce was enough."

I leaned back in my chair, my fists tightening on the armrests. "Enough?" I repeated, disbelief creeping into my voice. "Stopping short of justice is never enough."

He sighed deeply, but his gaze didn't waver. "You're thinking like your mother. That's what scares me, Alex."

"Well, maybe she had it right," I shot back, my voice firm. "We all take risks in this job, Shaw. It comes with the territory. If we let fear or politics stop us, we're letting the criminals win. We're proving their threats work."

His jaw tightened, his expression unreadable. "And what happens when those risks get people killed?"

I stood, pushing back my chair with more force than necessary. "Then we mourn them, and we keep fighting. Because the alternative is letting people like Pierce and Whitaker run free. Is that a risk you're willing to take?"

The silence that followed was deafening. Shaw didn't answer, and for the first time, I wondered if he wasn't sure himself. I felt a flicker of sympathy for him. But, there was still something gnawing at the edges of my mind.

"Was it you?"

He frowned, confused. "What are you talking about?"

"The file box. The one with my mother's notes. It disappeared from my office, and then, like magic, it turned up again. Was it you?"

Shaw's jaw tightened, and for a moment, he looked away. That was all the confirmation I needed, but I waited for him to say it out loud.

"Yes. It was me."

Anger and frustration flared in my chest. "Why would you do that? Were you trying to hide something?"

"I wasn't trying to hide anything that you couldn't have found on your own," he said, his tone defensive but not angry. "I panicked, Alex. When I saw the box, I realized what it was. And yes, I took it. I thought I was protecting you."

"Protecting me? By stealing evidence from my office?"

"Listen to me," Shaw said, leaning forward, his voice sharper now. "I saw firsthand what happened when Katherine got too close. All I could think was that if you started digging into it, you'd end up on the same path."

I opened my mouth to argue, but he held up a hand to stop me.

"And then I realized that taking it wouldn't stop you. It would only make you more determined to find out what was inside. I'd already failed your mother by not doing enough to protect her. I wasn't about to fail you too."

"So you put it back."

"I did. You'd find it eventually, one way or another. And it wasn't my place to keep it from you. You have a right to know what happened to her. And if anyone can get to the bottom of that case, it would be you."

I studied him, trying to gauge the sincerity in his expression. For all my doubts and suspicions, there was no mistaking the guilt and regret etched into his face. This wasn't a man trying to cover his tracks. This was a man haunted by his past decisions.

"Why didn't you just tell me the truth?" I asked, my voice softer now.

"Because I thought I could still keep you out of it," he said. "But I should have known better. You're just like her."

The tension in my chest loosened, but only slightly. I still had questions, still had doubts, but for now, some of my anger dissipated.

I sat back in my chair. "I guess the only way to move forward is to figure out where this all leads."

Shaw nodded. "Agreed."

I hesitated, debating whether to take the next step. Finally, I decided to tell him. "There's something else."

His eyebrow lifted, his focus sharpening. "What is it?"

I reached into my bag and pulled out my notebook, placing it on the desk between us. "I've been getting anonymous calls. They started just before I came back to the DA's office."

Shaw's expression shifted, a mix of concern and curiosity. "What kind of calls?"

I flipped open the notebook, revealing the notes I'd jotted down. "The voice is distorted, but whoever it is, they know things. They told me my mother's disappearance wasn't an accident. That she might still be alive. That I'm getting close to something dangerous."

Shaw leaned forward, scanning the notes with a furrowed brow. "And you think this is connected to the trial?"

"I don't know. But the woman in the courtroom—she's been at every key moment."

Shaw's brows furrowed. "What woman?"

I hesitated, gripping the notebook tightly. "She was at the press conference, jury selection, and now the trial. I think she's the one making the anonymous calls, or she at least knows something about them."

His eyes narrowed, his expression unreadable. "You're telling me the reason you got distracted during opening is because of some woman in the audience?"

"She's not just *some* woman. I've seen her at all these critical moments. There's something about her ... I can't explain it, but I think she's connected to this case."

Shaw leaned back in his chair, crossing his arms. "And you really think she's the one making the calls?"

"It makes sense. She always seems to appear when something significant is happening. She's dodgy, like she doesn't want to be noticed but still wants to be there. And the timing ... it can't be a coincidence."

"Have you tried to approach her?"

"Lisa did, but she slipped away before we could talk to her."

Shaw drummed his fingers on the desk, his eyes narrowing as he mulled it over. "If she's the caller, she could have valuable information. But if she's connected to the trafficking ring in some way, she could also be dangerous."

"I know," I said, nodding. "That's why I'm telling you."

"Turner might be able to help. He's good at finding people who don't want to be found."

I hesitated, my earlier suspicions about Turner resurfacing. "I don't know if I trust him."

Shaw's gaze hardened. "Turner's under a lot of pressure from his chain of command, just like the rest of us. He's pushing this case hard because he knows what's at stake. You might not like his methods, but he's not your enemy."

His words made sense, even if I didn't want to admit it. I nodded slowly. "Alright. If she shows up again, we'll loop Turner in."

"No, we should get him up to speed as soon as possible. He should know." Shaw leaned forward, his expression serious. "Alex, if these calls are part of some larger setup, we need to tread carefully. Whoever's behind this clearly has a vested interest in keeping us off balance."

Swallowing hard, the weight of his words settled over me. "I'll be careful."

For the first time, I felt like I could trust him. Whatever had happened in the past, Shaw wasn't my enemy either. If anything, he seemed determined to make sure I succeeded where my mother had been stopped.

As I stood to leave, I met his gaze. "Thanks for being honest."

Shaw nodded, his voice quiet but firm. "We're in this together, Hayes. Let's make sure we get it right."

CHAPTER THIRTY-SIX

THE ASSIGNED counsel room smelled of stale coffee and paper—a mix of long working hours and even longer nights. Shaw leaned back against the side of the table, arms crossed, while Lisa perched on the edge of a chair, her foot tapping against the floor. Turner, standing in the corner with his notepad in hand, looked visibly uncomfortable.

"So let me get this straight," Turner said, his voice laced with skepticism. "You've been getting anonymous calls about this case, and now you think this mystery woman is connected to them?"

"Not think," I corrected, folding my arms as I leaned against the wall. "I'm sure of it. She's always hovering just on the periphery of everything."

Turner's brows furrowed, and he exchanged a glance with Shaw. "That's a lot to take in."

"Which is why we're telling you now," Shaw replied, his tone even but laced with something heavier—guilt, maybe even regret. "If she's connected to the calls, she could be a key witness—or a threat."

Turner's gaze flicked to him. "What exactly do you mean by a threat?"

"Years ago, I worked on a case with Alex's mother. It involved a trafficking ring—one that Pierce is likely connected to." Shaw sighed, leaning back against the table, his arms crossing tightly over his chest. "These people are dangerous. They don't leave loose ends."

I swallowed hard, trying not to think of my mother as a "loose end."

Turner sighed, running a hand down his face. "Alright, assuming this mystery woman shows up again, what's the plan?"

Lisa straightened, speaking up. "I'll sit in the back of the room and keep an eye out. If she appears, Turner and I will follow her. She's slippery, but we might get lucky."

"And you're sure you'll recognize her?" Turner asked.

Lisa nodded. "Absolutely. I've got her face burned into my memory."

Shaw gave a curt nod. "Good. Let's move quickly. We can't afford to let her slip away again."

Turner glanced at me, still looking uneasy. "You sure about this, Hayes? I mean, this feels … out there."

I met his gaze, my tone firm. "Trust me, Turner. If you'd gotten those calls, you'd be as sure as I am."

He nodded slowly, the hesitation still evident but less pronounced. "Alright."

Lisa and Turner filed out, leaving Shaw and me alone in the room. The silence was heavy, broken only by the faint sound of muffled footsteps in the hallway.

Shaw finally spoke, his voice low. "You're still thinking about Matthews and Ellis, aren't you?"

I turned to him, my brow furrowing. "How could I not?"

Shaw sighed, rubbing the back of his neck. "Maybe I was wrong to dismiss it, but you can't seriously think Tom's involved in any of this."

"Why not? Whitaker's name keeps coming up, and now he's here, cozying up with Tom and Ellis? It's suspicious as hell."

Shaw's jaw tightened, and for a moment, I thought he might snap at me. But instead, he held up a hand. "Alright. I'll ask him. Directly."

I studied him for a moment, trying to gauge his sincerity. His face was calm, but there was a flicker of uncertainty that made me wonder if he was as convinced as he claimed.

"Fine," I said finally. "But don't let him wiggle out of it."

Shaw gave a small nod, his lips twitching slightly as if fighting back a smile. Under his breath, he muttered, "Just like your mother."

I froze for a beat, caught off guard. "What's that supposed to mean?" I asked, narrowing my eyes.

As he glanced at me, the ghost of a smirk tugged at the corner of his mouth. "Stubborn. Relentless. Always pushing, no matter the odds."

I rolled my eyes, but there was a flicker of warmth in my chest despite myself. "Yeah, well, I'll take that as a compliment."

"And you should. She'd be proud."

The unexpected sincerity in his voice left me momentarily speechless. Shaw didn't wait for a response, though. He pushed off the table and adjusted his tie. "Let's get to court. It's going to be a long day."

———

The courtroom was already filling when we entered. The bailiff was preparing the room, and Pierce sat at the defense table, his expression as eerily calm as ever. It still unnerved me, the way he carried himself as if he were untouchable.

Shaw and I took our seats at the counsel table, and I stole a glance at the gallery behind us. Lisa had slipped into a seat near the back, her eyes scanning the room. Turner sat beside her, looking equally alert.

The judge entered, and everyone rose. Once she was seated, the jury filed in, a mix of anticipation and weariness on their faces. As the trial began, Shaw called our first witness for the day: Detective Nathan Reyes, a seasoned detective who arrived shortly after Officer Briggs secured the scene.

Detective Reyes was a solid witness on paper—experienced, reliable, and professional. But as he took the stand, his nervous energy was palpable, likely due to the way Ellis had dismantled Briggs during the cross examination the other day.

Shaw began direct examination, guiding Reyes through the discovery of the bodies and the grim details of the scene.

"The bodies were buried in layers," Reyes began, his voice steady but tinged with discomfort. "Some were dismembered, others showed signs of strangulation. It was clear this wasn't a single incident."

The jury leaned in, their expressions a mix of horror and fascination. I watched them closely, noting the way some avoided looking at Pierce entirely, while others stole glances at him, as if trying to reconcile his calm demeanor with the atrocities being described.

Shaw wrapped up his direct with a series of pointed questions designed to underscore the brutality of the crimes and Pierce's proximity to the burial site. "Detective, in your professional opinion, would it be possible for someone to bury over forty bodies on that property without the owner noticing?"

"No, sir," Reyes replied. "It would be impossible."

As Shaw returned to his seat, I leaned over and whispered, "That went well."

He nodded slightly, but his eyes didn't leave the witness stand. Marcus Ellis was already on his feet, buttoning his jacket as he prepared for cross-examination.

Ellis's approach was methodical and unnervingly smooth. He began by picking apart small inconsistencies in Reyes' report, such as the timeline of when certain bodies were discovered and minor discrepancies in his notes.

"Detective," Ellis began, his tone light, almost conversational. He stepped closer to the witness stand, his hands clasped behind his back. "You've testified that the burial site was in a remote part of the property. Isn't it possible that someone could have used that area without the owner's knowledge?"

Reyes straightened in his seat, his eyes narrowing slightly. "It's possible, but highly unlikely."

Ellis smiled, like a teacher gently correcting a student. "Possible, though. Let's focus on that. You're saying it's not entirely outside the realm of possibility?"

Reyes hesitated, glancing at Shaw and me at counsel's table. "Yes, it's possible, but given the size of the operation—"

"Let's not get ahead of ourselves, Detective. You just acknowledged that it's possible. Thank you for your honesty."

Reyes frowned but didn't respond. Ellis seized the pause, pacing a few steps as he addressed the jury. "Now, Detective, you also testified earlier that this burial site contained multiple remains, buried over an extended period of time. Is that correct?"

"Yes," Reyes replied.

Ellis nodded, as if commending him for getting the answer right. "So, if it's possible that someone could use this part of the property without the owner's knowledge, how exactly would the owner be expected to notice if it occurred sporadically over years?"

Reyes' mouth opened, then closed again, clearly grappling for the right response. "The area is remote, but the scale of the activity makes it highly improbable that the owner wouldn't notice."

"Highly improbable, but not impossible?"

Reyes' jaw tightened, his hesitation stretching in the silent courtroom. "I suppose not impossible."

Ellis stopped pacing, his tone sharpening as he turned back to the detective. "So, Detective, your testimony boils down to this: It's entirely feasible that someone else could have buried these bodies without the owner of the property ever knowing about it."

"Objection!" Shaw stood, his voice cutting through the courtroom. "Badgering the witness and mischaracterizing testimony."

The judge's gavel hit the desk lightly. "Sustained. Mr. Ellis, rephrase or move on."

Ellis gave the judge a disarming smile. "Of course, Your Honor." Turning back to Reyes, his voice regained its calculated calm. "Detective, I'll make this simple. You've testified that while it's unlikely, it's not impossible for the owner to have been completely unaware of these burials. Is that correct?"

Reyes exhaled, his expression strained. "Yes. That's correct."

Ellis paused, letting the words sink into the jury before saying, "No further questions, Your Honor."

Turning he strutted back to the defense table with a self-assured gait, leaving the courtroom in a tense silence. I glanced at the jury, my stomach sinking as I read the expressions on their faces. Confusion. Doubt. The seeds Ellis had planted were already taking root.

Shaw leaned closer to me, his voice low. "We're going to need to undo that damage in redirect."

I nodded, my mind racing. Reyes was one of our strongest witnesses, and Ellis had just dismantled him with surgical precision.

The judge turned her attention to Shaw. "Redirect, Mr. Shaw?"

Shaw stood, buttoning his jacket and walking toward the witness stand with measured confidence. "Detective Reyes," he began, his voice steady, "you testified that while it's theoretically possible for someone to use the burial site without the owner's knowledge, it is, in your professional opinion, highly unlikely. Can you elaborate on why that is?"

Reyes sat a little straighter, clearly relieved to be given a chance to explain. "Yes, sir. The burial site required significant activity over a long period—digging, moving soil, and transporting bodies. It's not something that could go unnoticed without deliberate effort to conceal it."

Shaw nodded, gesturing for Reyes to continue. "And the tools and resources required—are those something that might raise suspicion?"

"Absolutely. There were indications of heavy machinery use, as well as evidence of chemicals to suppress decomposition smells. These would have required storage and frequent use, which would be hard to miss for anyone living on the property."

Shaw paced, letting the jury absorb the detective's words. "So, Detective, to clarify, while you acknowledged the possibility, your professional conclusion is that it would be extremely difficult—nearly impossible—for someone to operate a burial site of this scale without the property owner being aware. Is that correct?"

"That is correct."

Shaw stopped in front of the jury, his voice firm. "Thank you, Detective. No further questions."

As Shaw returned to the counsel table, I allowed myself a small breath of relief. He had done what he could to restore credibility, but the damage Ellis had done still loomed large. The jury's faces were mixed—some nodding slightly, others still skeptical.

"Witness dismissed," the judge said, her tone clipped. She turned to Shaw. "Next witness?"

But before Shaw could rise, a small commotion in the back of the courtroom drew everyone's attention. The sound of footsteps shuffling against the floor was followed by muffled voices.

The judge's gavel came down sharply. "Order! What is going on back there?"

I turned, my heart pounding. Lisa and Turner were both on their feet, moving quickly toward the exit.

The judge's face was a mixture of annoyance and curiosity as she addressed the courtroom. "Counsel, please maintain decorum. We'll take a ten-minute recess."

As the gavel struck, signaling the recess, Shaw leaned toward me, his voice low and urgent. "What's going on?"

"I think she's here."

THE GAVEL STRUCK AGAIN, and the judge dismissed us for a ten-minute recess. I turned to Shaw. "I'm going to find Lisa and Turner."

He gave me a sharp look, then nodded reluctantly. "Go. I'll hold the fort."

Without another word, I slipped out of the courtroom and into the hallway. The buzz of voices and footsteps echoed off the marble walls, the courthouse alive in its usual chaos. My heart raced as I glanced left, then right. No sign of Lisa or Turner.

Damn it.

I hesitated, glancing back toward the courtroom door. Ten minutes wasn't a lot of time, and Shaw wouldn't be happy if I missed the start of the next session. But something in my gut told me this was too important to let go. The crowd was thicker than I anticipated. Attorneys stood in tight clusters, talking over one another in rushed voices. Court staff wheeled carts of case files, their clattering wheels drowning out snippets of conversation. A couple of jurors wandered aimlessly, holding coffee cups and looking a little lost. I tried to maneuver through the chaos, muttering quick apologies as I bumped shoulders and dodged elbows.

Every second felt like an eternity. My heart was pounding so hard it drowned out everything else—the hum of the fluorescent lights, the tap-tap of hurried heels on the sleek tile floor. Glancing at my watch,I cursed under my breath. Seven minutes left before the recess ended. Seven minutes to find Lisa and Turner—and the woman—then get back to the courtroom.

I kept moving, scanning every face I passed. Nothing. No sign of Lisa, Turner, or the woman. Doubt started to creep in, tightening its grip on my resolve. What if I'd chosen the wrong direction? What if they'd gone deeper into the building, to some other exit? Or worse, what if they were already heading back to the courtroom while I wandered aimlessly?

I stopped at an intersection of hallways, indecision gnawing at me. Left would take me toward the elevators and offices. Right led to the side exits, less crowded but just as plausible. Straight ahead was the main lobby and the courthouse's primary exit.

Think, Alex.

My instincts pulled me forward, toward the main exit. If the woman was nervous enough to leave, she'd likely aim for the most obvious way out. I set off again, weaving through the thickening crowd.

Halfway to the lobby, a large group of attorneys spilled out of a conference room, blocking the hallway entirely. I came to an abrupt stop, my frustration boiling over as I waited for them to move. They didn't. Their animated discussion seemed to take priority over anyone else trying to get past. I clenched my fists, biting back a sharp remark. Wasting time wasn't an option.

"Excuse me," I said, squeezing between two of them. One muttered something about manners, but I ignored it, breaking free of the bottle-neck and hurrying toward the lobby. My shoes echoed sharply against the tile as the crowd began to thin.

The lobby came into view, its high ceilings and wide windows casting harsh sunlight across the polished floor. I scanned the space quickly, my gaze darting from one face to the next.

And then I saw them.

Near the main doors, Lisa and Turner stood close together, speaking to someone I couldn't quite see. My heart leapt into my throat. I quickened my pace, my shoes slipping slightly on the freshly waxed floor.

As I got closer, the woman came into view. She was exactly as I remembered—her headscarf tied tightly around her head, her posture stiff and defensive. Looking like she wanted to bolt at any second, her eyes darted around the lobby, searching for an escape. Lisa was speaking to her softly, her hands raised as if trying to calm a skittish animal. Turner stood a step behind her, his broad frame imposing, but his demeanor surprisingly gentle.

I slowed my approach, not wanting to spook the woman further. My pulse hammered in my ears as I watched her. With her arms crossed tightly over her chest, her fingers gripped her sleeves like a lifeline. As she looked up, her eyes locked on mine for the briefest moment. Recognition flickered in her expression. A chill ran down my spine.

Lisa noticed me first, her gaze flicking to mine, relief flashing across her face. Turner glanced over his shoulder, his expression one of caution. The woman didn't move. Her eyes stayed on me, wide and uncertain.

I kept my hands at my sides, trying to project calm even as my mind raced. "Hi," I said softly, my voice steady despite the adrenaline coursing through me. "Do you know who I am?"

The woman hesitated, her gaze darting between Lisa and Turner as if seeking reassurance. Finally, she nodded. "Yes," she murmured, her voice barely above a whisper.

My heart skipped a beat. I swallowed hard, the weight of the moment pressing down on me. "Will you talk to me?" I asked gently. "Help me with this case?"

Her eyes darted around the room again, her nerves palpable. She seemed to be weighing something, her lips pressing into a thin line. I held my breath, waiting, hoping.

After what felt like an eternity, she gave a small, hesitant nod. "Okay."

Relief swept through me, but I knew better than to show it. The four of us moved down the hall, the tension thick enough to cut with a knife. Turner led the way, his strides purposeful but not rushed. He scanned the corridor ahead like a sentinel, his sharp eyes missing nothing. Behind him, Lisa walked alongside the woman, speaking in a low, calming voice. The woman's shoulders were hunched, her head down, as if she were trying to disappear into herself.

I followed a step behind, my heart pounding in time with each footstep. My gaze stayed fixed on the woman. Every movement she made—her quick glances to the side, the way her fingers twitched at her sides—felt like a clue, something to decipher. Nerves radiated off her like static electricity.

Turner reached a witness room and opened the door, stepping aside to let us in. He gestured for Lisa to lead the way, his posture careful but firm. Lisa guided the woman inside with a reassuring smile. "Right this way," she said softly, her voice as steady as a heartbeat.

The woman hesitated at the threshold, her eyes darting toward the exit as if calculating the distance. For a moment, I thought she might bolt. But then she took a shaky breath and stepped inside, her movements stiff and deliberate.

Lisa followed close behind, positioning herself next to the table. Turner entered last, closing the door with a quiet, decisive click. He leaned back against it, his arms crossed over his chest, his broad shoulders making it clear that the exit was no longer an option. I wondered briefly if he was trying to keep her in or keep someone else out.

The room was small and sparsely furnished—a rectangular table, a few mismatched chairs, and a dusty artificial plant in a corner. The fluorescent lights buzzed faintly, casting a cold, clinical glow over the space.

The woman moved toward one of the chairs but didn't sit right away. She stood there, gripping the backrest, her knuckles white. Her eyes flitted around the room, taking in every corner, every shadow. Finally, with a visible effort, she lowered herself onto the edge of the chair, her knees pressed tightly together, her hands gripping them as if they were the only things keeping her grounded.

Lisa perched on the edge of the table, her hands resting loosely in her lap. Her expression was open, inviting, but I could see the subtle tension in her shoulders. "Take your time. We're just here to talk."

Turner remained at the door, shifting his weight slightly as he crossed one ankle over the other. As he looked at the woman, his expression unreadable, his presence alone filled the room with a quiet authority.

I stayed standing for a moment, watching her. But she didn't meet my eyes. Her focus was on her hands, her fingers tracing anxious patterns over her knees. Her shoulders were drawn in tight, as though she were bracing for impact.

Finally, I pulled out a chair across from her and sat down, the scrape of the metal legs against the floor loud in the otherwise silent room. Leaning forward slightly, I tried to appear as nonthreatening as possible.

For a moment, no one spoke. The air was thick with unasked questions and unresolved tension. The woman's breathing was shallow, her chest rising and falling quickly.

"Who are you?" I asked quietly, the words carrying the weight of all my questions.

She met my eyes, her voice trembling but clear. "I'm a friend of your mother's."

CHAPTER
THIRTY-EIGHT

THE WOMAN'S words echoed in my mind, each syllable unraveling my composure.

A friend of your mother.

My stomach lurched as my mind struggled to process the admission. Hands trembling, I clenched them into fists on the table, willing myself to stay grounded. I looked up at Lisa, hoping for some kind of anchor, and she met my gaze with a steadying nod.

The air in the room felt heavy, pressing down on me as Lisa began to speak, her voice soft and calm. My fingers fidgeted with the edge of my notebook, the worn leather suddenly fascinating. Wanting to look up, to participate, to take control of the situation, I was frozen.

"Okay," Lisa began. "Let's start with something simple. Can you tell us your name?"

The woman's gaze darted around the room, her body tense like a cornered animal. She licked her lips, her fingers digging into the edge of the chair. "It's ... it's Lydia," she said, her voice barely audible, almost swallowed by the silence. "Lydia Kane."

Lisa nodded, her tone softening. "Alright, Lydia. It's good to meet you. Can you tell us how you knew Alex's mother?"

Lydia's eyes flicked to me for a split second, and I thought I saw a flash of guilt—or maybe it was fear. Then her gaze dropped, and her hands tightened on the table's edge, her knuckles going white. "She helped me," Lydia said, her voice trembling. "A long time ago. I was ... involved in something bad, and she was trying to get me out."

As I shifted in my chair, the wood creaked beneath me. My hand went to my face, brushing an imaginary strand of hair away, anything to keep from giving away the storm of emotions surging through me. My mother had always been the type to help people, even when it meant putting herself at risk. But hearing it from Lydia—a stranger— made it feel real in a way that knocked the air out of my lungs.

Lisa leaned forward, her movements slow, as though she was afraid to startle Lydia. "Was this related to the trafficking case she was investigating?"

Lydia nodded, pressing her lips into a thin line, as if the words she wanted to say were physically painful. "Yes. She was trying to expose them. The people behind it. But they found out she was getting too close."

My nails dug into my palms as my hands fisted. The room seemed to tilt slightly, the fluorescent lights above casting harsh shadows.

Lisa glanced at me, her expression filled with quiet concern. I felt the pull to say something, to take over the conversation, but my throat had closed up. I traced the edge of the table with my thumb, focusing on the tactile sensation to ground myself.

"What happened when they found out?" Lisa asked, her tone still calm but carrying a note of urgency.

Lydia hesitated, her gaze darting to the door, Turner's bulk leaning casually against it. She looked like she was debating whether to answer at all.

"They warned her," Lydia said finally, her voice barely above a whisper. "But she didn't stop. She kept going. And then one day, she was just ... gone."

The words hit me like a physical blow, the air leaving my lungs. I blinked rapidly, staring down at my lap. My mother's disappearance had been a mystery for so long, a gaping wound I had learned to live with but never healed. Now, here was a stranger who might be able to fill in the pieces of the puzzle, and I didn't know how to process it.

Lisa pressed forward, her voice steady but laced with urgency. "Do you know who was behind it? The people she was investigating?"

Lydia hesitated, her hands gripping the edge of the table so tightly that her knuckles turned white. Her lips pressed together, and for a moment, I thought she might refuse to answer. But then she exhaled shakily, her shoulders sinking as if she'd been carrying the weight of the question for years.

"I do." Lydia lifted her gaze, meeting Lisa's eyes, then mine. "I know all of it. Who they are, how they operate, everything."

The room went still. I straightened in my seat, my pulse quickening. "What do you mean, everything?" I asked, my voice sharper than I intended.

Lydia swallowed hard, her gaze darting between the three of us. "Pierce. Whitaker. Scorpion, Slim, Lighthouse Ventures, Maria Alvarez and the others. I know how they're all connected. How it all fits together."

The air in the room felt electric, charged with the weight of her admission. Lisa glanced at me, her expression unreadable, but her grip on the edge of the table mirrored Lydia's.

I leaned forward. "Then why now?" I demanded, my voice rising. "If you've known all of this, if you could've helped my mother, why are you coming forward *now*? Why not years ago, when it might have actually made a difference?"

Lydia flinched at my words, her body curling inward like she was bracing for a blow. "Because …" She took a deep breath, her eyes glistening with unshed tears. "Because you're getting too close, just like she did."

I stared at her, my frustration mounting. Lisa shot me a warning glance, silently urging me to keep my tone even.

"You still haven't answered the question," I said, forcing myself to steady my voice. "Why didn't you say anything before? Why let this go on for so long?"

Lydia shook her head, her gaze fixed on the floor. Her hands twisted together in her lap, trembling. "Because it wouldn't have mattered. This ring, it's too big. Too powerful. It's not just in Houston, not even just in Texas. It's everywhere. They have people in law enforcement, politics, the courts. They make people disappear, and no one even notices."

Her words hung in the air, heavy and suffocating. A chill ran down my spine as the enormity of what she was saying sank in. Lisa leaned forward, her tone gentle but insistent. "But if it's that big, if it's everywhere, then why now? Why come forward at all?"

Lydia's eyes finally met mine, and the raw fear in them made my stomach twist. "I didn't want the same thing to happen to you," Lydia continued, her voice trembling. "I couldn't live with that. Your mother was so brave, but she didn't know when to stop. I don't want to see you end up like her."

The silence in the room was deafening. I looked at Lisa, hoping she had something to say, but her expression was just as conflicted as I felt. My mind raced, trying to piece together what Lydia was hiding and why she seemed so terrified.

Finally, I forced myself to speak, my voice low but firm. "Lydia," I said, locking eyes with her. "Have you been calling me?"

CHAPTER
THIRTY-NINE

TURNER CLEARED HIS THROAT, the sound cutting through the thick tension in the room. "The trial's about to resume," he said, his tone sharp but quiet. "We need to get back."

I turned my head sharply toward him, glaring.

Turner didn't flinch, his expression calm and unreadable as always. "We have a courtroom full of people waiting on us, Alex. They can't wait forever."

I sat there for a moment, my jaw clenched as I tried to suppress the frustration boiling inside me. Lydia's gaze darted toward the door, her nervousness escalating with the mention of time running out. She wasn't going to say anything else, not now. The moment was gone.

Exhaling sharply, I turned to Lisa, my voice softer now. "Will you stay with her?"

Lisa nodded without hesitation. "Of course."

I shifted my focus back to Lydia, trying to steady my tone. "Lydia, I need you to trust us. Whatever you know, whatever you've been keeping inside, it's time to let it out. I need you to tell Lisa everything about this trafficking ring—about Pierce, Whitaker, Slim, Scorpion, all of it." I paused, swallowing hard as my voice threatened to waver. "If you want to repay my mother for what she sacrificed for you, this is how you can do it. This is your chance."

Lydia's hands gripped her knees tightly, her knuckles white, but she didn't speak. Her eyes flicked between me and Lisa, her lips pressing into a thin line.

I held her gaze, willing her to see how much this mattered. She didn't respond, but something in her expression shifted. A flicker of resolve, maybe. It wasn't much, but it was enough for me to sense that she would help—eventually.

I stood slowly, the weight of the conversation heavy on my shoulders. As I moved toward the door, I glanced back at Lisa. "Text me if anything happens."

Lisa nodded, giving me a reassuring look. "Go handle court."

I met Turner's gaze as he held the door open for me. His usual calm felt grating, but I pushed down my irritation. The door closed behind me with a quiet click. Turner stood in the hallway, arms crossed, waiting. I shot him a glare, my frustration barely contained.

"Why would you interrupt at a moment like that?" I hissed as I approached.

Turner didn't flinch. His expression was calm, unreadable. "The trial's about to resume," he said simply. "This isn't the time or place to have those kinds of discussions, Alex. You should know that."

I stopped short, narrowing my eyes at him. "Don't patronize me, Turner. She was about to tell me everything, and you cut her off."

He held my gaze for a moment, then sighed. "You're running on emotion right now. I get it. But you need to focus. Lydia will still be there when the day ends. Right now, you've got a courtroom full of people waiting for you."

I clenched my fists at my sides, biting back the retort on the tip of my tongue. Shaw's words about Turner being under pressure came back to me, urging me to give him the benefit of the doubt. But it wasn't easy.

"Fine," I said through gritted teeth. "But this better not be some tactic to stall her."

Turner didn't respond, just turned and started walking toward the courtroom. I followed, weaving through the small clusters of people still lingering in the hallways. The noise of the courthouse seemed amplified now—every footstep, every hushed conversation grated on my nerves.

By the time we reentered the courtroom, the judge and jury were already beginning to file in. I slipped into my seat beside Shaw, who leaned over and asked in a low voice, "What happened?"

"We got her," I whispered back, keeping my eyes on the front of the room. "We'll discuss later."

Shaw nodded, his focus shifting as the judge called the session back to order. He stood smoothly when prompted and adjusted his jacket. "Your Honor, the State calls Dr. Sarah Milton to the stand."

Dr. Milton, the forensic pathologist, made her way to the witness stand with practiced ease. She was a composed woman in her early forties, with neatly tied-back dark hair and glasses perched on her nose. She was the kind of expert witness who could hold her own, and I silently prayed she wouldn't buckle under Ellis's scrutiny.

Shaw began his direct examination with a calm, measured tone. "Dr. Milton, could you please state your name and occupation for the record?"

"Dr. Sarah Milton," she said, her voice steady. "I'm a forensic pathologist with the Harris County Medical Examiner's Office."

"And how long have you held that position?"

"Ten years."

Shaw nodded. "Now, Dr. Milton, you performed autopsies on several of the victims in this case, is that correct?"

"Yes, I did."

Shaw stepped closer to the jury, his hands clasped behind his back, projecting calm authority. "Dr. Milton, could you describe your findings for the court?"

Dr. Milton adjusted her glasses, her tone professional but somber. "The victims suffered extensive trauma, consistent with homicide. The injuries included signs of asphyxiation, blunt force trauma, and, in some cases, sharp force injuries. The times of death varied across the victims, but the evidence suggests they were buried in the same location over a span of several years."

Shaw nodded, letting the gravity of her words sink in for the jury. "And were you able to ascertain anything about the tools or methods used to commit these murders?"

"Yes," she replied, her voice steady. "The blunt force injuries suggest the use of a heavy object, potentially a hammer or something similar. The sharp force injuries indicate a knife with a serrated edge. Additionally, the asphyxiation marks are consistent with the use of ligatures, such as ropes or cords."

A murmur of unease rippled through the jury. I studied their faces. A man in his sixties on the far left rubbed his chin, his eyes narrowing. A younger woman in the front row winced, her hands clenched tightly in her lap. I mentally cataloged these reactions, knowing Shaw would want to leverage them in closing arguments.

Shaw moved in for the next question. "Dr. Milton, based on your analysis, do these tools and methods suggest anything about the perpetrator? Their level of planning, for example?"

Dr. Milton hesitated for a moment. "The injuries are consistent with deliberate actions, indicating a perpetrator who planned these attacks. The range of injuries and tools used suggest familiarity with violence."

Shaw paused, letting her words hang in the air before continuing. "And given the burial site's location, do you believe it would have been possible for someone to bury these bodies without the property owner's knowledge?"

Dr. Milton folded her hands in her lap, maintaining her calm demeanor. "It would have been difficult, but not impossible. The burial site is remote, which could allow for concealment. However, the frequency and volume of activity required to bury this many bodies over such an extended period make it highly improbable that the property owner was unaware."

I felt a flicker of hope at her answer. Shaw's question was critical, and she had landed it in our favor. Shaw nodded approvingly. "Thank you, Dr. Milton. I have no further questions at this time."

As Shaw took his seat, Ellis rose smoothly, his expression calculated. His confidence was palpable as he approached the witness stand, adjusting his tie as though he were preparing for a show. "Dr. Milton," he began, his tone almost conversational, "you testified that the burial site is remote. Is that correct?"

"Yes."

"You also stated that it would have been difficult, but not impossible, for someone to bury the bodies without the property owner's knowledge?"

"That's correct."

Ellis nodded, pacing in front of the jury. "Difficult but not impossible. So, it's within the realm of possibility that someone other than the property owner could have buried those bodies?"

Dr. Milton hesitated before replying. "As I said, it's possible, but highly improbable."

"And in the course of your investigation, were you able to recover any of Mr. Pierce's DNA from any of the victims' bodies?"

"No," she admitted, her voice steady but quieter.

"How about from the tools you mentioned? The hammer, the serrated knife? Did any of Pierce's DNA show up on those?"

Dr. Milton shook her head. "No, none of the evidence presented to me contained DNA conclusively linking Mr. Pierce to the crimes."

Ellis turned to the jury, spreading his hands in a gesture of mock sympathy. "Thank you, Dr. Milton. That will be all."

The weight of his words settled over the room. I clenched my jaw, frustration mounting. Ellis had turned the absence of evidence into his weapon, twisting the narrative to plant doubt in the jury's mind.

Shaw stood, buttoning his jacket as he prepared for redirect. His movements were measured, deliberate. "Dr. Milton, given the nature of these crimes and the number of victims involved, would it be reasonable to assume that the perpetrator had experience in committing these acts?"

"Yes," Dr. Milton replied. "The consistency of the injuries and the efforts taken to conceal the bodies suggest a level of experience and planning."

Shaw leaned in slightly, his voice calm but firm. "And would someone with such experience likely understand how to avoid leaving evidence—such as DNA—behind?"

Ellis shot to his feet. "Objection, Your Honor. Speculation."

Shaw turned to the judge, his tone measured. "Your Honor, this question is within the scope of Dr. Milton's expertise. As a forensic pathologist, she can speak to patterns of criminal behavior based on evidence, or the lack thereof."

The judge considered for a moment before nodding. "Overruled. You may answer, Dr. Milton."

Dr. Milton adjusted her glasses. "Yes. It's reasonable to conclude that someone experienced enough to commit and conceal multiple murders over an extended period would also know how to eliminate or minimize forensic evidence."

Shaw stepped back, satisfied. "Thank you, Dr. Milton. No further questions."

He returned to his seat, his expression controlled but tinged with irritation at the effort it had taken to salvage the testimony. As he sat down, he leaned toward me. "Damage control, but it'll hold."

I nodded, though the unease in my chest remained.

The judge glanced at the clock. "We'll adjourn for the day."

I forced myself to stay seated, but my nerves were already buzzing. As the last juror exited and the judge left the bench, my gaze shifted back to the defense table. Pierce was staring directly at me, his expression eerily calm, his eyes unblinking.

CHAPTER FORTY

THE COURTHOUSE HALLS felt oppressively quiet as we walked toward the witness room. My heels echoed on the polished floors, the sound too sharp and too loud. Turner walked ahead, his posture stiff, while Shaw stayed just behind, flipping through his notepad with practiced nonchalance. But I could feel the tension radiating off him, matching my own.

I couldn't stop the questions racing through my head. Had Lydia stayed? Did Lisa manage to convince her? Or had the woman bolted, leaving us to pick up the pieces of a fragile plan? My stomach churned at the thought of walking into an empty room.

Turner glanced back at me. "You're quiet."

I shrugged, my voice tight. "Just thinking."

My breath caught as I stepped inside. Lydia was still there, sitting at the small table with Lisa. They were deep in conversation, Lisa leaning slightly forward, her hands moving animatedly as she spoke. Lydia nodded along, her shoulders a little less hunched than before.

Relief washed over me, but it didn't entirely settle the knot in my chest. They looked so at ease, as if they'd known each other for years instead of hours. It should have reassured me, but instead, it made me feel uneasy. Lydia's demeanor was too polished, too cooperative for someone who had just stepped into the middle of a high-stakes legal case.

Shaw cleared his throat, breaking the moment. Lisa looked up and waved us in. "She's still here," she said, her voice bright but edged with tension. "Ready to talk."

I nodded, forcing a tight smile. "Good."

Turner closed the door behind us, and for a second, the small room felt cramped. Lydia shifted in her seat, her gaze darting toward Shaw, then to me. She looked nervous, but there was something else there, too. Calculating. Or maybe I was imagining it.

Turner's voice broke through my thoughts. "If we're going to keep talking, I suggest we move to your office," he said, gesturing his head toward Shaw.

Lydia hesitated, glancing at Lisa for reassurance. Lisa gave her a small smile and stood, motioning for her to follow. "It's just down the street," she said softly. "You'll be more comfortable."

Lydia nodded, her movements hesitant but compliant. The five of us left the room together, filing into the hallway and heading toward the courthouse exit. The crisp air outside hit me as we stepped onto the street, and I adjusted my bag on my shoulder, glancing at Lydia. She walked slightly behind Lisa, her scarf pulled tighter around her neck as if trying to shield herself from more than just the wind.

The walk to the DA's office was quiet, each of us absorbed in our own thoughts. Turner led the way, posture rigid, while Shaw walked beside me, flipping through his notepad like he was already mentally drafting arguments. I found myself trailing slightly behind, watching Lydia out of the corner of my eye. Her fingers fidgeted with the edge of her scarf, her movements nervous but controlled. It didn't match the fear I expected from someone in her position. Instead, it felt deliberate —like she was measuring each step, each breath.

The ride up the elevator to our floor was silent and so was the walk down the hallway. When we reached the office, the building was dimly lit, the faint hum of fluorescent lights echoing in the quiet hallway as we made our way to his office. Shaw unlocked the door and held it open, motioning for everyone to file inside.

"Let's get started," Shaw said, his tone sharp but steady, as he gestured for everyone to take a seat.

The air in Shaw's office felt heavy, a mix of tension and anticipation settling like a fog over the room. Lydia sat stiffly in the chair across from his desk, her hands folded tightly in her lap. Lisa perched on the edge of a side table, Turner stood by the door with his arms crossed, and Shaw leaned against his desk, still holding his notepad.

Sinking into the chair beside Lydia, my legs crossed but restless, I bounced my foot against the carpet. My mind buzzed with everything that had happened in the courtroom today—and now this. It was too much, and yet it felt like the exact moment we'd been waiting for.

"All right," Shaw said, breaking the silence. "Lydia, you've claimed to have information that can directly implicate Pierce and others connected to the trafficking ring. We need you to start from the beginning."

Lydia took a shaky breath, her hands gripping the edge of the chair. "They recruited me when I was nineteen. Lighthouse Ventures approached me with a job offer as a personal assistant. It was too good to be true, but at the time, I didn't realize it. I wasn't far out of high school, and I needed a job."

I caught Lisa's eyes from across the room. The mention of Lighthouse Ventures hit too close to home after what we'd learned about Maria Alvarez's involvement.

"They promised me a career, financial security, everything I needed to escape the mess my life had been," Lydia continued. Her voice wavered, but she pressed on. "On my first day, they took me to a party. That's where it all started."

Shaw scribbled something in his notepad. "What kind of party?"

Her jaw tightened. "The kind where women are treated like property, passed around, and told they belong to whoever pays the most." She looked down at her hands, her voice softening. "Whitaker was there. Scorpion too. They were … watching."

Turner shifted against the door frame, his face impassive but his posture tense.

"What about Pierce?" Shaw asked.

Her gaze flicked up to meet his. "Pierce wasn't at the parties. Not usually. He … he came in later, when they needed him to clean up their messes." Her lips pressed into a thin line. "The women who stopped cooperating but knew too much—he was the one who made them disappear."

Lisa inhaled sharply. Shaw straightened, his pen hovering above the page.

"He killed them?" I asked, my voice quieter than I intended.

Lydia nodded. "I saw him once, dragging a woman into a car. She was begging for her life. I thought … I thought I was next."

The room fell into an uneasy silence, everyone processing her words. My stomach twisted, but not entirely because of the gruesome imagery.

Shaw cleared his throat. "And Whitaker's role?"

"He's the leader," Lydia said immediately. "He manages everything from the top. He funds the operations, keeps the network protected, and recruits men like Scorpion and Slim to do the dirty work."

"And Lighthouse Ventures?" Lisa prompted.

"It's a front," Lydia said. "They lure women in with fake jobs, just like they did with me. Some are trafficked here in the States, others overseas."

I studied Lydia closely as she spoke. Her hands trembled, but her voice remained steady. The details were damning, but they were also perfect. Too perfect.

"And Pierce?" Shaw pressed.

"He's guilty," Lydia said firmly. "I know he is. He's a monster."

Her words lingered in the air, heavy and definitive. Everyone else seemed to take them at face value. Turner nodded slightly, Lisa leaned back as if she was letting out a breath she'd been holding, and Shaw jotted more notes in his pad.

But I couldn't shake the unease creeping up my spine.

"Lydia," I said carefully, leaning forward. "What do you know about my mother?"

Her eyes widened slightly, and she hesitated for the first time since we'd started. "Your mother … Katherine Hayes?"

I nodded.

"Pierce was going to kill me. I'd stopped cooperating, and they decided I was a liability. Your mother convinced them I wasn't a threat. She … she risked everything for me."

My chest tightened, the weight of her words settling heavily. My mother. Risking everything. For her.

"And now?" I asked, my voice quieter. "Do you know where she is now?"

Lydia shook her head slowly, her expression pained. "I don't. I wish I did. But if she's alive ..... She paused, glancing around the room. "If she's alive, it's because they're forcing her to do their bidding. Just like they did with me."

The room fell silent again. I could feel everyone's eyes on me, waiting for my reaction, but I didn't trust my voice enough to speak. My mind raced with questions I didn't even know how to ask.

Turner broke the tension. "We're going to need corroboration for all of this. Details. Evidence. Something to back up your testimony."

He was right. As much as Lydia's story aligned with what we already suspected, it was just that—a story. I felt a flicker of respect for Turner, who didn't seem entirely swept up in Lydia's narrative.

Shaw, on the other hand, seemed less concerned. "She's going on the stand," he said, his tone leaving no room for debate.

I met Turner's gaze briefly, seeing my own skepticism reflected in him. But I kept my mouth shut. For now.

CHAPTER
FORTY-ONE

THE NEXT MORNING FELT HEAVY, the kind of weight that pressed against your chest and made it hard to breathe. Clouds hung low in the sky, dulling the sunlight and reflecting the apprehension I couldn't shake.

My nerves felt frayed, a product of both exhaustion and the nagging doubt I couldn't shake about Lydia. The DA's office was buzzing when I'd arrived, but the energy was split between focused intensity and barely concealed tension. Everyone knew today could make or break the case.

Shaw and I didn't exchange many words on the walk to the court-room. He carried himself with the same confidence as always, his stride purposeful, his expression unreadable. I envied that composure. In contrast, my thoughts churned endlessly, still looping through everything Lydia had said. Every detail of her testimony sounded airtight, but that was part of what bothered me—it was all a little too perfect.

We entered the courtroom together, the heavy oak doors groaning as they closed behind us. The jury box stood empty for now, the judge's bench vacant. The gallery buzzed quietly, filled with observers whispering to each other in anticipation. I glanced toward the defense table, where Marcus Ellis leaned over to whisper something to Pierce. Pierce, as always, looked calm.

As we settled at our table, Shaw began sorting through his notes with the same sharp efficiency he always did. I, on the other hand, couldn't keep still. Bouncing my knee beneath the table and fidgeting with the edge of my notebook.

Lydia Kane. Her name was like a mantra in my mind, swirling with uncertainty.

I had fought to bring her forward, chasing her down, insisting she was the missing piece. And yet, now that she was here, about to testify, a deep unease gnawed at me. Sure, we'd gotten the short version of her story yesterday, but that was just a summary—a handful of pieces to a puzzle we hadn't finished assembling. What if there were gaps? Inconsistencies? Lies?

She hadn't been coached properly for this. We hadn't rehearsed her answers or drilled her on potential questions. We hadn't prepared her for Marcus Ellis, who would pounce on any hesitation, any misstep, like a predator sensing weakness. The first lesson they drill into your head in law school is never to ask a question if you don't already know the answer. And here we were, about to violate that cardinal rule in a very big way.

My mind raced with scenarios of how this could go wrong. What if she froze? What if her story unraveled under cross-examination? What if Ellis tore her credibility apart in front of the jury? This case was already tenuous, and the jury's attention was hanging by a thread. Could we afford to gamble everything on a witness we barely knew?

And then there was Lydia herself. It wasn't just the lack of preparation or the risk of Ellis shredding her that had me on edge. It was *her.* She'd spent so much time running from us, evading questions, dodging answers. And yet, the moment we cornered her, the moment we truly got to her, not only did she fold, but she offered everything. Names, details, promises to testify. It was too easy.

Was I making another mistake? Had I let my desperation cloud my judgment again?

I glanced over at Shaw. Reviewing his notes, his pen tapped rhythmically against the yellow legal pad in front of him. Of course, he looked at ease. He'd handled unprepared witnesses before. He thrived in the chaos and unpredictability of the courtroom. Shaw lived for moments like these, where quick thinking and instinct could outshine meticulous planning.

But I wasn't Shaw. And this wasn't just another trial to me.

I smoothed my hands over my skirt, trying to ground myself, but my nerves refused to settle. This wasn't just about the case. This was about Pierce. About Whitaker. About the faceless, shadowy network that seemed to pull strings no one else could see.

It was also about my mother—a puzzle piece I couldn't quite fit but couldn't stop trying to place.

Leaning back slightly, I stared at the ceiling for a moment, as if the plaster patterns might somehow provide clarity. They didn't.

I fiddled with the edge of my notepad, flipping it open and scribbling a few disjointed words: *Lydia, testimony, Pierce, Whitaker.* Crossing them out, the pen pressed deep into the paper. My head was too crowded with what-ifs and second-guesses. I glanced at Shaw again, hoping to absorb some of his steadiness, but it only made me feel more out of place. He thrived in unpredictability, but I lived in preparation. And right now, I felt unmoored.

My eyes shifted to the door, half-hoping Lisa would appear with some reassuring word or sign. She wouldn't—she was likely still with Lydia, prepping her as best they could in the short time we'd been given. A short, humorless laugh almost escaped my lips. Prepping. What could Lisa even do in such a short time?

Shaw didn't seem to notice my growing tension, or if he did, he didn't show it. He flipped a page of his notes, his pen tapping once before it stilled. I envied his composure, but I couldn't mirror it. This case wasn't Shaw's life. It wasn't his past clawing its way into his present.

It was mine.

"Good morning, Counsel," Judge Elaine Carter said as she swept into the courtroom. Her presence was commanding, her sharp black robes flowing as she took her place behind the bench. She adjusted her glasses, her piercing gaze scanning the room. "Are we ready to proceed?"

"Yes, Your Honor," Shaw said, standing and buttoning his jacket.

"Very well." She gestured for the bailiff to bring in the jury.

As the jurors filed in, I studied their faces. Some looked tired, others curious. They were trying to piece this puzzle together, just like we were.

Judge Carter addressed Shaw again. "Does the prosecution rest?"

Shaw stepped forward, his tone confident. "No, Your Honor. The state requests permission to call a witness not included on our original list."

A murmur rippled through the gallery. Ellis stiffened, his head snapping toward us. He was on his feet in seconds. "Objection, Your Honor! This is a blatant violation of discovery rules. The defense has had no opportunity to prepare for this witness."

Judge Carter raised a hand to silence him, then motioned for Shaw and Ellis to approach. She signaled to the clerk, who turned on the white noise that blocked the jury from overhearing conversations at the bench.

I stood, despite not being explicitly invited, and followed behind Shaw.

"Mr. Shaw," Judge Carter said, her tone and expression coated in annoyance. "Explain."

Shaw didn't flinch. "The witness came forward only yesterday, Your Honor. Her testimony is crucial to this case and can provide direct evidence linking the defendant to the murders."

Ellis's scoff was loud enough to carry across the room. "Direct evidence? This reeks of desperation."

Judge Carter's sharp gaze pinned him in place. "You'll have your chance to respond, Mr. Ellis. For now, both of you, follow me to chambers."

The short walk to Judge Carter's chambers was silent, the tension almost suffocating. Once inside, she seated herself behind her imposing oak desk and we all took our seats.

"Mr. Shaw," she began, "you understand the gravity of calling an undisclosed witness at this stage of the trial?"

"Yes, Your Honor," Shaw said. "But given the nature of this case and the witness's firsthand knowledge, we believe it's essential for justice."

Ellis leaned forward, his voice dripping with skepticism. "Essential? This is trial by ambush, plain and simple. We don't even know if this witness is credible."

He paused, letting the weight of his words settle over the room, then added, "And let's not forget, Your Honor, the last time this District Attorney's office prosecuted a big murder case, they pulled the same stunt. A surprise witness at the eleventh hour? Once is coincidence, twice is a pattern."

"This isn't about spectacle," Shaw countered. "It's about presenting the truth. The jury will determine credibility. Our job is to present the evidence."

"Evidence you've had less than twenty-four hours to verify," Ellis shot back.

Judge Carter held up a hand. "Enough. Mr. Shaw, does this witness's testimony align with the evidence presented thus far?"

"It does, Your Honor," Shaw replied. "And we've provided the defense with a summary of her statements this morning."

Ellis crossed his arms, his jaw tight. "A summary isn't sufficient preparation, Your Honor. This is highly prejudicial."

Judge Carter tapped a pen against her desk, her expression thoughtful. "Mr. Ellis, you'll have the opportunity to cross-examine the witness. I'll allow the testimony."

Ellis opened his mouth, but she silenced him with a glare. "That's my ruling. Court will reconvene in ten minutes."

We returned to the courtroom, the air electric with anticipation. Shaw's confidence didn't waver as he resumed his seat, but I couldn't shake the growing knot in my stomach. I glanced toward the witness stand, imagining Lydia seated there, her words shaping the course of this trial.

"Feeling nervous?" Shaw asked quietly, his voice breaking through my thoughts.

I hesitated. "No more than usual," I lied.

He gave me a knowing look but didn't press further. Judge Carter reentered the courtroom, and the jury settled back into their seats. My heart pounded as Shaw rose, his voice clear and steady.

"The State calls Lydia Kane to the stand."

CHAPTER
FORTY-TWO

THE ROOM SHIFTED SLIGHTLY, an almost imperceptible ripple of movement as all eyes turned toward the doors leading to the witness room. My stomach clenched as the bailiff escorted Lydia in. She walked slowly, her headscarf drawn tight around her head, her hands clasped in front of her like a shield. Her demeanor was measured, almost too calm.

I adjusted in my seat at the counsel table, brushing invisible lint off my skirt and willing my nerves to settle. This was it—the moment Shaw had argued for, the witness who could potentially tie everything together. Or cause everything to crumble.

Lydia took her oath and settled into the witness stand, and I tried to silence the nagging doubt that gnawed at the edges of my mind.

Shaw wasted no time diving into his direct examination, his voice steady and authoritative. "Ms. Kane, can you state your full name for the record?"

"Lydia Kane," she answered, her voice soft but clear. She clasped her hands tightly, her knuckles white against the dark wood of the witness stand.

"And can you tell the court how you are connected to this case?" Shaw asked, his tone even, deliberate.

She hesitated for the briefest moment, her eyes flicking toward the jury before returning to Shaw. "I was part of the trafficking ring," she began. "They recruited me when I was young. They promised me a better life, a job. But it wasn't what they said it would be."

A murmur rippled through the courtroom, a low hum of disbelief. I glanced at the jury. One juror, a man with salt-and-pepper hair who had been relatively stoic throughout the trial, shifted uncomfortably in his seat. A young woman in her twenties, leaned forward slightly, her notepad untouched in her lap as she stared at Lydia with rapt attention.

Shaw nodded, encouraging her to continue. "Ms. Kane, can you describe what happened after you were recruited?"

Lydia swallowed, her throat bobbing. "At first, it seemed legitimate," she said, her voice trembling slightly. "An office job. They gave me a place to stay, said I'd be working with professionals. But it changed quickly. They took my phone, isolated me, controlled everything I did. And then ..." She paused, her hands gripping the edge of the stand as though for support. "Then they started forcing me to do things I didn't want to do. Things I couldn't escape from."

My chest tightened, my breathing shallow. The words were damning, haunting, but something in her delivery gnawed at me. Her story was compelling and also composed. My gaze flicked to Shaw, who gave a slight nod, his expression somber but focused.

"Ms. Kane," Shaw said gently, his voice softening. "You mentioned that there were individuals who controlled this ring. Can you tell us their names?"

Lydia hesitated, her gaze darting to the jury again. "Sam Whitaker was one of the leaders. He managed everything behind the scenes, kept it all running. Then there were men like Slim and Scorpion—they handled the logistics, made sure the women stayed in line."

"And Randall Pierce?" Shaw's tone sharpened slightly, and the room seemed to hold its collective breath.

Lydia's hands tightened further on the stand, her knuckles white. "He was one of the enforcers," she said, her voice cracking. "He was the one who ... disposed of the women."

A sharp intake of breath rippled through the courtroom, followed by the quiet rustle of jurors shifting in their seats. My stomach turned. I forced myself to glance at the jury. The man with salt-and-pepper hair had his arms crossed tightly, his frown deepening. The young woman in the front row scribbled something furiously on her notepad, her expression a mix of horror and focus.

Shaw pressed forward. "When you say he disposed of the women, what do you mean by that?"

Lydia's gaze dropped to her lap, her voice faltering. "If a woman ... if she couldn't keep up, if she caused problems, or wasn't useful anymore, he killed her. And then buried her."

"Where?" Shaw asked, his voice as cold and sharp as a knife.

"On his property."

The air in the courtroom grew heavier, the weight of her words settling over everyone like a dark cloud. I shifted in my seat, my fingers gripping the edge of the table. This was it—the testimony we needed to tie Pierce to the murders definitively. It should have felt like a victory, but instead, my apprehension increased.

"Ms. Kane," Shaw continued, "can you tell the court how you managed to escape?"

Lydia's gaze lifted briefly, her eyes locking onto mine for a split second. I felt a jolt, something visceral and unsettling in the way she looked at me. "I was supposed to be killed," she said, her voice softer now. "Pierce was going to kill me. But someone helped me escape."

Shaw tilted his head. "And who helped you, Ms. Kane?"

She hesitated, her hands trembling slightly now. "Someone who knew it wasn't right. Someone who believed I deserved a second chance."

The hairs on the back of my neck rose as she glanced at me again, a flicker of something unreadable in her eyes. Gratitude? Guilt? It was impossible to tell, but it made my unease deepen.

Shaw stepped back, his tone growing more focused. "Ms. Kane, can you confirm for this court that Randall Pierce is the man responsible for these crimes?"

"Yes. Randall Pierce is the one who killed those women. I saw him do it many times."

The finality of her statement sent a shiver down my spine. I glanced at the jury again. They were riveted, their attention glued to Lydia.

Even the salt-and-pepper-haired juror, who had seemed skeptical at times, looked troubled.

Shaw nodded once, his expression composed but satisfied. "No further questions, Your Honor."

Judge Carter nodded toward Marcus Ellis, who rose from his seat with an air of measured confidence. "Defense may cross."

Ellis approached the podium slowly, his steps deliberate. He regarded Lydia with a calm, almost disarming expression. "Ms. Kane," he began, his voice smooth. "You've given a very detailed account of this alleged trafficking ring. But I only have a few questions for you."

Lydia straightened, her hands still gripping the stand. "Okay," she said softly.

Ellis leaned on the podium, his posture casual but calculated. "When exactly did you become involved in this ring?"

"About ten years ago."

"And during that time, how many interactions did you have with Randall Pierce?"

"Several," she said, her voice firm.

"Several." Ellis tilted his head, his gaze sharpening. "Yet you have no physical evidence—no photographs, no recordings—tying him to these murders. Isn't that correct?"

Lydia hesitated, glancing at Shaw as if seeking reassurance. "I was a victim. I didn't have access to those things."

Ellis nodded slowly, his expression almost sympathetic. "Of course. But you understand that without corroboration, your testimony is just words. Isn't that correct?"

Shaw rose to his feet. "Objection, Your Honor. The witness's credibility is a matter for the jury."

"Sustained,"

Ellis didn't push further. Instead, he gave Lydia a small nod and returned to his seat. "No further questions."

I exhaled slowly, realizing I'd been holding my breath. Shaw sat back down, his expression unreadable.

The judge addressed the jury. "We'll take a short recess before continuing with the next phase of the trial. Please remember the admonitions during this break."

As the jury filed out, I leaned closer to Shaw. "That felt off."

Shaw didn't respond immediately. He gathered his notes, his movements deliberate. Finally, he said, "We'll talk after the recess."

I glanced toward the witness stand. Lydia was being escorted out by the bailiff, her expression calm.

OUTSIDE SHAW'S OFFICE WINDOW, the Houston skyline glittered against the darkening sky, a stark contrast to the institutional gloom of the DA's building after hours. I wore a trail through the carpet as I paced, unable to stay still despite the exhaustion seeping into my bones.

Shaw lounged in his chair, his tie loosened, and sleeves rolled up, a picture of ease that only irritated me more. "We've got enough to move on Whitaker," he said, tapping his pen against the legal pad in front of him. "Lydia's testimony ties everything together. The trafficking ring, Pierce, the bodies—it's all there."

I stopped pacing, bracing my hands against the back of the chair across from his desk. "Don't you think it's a little too perfect?"

"Too perfect?" Shaw's brow furrowed. "Christ, Alex. You've been chasing this woman for weeks, convinced she was the key to everything. Now she shows up, gives us exactly what we need, and you're suspicious?"

"That's exactly my point," I said, my voice sharper than I intended. "She gives us *exactly* what we need. Everything fits together like a neat little puzzle. When has anything in this case been neat?" I pushed away from his desk. "Think about it, Shaw. We've been desperate for evidence for months. DNA tests came back inconclusive. The knife you found had trace evidence that went nowhere. Forty-four bodies in a pit, and somehow we couldn't get a single solid forensic match to Pierce."

I started pacing again. "We couldn't even get a witness to place him at the scene. Turner and his team interviewed everyone within a five-mile radius of that property, and nobody saw a thing. Not one person noticed someone burying forty bodies?" I stopped, turning back to face him. "And then suddenly this woman appears, and she doesn't just give us Pierce—she gives us the whole operation. Whitaker, Slim, Scorpion, the trafficking ring, everything wrapped up in a perfect package with a bow on top."

Shaw leaned back in his chair, watching me with that maddeningly calm expression. "Sometimes cases break like that."

"No," I shot back, "they don't. Cases don't just magically solve themselves. Evidence doesn't materialize out of thin air. We've been working this for months, Shaw. Months of dead ends and false leads. Remember Maria Alvarez? I thought she'd give us something concrete, but all we got were vague references and street names. The warehouse case? More circumstantial evidence that didn't quite connect. Even Rachel Saunders could only give us pieces of the puzzle."

I braced my hands on his desk, leaning forward. "But now Lydia shows up, and suddenly every gap is filled? Every loose end tied? She knows exactly who did what, when they did it, and how they did it? It's too clean. Too convenient."

"Or maybe," Shaw said, his voice taking on an edge, "it's exactly what we've been waiting for. The break we needed. She was a victim. It makes sense that she would know those things."

I straightened, shaking my head. "When have you ever seen a case like this break clean? Real evidence is messy. Real witnesses are unreliable, their stories full of holes and inconsistencies. But Lydia?" I let out a bitter laugh. "Her story is perfect. Like she rehearsed it."

"Or like she's telling the truth," Shaw countered, but I could see a flicker of uncertainty in his eyes.

"The truth is never this neat."

Shaw leaned forward, rubbing his temples. The dim light from his desk lamp cast deep shadows under his eyes. "You know what your problem is, Hayes? You can't accept a win. You're so used to looking for conspiracies that you can't recognize when something actually goes our way."

"That's not fair."

"Isn't it?" He stood, walking to his window. "I get it. This case is personal for you. Your mother—"

"Don't," I cut him off. "This isn't about my mother. This is about making sure we're not being played."

He turned back to face me, his expression softening. "Alex, you brought her to us. You insisted she was crucial to this case. Now you want to what—throw away her testimony because it feels too convenient?"

Sinking into the chair, the leather creaked under my weight. "I just … something feels off. The way she talks about Pierce, about Whitaker. It's like she's giving us exactly what we want to hear."

"Or maybe," Shaw said, returning to his desk, "she's telling the truth. Maybe it all fits because that's how it actually happened."

I stared at the ceiling, watching the shadows dance across the tiles. "Maybe," I conceded, though the doubt still gnawed at me. "But if we're wrong about her—"

"Then we'll deal with it. But right now, we have a witness willing to testify against both Pierce and Whitaker. That's not nothing."

I nodded, pushing myself to my feet. My bag felt heavier than usual as I slung it over my shoulder. "I should head home."

Shaw watched me gather my things, his expression unreadable. "Get some rest, Hayes. Maybe things will feel better on Monday."

"Yeah," I muttered, "We'll see."

The drive home was quiet, the radio turned low as I navigated the familiar streets. My phone rested on the passenger seat, its screen dark except for the occasional streetlight that caught its surface.

As I stopped at a red light, I picked it up and tapped out a quick message to Lisa. Maybe she could offer insight into where I was coming up blank. *Hey, any thoughts on today's testimony?*

Back home, my father's truck sat in the driveway, and warm light spilled from the kitchen windows. The sight of it—so normal, so steady—made my throat tight.

Inside, I found him at the kitchen table, a half-empty cup of coffee in front of him despite the late hour. He looked up as I entered, his eyes crinkling with concern. "Rough day?"

I dropped my bag by the door and collapsed into the chair across from him. "You could say that."

He pushed his coffee aside, folding his hands on the table. "Want to talk about it?"

The question hit me harder than it should have. I opened my mouth to give my usual deflection—I'm fine, just tired, nothing to worry about—but something in his expression stopped me. He was looking at me the way he used to when I was little, when I'd come home from school, trying to hide that I'd had a bad day. That same patient, knowing look that said he could see right through me.

My throat tightened. I'd been holding everything in for so long— the calls, the doubts, the growing unease—trying to be the composed professional everyone expected. Shaw, Turner, Tom ... they all wanted certainty, conviction. They didn't want to hear about gut feelings and nagging suspicions. But sitting here in our kitchen, with the familiar smell of coffee and the quiet hum of the refrigerator, those carefully constructed walls began to crack.

"Dad, I—" My voice caught, and I looked down at my hands, surprised to find them trembling slightly. "I've been getting these calls."

He didn't say anything, just waited. The silence stretched between us, not uncomfortable but heavy with understanding. When I looked up again, his eyes were soft with concern, and something in me finally broke.

The words came flooding out in a rush—about the anonymous caller with their distorted voice and cryptic warnings; about Lydia appearing like a ghost in the courtroom; about her testimony that seemed too perfect, too rehearsed. My voice shook as I described the growing certainty that something wasn't right, that we were all being played somehow, but I couldn't prove it.

"And the whole time," I said, running a hand through my hair, "I keep thinking about Mom. About her case, about how she disappeared just when she thought she was getting close to something big. What if —" I stopped, swallowing hard. "What if I'm missing something obvi- ous? What if I'm walking right into the same trap?"

My father listened to all of it, his expression shifting between concern and understanding as I laid out every doubt and fear that had been building for months. When I finally ran out of words, the kitchen felt quieter than before, as if the very air was holding its breath. My father sat there for a moment, his coffee long forgotten, just watching me with an expression I couldn't quite read.

"And now Shaw thinks I'm paranoid," I finished, my voice barely above a whisper. "Maybe I am. Maybe I'm seeing shadows where there aren't any."

My father was quiet for a moment, studying me with the kind of careful attention that made me feel like a kid again. "What's your gut telling you?"

I let out a slow breath, considering. "That I need to dig deeper. That there's something we're missing."

He nodded, as if he'd expected nothing less. "Then dig deeper."

"Even if it means potentially compromising the case? Even if I'm wrong?"

Reaching across the table, his hand covered mine. The gesture was so unexpected, so gentle, that I felt tears prick at my eyes.

"Your mother always said that the truth matters more than the conviction. Even when it's messy, even when it's not what we want to hear."

I swallowed hard. "I don't want to let her down."

"Alex," he said softly, "the only way you could let her down is by ignoring your instincts. If something feels wrong, figure out why. That's what she would have done."

I nodded, wiping quickly at my eyes. "I just wish …" I trailed off, not sure how to finish the thought.

"I know," he said, squeezing my hand. "I know."

We sat there in comfortable silence, the kitchen clock ticking softly in the background. Outside, a car passed, its headlights sweeping across the walls. Finally, I stood, my chair scraping against the floor.

"Thanks, Dad."

He smiled, though it didn't quite reach his eyes. "Get some sleep. Whatever you decide to do tomorrow, you'll need your head clear."

CHAPTER
FORTY-FOUR

MY FATHER HAD GONE to bed hours ago, but I couldn't sleep. The kitchen table had once again become my war room, case files and photographs spread across its weathered surface in a maze of evidence. A half-empty mug of tea sat forgotten by my elbow, gone cold in the quiet of the night.

Dad's words echoed in my head, *Your mother always said that the truth matters more than the conviction.*

I rubbed my eyes, trying to focus through the exhaustion. It was all there, scattered across the table like puzzle pieces from different boxes, but they weren't fitting together.

Lydia's testimony played on repeat in my mind. *He killed those women. The ones who didn't cooperate.* The women. Always the women. I shuffled through the autopsy reports again, my finger trailing down the list of victims. Forty-four bodies total. Forty-three female.

And one male.

I sat up straighter, my chair creaking in the silence. The sound seemed too loud in the sleeping house. How had we glossed over this? Who was he, and why bury him in a mass grave filled with women?

"Come on, Alex," I muttered. "Think."

I pushed back from the table, my chair scraping against the floor. The sound made me wince—Dad was a light sleeper. I needed to move and padded around the kitchen. The linoleum was cold under my bare feet as I paced.

"This doesn't make sense," I whispered to myself, pausing and reaching for my laptop. "Pierce killed women who threatened Whitaker's operation, but there's a male body in that pit. A teenager."

I pulled up Pierce's background check, the screen's blue glow harsh against the warm lamplight. Divorced father of two. Ex-wife, Judy Pierce. Daughter, Jessica Pierce, age nineteen, attending college in Austin. And son, Timothy Pierce, deceased at sixteen. I frowned, scrolling through the records. The divorce was finalized just months after Timothy's death.

I dug deeper into local news archives, searching for any mention of Timothy Pierce's death. There was an obituary, brief and vague. No cause of death listed. No mention of where he was buried. Just "tragic circumstances" and "gone too soon."

Through the kitchen window, moonlight silvered the backyard where Dad had been working earlier. The half-finished landscaping project seemed frozen in time, like everything was holding its breath, waiting for dawn. I turned back to the crime scene photos spread across the table, studying them in the lamp's glow. The pit was methodical, bodies arranged in layers. I squinted, pulling one photo closer. The male body was different. Positioned with more care, almost protected by the earth packed around it.

My heart started pounding as pieces clicked into place. I pulled up the forensics report on my laptop, scanning for Dr. Milton's analysis of body decomposition. According to her findings, the bodies had been buried in layers over approximately four years, with the deepest remains showing the most advanced decomposition.

I grabbed Timothy Pierce's death certificate, my hands shaking as I compared the dates. Timothy had disappeared four years and two months ago—right when Dr. Milton estimated the first bodies were buried. A chill ran down my spine as I dug deeper into the forensics data. The male body had been found in the lowest layer of the pit, among the first victims.

"Son of a bitch," I breathed, the realization hitting me like a physical blow.

I sank back into my chair, the old wood groaning under my weight. My mind raced. Pierce was supposed to be our killer, our monster who disposed of bodies without remorse. But what kind of monster would bury his own son in a mass grave? What father would throw his child away like garbage?

"He wouldn't," I answered myself, my voice barely a whisper. "No father would."

Which meant Pierce wasn't our killer.

Someone else had put Timothy in that pit.

The house creaked, settling in the night's quiet. From upstairs came the faint sound of my father turning over in his sleep. I grabbed my phone, scrolling through contacts until I found Turner's number. My thumb hesitated over the call button. Turner had been skeptical of Lydia too, watching her testimony with the same guarded expression I'd worn. He might be the only one willing to listen without dismissing me outright.

The phone rang three times before he answered, his voice rough with sleep. "Hayes? Do you know what time it is?"

"I need to talk to you," I said, the words tumbling out. "I found something about Pierce, about the bodies. Something that changes everything."

"It's"—I heard rustling, probably him checking the time—"almost midnight, Hayes."

"I know, but—"

"Precinct. Tomorrow morning," he cut me off, though his tone was gentler than usual. "Whatever you found will still be there in six hours. Get some sleep."

I wanted to argue, to insist that this couldn't wait, but exhaustion weighed heavy on my shoulders. Maybe he was right. "First thing?" I pressed.

"First thing. And Hayes? Make sure you bring everything you've got."

The line went dead. I stared at the scattered files across the kitchen table, my mind still racing despite my body's protests. Everything we thought we knew about this case, about Pierce, about Whitaker's operation—it was built on Lydia's testimony. But if Pierce wasn't the killer she claimed he was, then what else had she lied about?

And more importantly, why?

I forced myself to organize the files into neat stacks, knowing I'd need them ready to go first thing in the morning. My movements were mechanical, driven more by habit than conscious thought. I scribbled a quick note for my dad. *Early meeting at precinct. Don't worry. -A*

The stairs creaked under my feet as I made my way to my room. I didn't bother changing, just kicked off my shoes and collapsed onto my bed. The ceiling fan spun in lazy circles above me, its shadows dancing across the walls in the dim light filtering through my window.

Sleep wouldn't come. Every time I closed my eyes, I saw the crime scene photos, the layers of bodies in that pit. Timothy Pierce's death certificate. The careful way his body had been positioned, while the others had just been disposed of. None of it made sense.

I rolled onto my side, watching the digital clock on my nightstand count off minutes that felt like hours. 12:17. 12:43. 1:22. My mind wouldn't shut off, spinning through theories and possibilities. What if Pierce wasn't working for Whitaker? What if someone else had access to that property? What if Lydia wasn't who she claimed to be at all?

By the time my alarm buzzed at 5:30, I'd managed maybe two hours of actual sleep. But it didn't matter. I was too close to something —something that could blow this whole case wide open. I just had to prove it.

Dawn was just starting to break as I showered and dressed, my movements quiet in the sleeping house. Whatever truth was buried in this case, I was going to dig it up. Even if it meant tearing everything apart to do it.

CHAPTER FORTY-FIVE

THE PRECINCT FELT different on weekends—emptier, quieter, the usual buzz of activity replaced by a hollow sort of echo. My footsteps rang against the tile as I made my way to Turner's desk, my bag heavy with files and a thermos of coffee that hadn't done much to chase away my exhaustion.

Turner sat at his desk, the harsh fluorescent lights casting deep shadows under his eyes. A half-empty cup of coffee sat among scattered papers, and his tie was already loosened despite the early hour. He looked about as tired as I felt.

"You look like hell," he said by way of greeting.

"Couldn't sleep." I dropped into the chair across from him, pulling out the files I'd organized in the middle of the night. "Too busy thinking about this."

I spread the documents across his desk: Timothy Pierce's death certificate, the forensics reports, the crime scene photos. Turner leaned forward, his expression sharpening despite his apparent fatigue.

"Walk me through it," he said.

I took a deep breath, trying to organize my scattered thoughts. "Lydia's testimony. She said Pierce killed women who threatened Whitaker's operation, right? But there's a male body in that pit. And not just any male." I tapped Timothy's death certificate. "Pierce's sixteen-year-old son."

Turner picked up the death certificate, his brow furrowing. "The timing matches?"

"According to forensics, he was among the first bodies buried. And look at this." I pulled out the crime scene photos, spreading them across his desk. "See how he's positioned? Different from the others. Protected almost."

Turner studied the photos, his jaw tightening. "You think Pierce wouldn't kill his own son?"

"Would you?" I asked quietly. "Would any father?"

He sat back, rubbing his chin. The precinct's silence pressed in around us, broken only by the distant hum of the heating system and the occasional ring of a phone from somewhere deep in the building.

"What are you thinking?" he asked finally.

I shook my head, frustration building in my chest. "I don't know exactly. But something about Lydia's story doesn't add up. If Pierce isn't the killer she claims he is—"

"Then what else is she lying about?" Turner was quiet for a moment, then started typing on his computer. "Pierce's ex-wife. Maybe she knows something."

I leaned forward as he pulled up an address. "You think she'll talk to us?"

"One way to find out."

The drive to Judy Pierce's house was quiet, both of us lost in thought. Houston sprawled around us, early Saturday morning traffic light as we wound through residential streets. Her neighborhood, when we found it, was modest but well-kept—small ranch houses with neat yards and basketball hoops over driveways.

Judy Pierce's house sat at the end of a cul-de-sac, its pale-yellow paint peeling slightly around the trim. Wind chimes tinkled softly on the front porch, and a worn welcome mat sat crooked by the door.

Turner knocked, his knuckles sharp against the wood. For a long moment, nothing. Then the door opened a crack, revealing a woman in her early fifties, her graying hair pulled back in a messy bun. Her eyes widened and she immediately tried to close the door.

I stepped forward, putting my hand against the door before it could shut. "Mrs. Pierce, please. We need to talk to you about Timothy."

She froze, her hand still on the door. Something flickered across her face—pain maybe, or fear.

"Please," I said again, softer this time. "We want to understand what really happened."

She stared at us for what felt like an eternity, then slowly opened the door wider. "Come in."

The living room was small but tidy, family photos covering one wall. Judy gestured for us to sit on a faded floral couch while she took the armchair across from us, her hands twisting in her lap.

"Why are you here?" she asked, her voice barely above a whisper.

I glanced at Turner, then back to her. "We found Timothy," I said gently. "In the grave outside of your ex-husband's house. With the others."

She closed her eyes, pain etching deep lines around her mouth. When she opened them again, they were bright with unshed tears.

"He got involved with bad people," she said, her voice shaking. "Timmy … he was always trying to prove himself. Too smart for his own good. He thought he could handle it, thought he was grown up enough to—" She broke off, pressing a hand to her mouth.

"What happened?" Turner asked, his tone softer than I'd ever heard it.

"He started bringing girls to the farm. Said he was helping them, giving them a place to stay. We didn't know. Didn't understand what was really happening. Not until it was too late."

The pieces started falling into place. I leaned forward, my heart pounding. "Your husband found out?"

She nodded, a tear slipping down her cheek. "He tried to help Timmy cover it up, to protect him. But these people, they don't let you just walk away. They killed our boy and then—" Her voice broke. "Then they told Randy if he didn't keep their secret, if he didn't let them keep using the property, they'd come for Sarah next. For all of us."

The room felt too small suddenly, the weight of her words pressing in like a physical thing. Turner shifted beside me, his notebook forgotten in his lap.

"Why didn't you come forward?" he asked.

Judy laughed, a hollow sound. "Who would believe us? And what would it matter? They'd kill us all." She looked directly at me, her eyes fierce despite her tears. "Randy didn't kill those women. He didn't even bury them. But he couldn't stop it. None of us could."

The pieces clicked into place with such force it felt like a physical jolt. That's why we couldn't find any DNA evidence linking Pierce to the murders. That's why every forensic test came back inconclusive, why my desperate search for physical evidence kept hitting dead ends. He'd never touched those bodies. Never buried them. Never killed them. He was just a man standing guard over a grave he was forced to keep, protecting what remained of his family with his silence.

A heavy silence followed, broken only by the gentle tinkling of wind chimes from the porch. Through the living room window, I watched a neighbor walk their dog past the house, completely unaware of the weight of the confession happening inside.

"Mrs. Pierce," I said carefully, "would you be willing to make a statement? Officially?"

She shook her head, fear flashing across her face. "I can't. They'll know. They always know."

Turner leaned forward and said softly, "We can protect you—"

"Like you protected Timmy?" Her voice cracked on her son's name. "Like you protected all those other girls?" She stood abruptly, wrapping her arms around herself. "I've said too much already. Please just go."

Turner and I exchanged glances. There was more we needed to ask, more we needed to know, but the tremor in her voice told us we'd pushed as far as we could.

"Thank you," I said softly, standing. "For telling us the truth."

She walked us to the door, her movements stiff like she'd aged years in the last hour. As we stepped onto the porch, she caught my arm. "Help him if you can," she whispered. "Randy's not perfect, but he's not a murderer. He's just a father who couldn't save his son."

The drive back to the precinct was quiet at first, both of us processing what we'd learned. Houston's streets were busier now, Saturday morning traffic picking up as we wound our way downtown. The sun had climbed higher, harsh and bright against the windshield.

"What are you thinking?" Turner asked finally, breaking the silence.

I kept my eyes focused on the road. "I'm thinking Pierce is guilty of obstruction, maybe accessory after the fact. But murder?" I shook my head. "He was protecting his daughter. His ex-wife."

"And Lydia?"

"Is lying." The words came out sharper than I intended. "About Pierce, at least. Which means she could be lying about everything else, too."

Turner nodded slowly. "Shaw's not going to like this."

"Shaw's going to have to deal with it." Turner turned onto the street leading to the precinct. "We can't prosecute a man for murders he didn't commit just because it's convenient. Not when the real killers are still out there."

"Whitaker," Turner said, his voice hard.

"And whoever else is involved." He pulled into the parking garage, killing the engine. "The question is, why is Lydia trying so hard to pin everything on Pierce? Who is she really protecting?"

Turner unbuckled his seatbelt but didn't move to get out. "We need to tell Shaw."

Anxiety felt like a ball of hot lead in my stomach. Shaw had been so certain about Pierce's guilt, so focused on getting this conviction. "He's not going to like having to change strategy this late in the game."

"No," Turner agreed, "but he needs to know. The whole case is built around Pierce being the killer. If he's not …"

The parking garage grew colder, the shadows between cars deeper and more threatening. Everything we thought we knew about this case, everything we'd presented to the jury—it was built on a lie. A lie that Lydia had handed us, perfectly packaged and precisely delivered.

"We need to talk to Shaw," I said finally, opening my door. "Today."

CHAPTER
FORTY-SIX

THE DA'S office felt different on Saturdays—almost abandoned, like a stage after the actors had gone home. My footsteps echoed through empty halls as Turner and I made our way to Shaw's office.

Shaw was already there when we arrived, wearing dark jeans and a light blue button-down with the sleeves rolled to his elbows—a jarring sight that made me do a double-take. In the six years I'd known him, I had never seen him in anything but precisely pressed suits, every button done up like armor. Even his tie was missing, the top two buttons of his shirt undone. It made him look more human somehow, less like the untouchable senior prosecutor and more like someone who had been dragged out of bed on a Saturday morning. Empty coffee cups littered his desk—evidence of his own early start. He looked up as we entered, his expression grim.

"Close the door," he said by way of greeting.

Turner shut it behind us, the click loud in the quiet building. I sank into one of the chairs across from Shaw's desk, the leather creaking beneath me. The morning sun slanted through the blinds, casting striped shadows across the floor.

"We need to talk about Pierce—"

Shaw held up a hand to stop me. "Wait," he said, turning his monitor toward us. "You need to see this first."

My stomach dropped as I read the subject line of the email. **NO**

INDICTMENT. The sender's address was a string of random numbers and letters.

"This came in this morning," Shaw said, his voice tight. "Looks like Whitaker's getting nervous."

I leaned forward to read, my hands gripping the arms of the chair.

Drop the indictment against Whitaker, or Katherine Hayes' role in our operation becomes public. Your predecessor wasn't just investigating us—she was helping us. And we have proof.

Attached files showed bank statements, emails, and photographs. My mother's signature was on documents I didn't recognize. Meeting dates. Location coordinates.

The room spun slightly. I felt Turner shift beside me, heard Shaw's sharp intake of breath, but I couldn't tear my eyes from the screen. From my mother's name, from the evidence that threatened to destroy everything I thought I knew about her.

"Alex," Shaw said softly, and something in his tone made me look up. "There's more."

I forced myself to keep reading.

Katherine Hayes helped traffic these women. She arranged transport, facil-itated deals, covered our tracks. If you proceed with this indictment, her legacy—and her daughter's career—will be destroyed. Every case Alex Hayes has ever touched will be called into question. Every conviction scrutinized. How many guilty men will walk free when the world learns her mother was a criminal?

The silence that followed was thick enough to choke on.

"It's bullshit," Turner said finally, his voice hard. "They're desperate. Making things up."

But Shaw was looking at me, his expression serious. "The documents look real, Alex. The signatures, the dates—they match other cases from that time period."

My mind raced, trying to reconcile the mother I knew with these accusations—the one who fought for justice, who disappeared trying to expose corruption. It didn't fit. It couldn't fit. Unless …

"What do you want to do?" Shaw asked quietly.

The question hung in the air between us. My career, my mother's legacy, every case I'd ever worked—all of it balanced on the edge of a knife. If we moved forward with the indictment, if we exposed Whitaker, they'd destroy everything. Not just my mother's reputation, but mine too.

Every defense attorney in Texas would file appeals on cases I'd prosecuted. They'd argue that I followed in my mother's corrupt foot-steps, that I inherited more than just her drive for justice—that I inherited her propensity to break the law, to manipulate evidence, to work both sides. They'd claim I used the same tactics, the same connections, the same dirty tricks. The Martin case would be scrutinized all over again. The mayor's corruption charges would be called into question. Every plea deal I'd ever negotiated, every witness I'd ever prepped, every piece of evidence I'd ever presented. It would all be tainted by association.

Years of work, hundreds of convictions. Rapists, murderers, traf-fickers—all of them could demand new trials. Their attorneys would argue that my involvement alone was grounds for appeal, that my mother's corruption had influenced every aspect of my prosecution strategy. The courts would be flooded with motions, the DA's office swamped with requests for review. Convictions I'd fought for, justice I'd secured—all of it could unravel.

And for Tom, his re-election campaign would implode. His oppo-nents would have a field day—the DA who not only hired the daughter of a corrupt prosecutor but let her handle major cases. They'd say he showed poor judgment, failed to vet his attorneys prop-erly, allowed a compromised prosecutor to jeopardize countless cases. His campaign slogan of "Tough on Crime" would become a punchline. The scandal would eclipse everything else—his conviction rates, his anti-corruption initiatives, even the success of the Martin case. His career would effectively be over, and he'd take half the office down with him.

My gaze shifted between Shaw and Turner, the weight of realiza-tion settling even heavier in my chest. Shaw had worked with my mother on these cases—how long before people started questioning his involvement too? They'd wonder what he knew, what he might have covered up.

And Turner, he had been my partner through this whole investigation. Would they assume he helped me bury evidence, manipulate witnesses? These men had families, mortgages, entire lives. Turner's daughter had just started medical school. Shaw's son was in high school, looking at colleges. Their careers, their reputations, their families' security—all of it could be collateral damage in this explosion. The ripples would keep spreading, destroying everything in their path.

The thought made my chest tight, my breath shallow. It wasn't just about me anymore. It was about every victim who had trusted me to get them justice, every family who had counted on me to put their loved one's perpetrator behind bars. If those convictions got overturned.

But then I thought about Pierce, an innocent man facing murder charges. About his ex-wife, living in fear. About Timothy, buried in that pit. About all the women who had died, who deserved justice. About my mother, who had disappeared trying to stop this—because she must have been trying to stop it. She must have.

The weight of it all pressed down on me, threatening to crack my ribs. My whole life, I'd tried to live up to her legacy, to be the kind of prosecutor she was. That legacy couldn't be a lie, could it?

"Before we decide anything," Turner said, his voice steady despite the tension in the room, "we need to tell you what we learned about Pierce."

I sank back in my chair, grateful for the momentary reprieve from my own spiraling thoughts. The weight of my mother's potential betrayal sat heavy in my chest, but Turner's words pulled me back to our other revelation—one that seemed both massive and insignificant in comparison to what we'd just read.

Turner walked Shaw through everything: Timothy Pierce's death, the male body in the pit, the visit to Judy Pierce. I watched Shaw's expression shift as Turner explained, the furrow in his brow deepening with each new detail. Outside, clouds drifted past the window, casting shifting shadows across Shaw's desk.

"The son was using the property," Turner continued, his voice grave. "Got involved with these people, started bringing girls there. When Pierce found out, he tried to protect his son, but "They killed him instead," Shaw finished, rubbing his temples. The morning sun caught the silver in his hair, making him look older somehow. More tired.

"And threatened to kill the rest of the family if Pierce didn't cooperate," I added quietly, my first words since reading the email. "That's why there's no DNA evidence linking him to the bodies. He never actually touched them. Never buried them."

Shaw leaned back in his chair, the leather creaking under his weight. "It fits," he admitted. "The timeline, the forensics, the gaps in our case. But"—He spread his hands on his desk—"We can't dismiss charges based solely on an ex-wife's statement. We need more."

Turner started to say, "The male body—"

"Proves the son was involved, maybe," Shaw interrupted. "But it doesn't prove Pierce's innocence. Defense attorneys make up stories all the time about their clients being coerced. Without concrete evidence …"

"So we just let an innocent man go to prison?" The words slipped out before I could stop them, sharper than intended.

Shaw's expression softened. "No. But we need to be smart about this. We have time—right up until the jury reaches a verdict. We need to verify Judy Pierce's story, find something to corroborate her claims."

The room fell quiet. Through the walls, I could hear the building's old pipes knocking, a steady rhythm like a ticking clock. Finally, Turner cleared his throat.

"And the email?" he asked carefully. "About Katherine?"

Both men's eyes were on me, but I kept my gaze fixed on the window, watching a bird circle the parking garage across the street. Everything felt surreal, like I was watching someone else's life implode in slow motion.

"Alex," Shaw said gently, "maybe you should take some time. Go home, rest. Think about how you want to handle this. Both of these," he added, glancing at his computer screen. "We don't have to decide anything today."

I wanted to argue, to insist that I was fine, that I could handle both revelations at once. But the truth was, I felt like I was drowning. My mother's possible corruption, Pierce's innocence, Whitaker's threats—

it was all too much, pressing in from all sides until I could barely breathe.

"Yeah," I managed, pushing myself to my feet. My legs felt unsteady beneath me. "Maybe you're right."

Turner stood too. "I'll walk you out."

I shook my head. "I need … I just need a minute. Alone."

They let me go, their concerned gazes following me to the door. As I stepped into the empty hallway, their voices dropped to murmurs behind me, discussing next steps, planning strategies. I should have cared more about what they were saying, about what they'd decide. But right then, all I could think about was getting out of that building, away from that email, away from everything I thought I knew about my life, my career, my mother.

The elevator doors closed behind me with a soft ding, and I let out a shaky breath. Whatever truth lay buried in all of this, I'd have to face it eventually. But not today. Today, I just needed to breathe.

CHAPTER
FORTY-SEVEN

THE HOUSE FELT empty when I got home, though I knew Dad was somewhere around. Probably in the backyard gardening, filling the empty hours with something productive—something that didn't involve other people's judgment.

I dropped my keys on the kitchen counter, the sound too loud in the quiet house. My bag felt heavier than usual, weighed down with copies of my mother's notes, old case files, and everything I'd grabbed from the office before leaving. Before running away, if I was being honest with myself.

My phone buzzed—a text from Turner. *You okay?*

I ignored it, just like I had ignored his last two messages. Just like I'd been ignoring the knot in my stomach since reading that email. My mother, working for the ring? It didn't make sense. But if she was—if she still is—then where has she been all these years?

The question burned in my throat like acid. If she was alive, if she had been working with them this whole time, why hadn't she tried to contact me? One phone call, one letter, one sign that she was still out there. I'd spent years imagining her dead in a ditch somewhere or buried in an unmarked grave because the alternative was too painful to consider: that she might be alive and choosing to stay away.

My fingers traced the edge of the kitchen counter, following the familiar chip in the granite from when I dropped a pot last month. I was eight when she disappeared. Eight years old, waiting up past bedtime because she'd promised to read me another chapter of *Charlotte's Web*. Dad had said she was just working late. Then days passed. Then weeks. Then years.

Did she think about me on my birthdays? When I graduated high school? Law school? Did she know I had become a prosecutor, following in her footsteps like some cosmic joke? All those milestones, all those moments when I'd needed my mother—was she out there somewhere, deliberately staying away? Or was she trapped in this web of trafficking and corruption, unable to reach out without putting me in danger?

The not knowing felt like an open wound, raw and festering after all these years. And now this email threatened to rip off whatever scabs had formed, forcing me to question everything I thought I knew about her. About us.

The back door creaked open, and Dad stepped inside, moving to the sink to wash the dirt from his hands. He took one look at my face and stilled.

"That bad, huh?"

I sank into a kitchen chair, the same one I'd sat in last night. Had that really just been hours ago? "Worse."

He studied me for a moment, then glanced at the clock. "Let's go to dinner."

"What?" The suggestion was so unexpected it pulled me from my spiral.

"Dinner. At Mario's."

I stared at him. Dad hadn't voluntarily gone out to eat since before prison. Too many stares, too many whispers from people who remembered his case.

"You hate going out," I said.

He shrugged, but I caught the tension in his shoulders. "Maybe it's time to stop hiding. Besides, you look like you could use a chocolate milkshake."

Mario's. Where we used to go every Sunday after church, before everything fell apart. Where I'd sit in the red vinyl booth and swing my legs, too short to reach the floor, while Mom and Dad argued over who would get the last French fry.

"Okay," I heard myself say. "Let me change first."

Twenty minutes later, we slid into a booth by the window. The diner looked exactly the same—chrome fixtures gleaming dully, neon signs humming against wood-paneled walls, the same worn menus with their faded photographs. Even our waitress was familiar, although her hair had gone completely gray now.

I pulled out my phone, typing a quick text to Lisa. *Grabbing dinner but still need to fill you in on things. Talk later?* I hit send, noticing that my earlier message to her was still unanswered. A flicker of unease crept in, but I pushed it aside.

"Your mother loved their patty melts," Dad said as the waitress brought our drinks. He ordered a chocolate shake for me without asking. Just like he used to.

"I remember." I stirred the shake with my straw, watching the whipped cream swirl into the chocolate. "Dad ... they're saying she worked for them. For the trafficking ring."

He was quiet for a long moment, studying his coffee. "You believe that?"

"I don't know what to believe anymore." The words came out more bitter than I intended.

"Your mother," Dad started, then paused as the waitress brought our food. He waited until she was gone before continuing. "She wasn't perfect, Alex. None of us are. But everything she did, she did to help other people."

I checked my phone again, apparently more interested in my messages than this conversation—still no response from Lisa. Probably busy with case prep for Monday.

"Alex." His tone softened, though his eyes remained steady on mine. "People will say anything to protect themselves. Look at what they said about me. They called me a thief, a cheat, a liar. None of it was true. It doesn't matter how much proof they say they have, people like Whitaker twist the truth to serve their own ends."

I looked down at the patty melt in front of me, the familiar scent mingling with the stale anxiety gnawing at my stomach. "But what if they're not twisting it this time? What if ..." I hesitated, unable to finish the thought. If she did help them, what did that make her? What did that make me?

"She didn't do what they're saying," Dad said firmly, his voice cutting through my spiraling thoughts. "Your mother loved you more than anything. She fought for people who couldn't fight for themselves. Don't let them rewrite her story."

"But even if she didn't, they're threatening to ruin everything—her reputation, my cases, all of it."

Dad's gaze didn't waver. "And what are you going to do about it?"

The question hung between us, heavy and unavoidable. I looked out the window, watching cars pull in and out of the parking lot, their headlights cutting through the growing dusk. "I don't know," I admitted finally, my voice barely above a whisper. "But I can't just let Whitaker walk free."

Dad's expression softened as he nodded, his shoulders relaxing. "That sounds like the Alex I know. Your mother would be proud of that answer."

When we got home, I spread my mother's notes across the kitchen table again. The same ritual as last night, but everything looked different now. Every word carried new weight, new possibilities.

I checked my phone again. Still nothing from Lisa. A tendril of unease curled in my stomach, but I pushed it aside. *Focus.*

My mother's handwriting filled page after page, her thoughts on the trafficking ring's structure, possible leaders, suspected locations. I'd read these notes a dozen times before, looking for answers about her disappearance, but tonight they felt different. Heavier somehow, like each word carried new meaning.

One name kept appearing throughout her notes. Slim. No physical description, just fragments about his role in the organization. *Handles recruitment. Controls day-to-day. All roads lead back.* My mother had underlined this last part twice, the pen strokes sharp and urgent.

I rubbed my eyes, fighting exhaustion. The ceiling fan light cast yellow circles on the scattered papers, and somewhere in the house, a clock ticked steadily. Dad had gone to bed an hour ago, leaving me alone with these ghosts of my mother's investigation.

Something about Slim's mentions nagged at me. The way my mother wrote about him—not just as muscle, but as someone central to the operation. Someone smart. Someone careful. I flipped through the pages faster now, looking for—*there*. A list of suspected properties, with the warehouse circled multiple times. And next to it, in my mother's precise handwriting. *Slim's base of operations? Women report being processed here before transport.*

Processed.

I sat back, the chair creaking beneath me. That word. Clinical. Detached. The kind of euphemism someone would use to distance themselves from what they were actually doing to these women.

My fingers traced over my mother's handwriting, following the loops and curves of her letters. *Processed.* Where had I heard that recently?

The trial transcript. I pulled my laptop closer, hands trembling slightly as I searched through the document. The screen's glow felt harsh in the dim room as I scrolled through Lydia's testimony. My heart started beating faster as I found what I was looking for.

There it was, Lydia, describing how the women were "processed" through various locations. The exact same word. Not "moved" or "transferred" or any other term. A detail that had seemed innocuous at the time, but now...

I stood, needing to move. The kitchen suddenly felt too small, too confined. We'd all assumed Slim was a man. Everything had been focused on finding a male suspect. I'd even convinced myself it was Hendrix, building a profile around him.

But had anyone actually confirmed that?

I walked to the window, staring out at the dark street beyond. My reflection looked pale, almost ghostly in the glass. *Think, Alex. Who had actually seen Slim?*

The victims—all dead or disappeared. Pierce's ex-wife had mentioned someone giving orders, but she'd never met them directly. Even my mother's notes never specified a gender.

No one had seen Slim.

No one except Lydia.

The pieces were clicking into place with sickening clarity. Lydia knew every detail about the operation—not just broad strokes, but intimate knowledge of how it worked. She appeared at exactly the right moments, always watching. Her testimony was perfect, rehearsed, designed to point us exactly where she wanted us to look.

And that word—*processed*. The same clinical, detached language my mother had noted years ago. The language of someone who saw these women as commodities, not people.

A car drove past outside, its headlights sweeping across the room. The light caught the pages spread across the table, illuminating my mother's warnings about Slim. *All roads lead back.*

"Oh god," I whispered, my voice sounding strange in the quiet house.

They led back to Lydia.

She wasn't just some confused victim.

She was Slim.

The one controlling everything from the shadows. The one my mother had been hunting all those years ago. That's how Whitaker knew about the indictment plans—Lydia had been in our office, in our meetings, watching our every move. The evidence against my mother had been sitting in an email, ready to deploy the moment we moved against them, because Lydia had orchestrated all of it. She wasn't just testifying in our case. She was controlling both sides, keeping us focused on Pierce while protecting the real operation.

My phone buzzed on the table—another message from Turner about tomorrow's witness prep. But there was still nothing from Lisa. The unease that had been building all weekend crystallized into something much darker.

Lisa, who had been digging into the fake ID case. Lisa, who hadn't answered any messages since Friday. Lisa, who would never just disappear without telling someone where she was going.

The unease in my stomach bloomed into full-blown panic as I dialed her number.

Straight to voicemail.

"No," I breathed, standing so abruptly my chair tipped over. "No, no, no."

I called Turner, my heart pounding. "When's the last time you saw Lisa?"

"Friday, after court. Why?"

"Has she responded to any of your messages this weekend?"

A pause. "No, but—"

"The warehouse," I cut him off, already grabbing my keys. "She's been looking into the warehouse case. If Lydia is Slim—if I'm right about this—" The words caught in my throat as images of my mother's disappearance flashed through my mind. "Turner, they make people disappear. That's what they do."

"Alex—"

"Meet me there," I said, already moving toward the door. "The old warehouse off Industrial."

"Don't you dare go in alone," Turner's voice was sharp with warning. "Wait for me. I mean it, Hayes."

But I was already running to my car. If I was right about Lydia, about all of it, then Lisa didn't have time for me to wait.

CHAPTER
FORTY-EIGHT

I PUSHED my car to its limits, the engine whining in protest as I took the industrial park's corners too fast, blazing through mazes of corrugated metal and chain link fences. Broken streetlights created pools of darkness between islands of sickly orange light.

My phone lit up with another call from Turner. This time I answered, putting it on speaker.

"I told you to wait."

"And I told you where Lisa is. How far out are you?"

"Five minutes. Alex, I mean it—don't go in alone."

I pulled up to the warehouse, killing the engine but leaving the keys in. The building loomed against the night sky, its broken windows like dead eyes staring down at me.

"I'm just going to look," I lied, already getting out of the car. The gravel crunched under my feet, the sound too loud in the empty lot.

"Hayes—" Turner started, but I ended the call.

The side door was unlocked. My fingers hesitated on the cold metal handle for a moment before I pushed it open. The hinges gave a long, protesting creak that echoed endlessly into the darkness, making my heart lurch. Every muscle in my body tensed as the door swung inward, revealing the void beyond.

Inside, the warehouse was vast and overpowering, a cathedral of shadows stretching higher and farther than I'd remembered. Moonlight spilled through the shattered skylights in jagged patterns, creating pale pools on the dusty concrete floor. The air was heavy with the smell of rust, mold, and something sickly sweet that churned my stomach. Somewhere in the distance, water dripped steadily, the sound loud in the oppressive silence.

"Lisa?" I called, barely above a whisper, the word catching in my throat. It echoed back to me, distorted and hollow, as though the building itself mocked my desperation.

Stepping into the space, my shoes crunched on scattered debris. The sharp sound made me flinch, each step feeling like a violation in the unnatural quiet. My phone's flashlight cut through the gloom in narrow beams, casting long, flickering shadows against the crumbling walls.

The warehouse was a graveyard of forgotten machinery and rotting pallets, each corner a potential hiding place. Massive, rusted beams rose like skeletal ribs from the floor to the ceiling, and I found myself imagining unseen eyes watching me from the rafters.

"Lisa?" I tried again, louder this time, my voice cracking slightly.

Still nothing.

A faint sound froze me in my tracks—a dull thump, so soft I almost convinced myself I'd imagined it. I held my breath, listening intently. There it was again, just ahead of me. A muffled, irregular noise, as though someone was struggling to move.

"Lisa?" I called once more, urgency creeping into my voice.

The sound came again, sharper this time. A spike of adrenaline shot through me, propelling me forward. My light swept across rusted chains hanging from the ceiling and jagged scraps of metal scattered like discarded bones. The farther I went, the louder the thumps became, leading me deeper into the cavernous space.

I followed the noise toward the small office tucked into the far corner of the warehouse. The grime-covered windows were opaque, blocking any view inside. My flashlight beam flickered over the door, slightly ajar, revealing darkness beyond.

My fingers closed around the doorknob, and I pushed the door open with a sudden burst of courage.

"Lisa?"

The beam of my phone flashlight landed on her. She was slumped in the corner, her arms bound tightly with duct tape, her legs curled beneath her. Another strip of tape covered her mouth, her wide, terrified eyes glinting in the dim light. She thrashed, her muffled cries urgent and pleading.

"Lisa!" I gasped, rushing forward, dropping to my knees in front of her. My hands fumbled to peel the tape from her mouth.

Her head jerked wildly, her eyes widening further. A warning.

Before I could process it, something hard and cold pressed against the back of my head—a gun barrel. My breath hitched, panic slamming into my chest like a freight train.

"Don't move."

CHAPTER
FORTY-NINE

THE COLD METAL of the gun barrel pressed harder against the back of my head, sending a shiver down my spine. My breaths came shallow, my pulse pounding in my ears as I stared at Lisa. Her muffled cries stopped as she froze in place, her eyes locked on mine.

"Move an inch, and this gets messy," the voice growled. It was rough and unrelenting, a rasp that scraped against my nerves.

I froze, every instinct screaming at me to run, to fight back, but I couldn't. Not with Lisa still bound in the corner, her terrified eyes locked on mine. The man's presence loomed over me, his breath hot against my neck.

"Well, well. Looks like we've got ourselves a little hero."

My stomach twisted, the words sending a fresh wave of unease through me. Before I could even begin to form a response, another voice cut through the tension, sharp and commanding.

"Drop the theatrics, Scorpion."

The gun on my head shifted as the man—Scorpion—let out a low chuckle. "Always gotta ruin my fun, don't you?"

Lydia stepped into view, emerging from the shadows like a predator stalking her prey, her scarf now gone, revealing sharp, angular features and eyes that gleamed with evil calculation. Her presence filled the room, the confidence she exuded making it clear that she was no victim.

"Lydia," I said, my voice trembling with barely controlled anger. "This was all you. The calls, the lies—everything."

She didn't flinch, didn't look away. Instead, her lips curled into a small, satisfied smile, as if she were savoring the moment. Her gaze locked onto mine, unwavering and cold. A predator's gaze.

"You're a sharp one, Alex," she said, her tone mocking. "I'll give you that. Took you longer than I expected to catch on, though."

The confirmation hit me like a blow, knocking the wind out of me. All the pieces I'd been scrambling to put together clicked into place, forming a picture so horrifying, I almost couldn't believe it.

"Slim."

Lydia's smile widened.

My mind raced, struggling to reconcile the woman I'd thought was a victim with the cold, calculating leader standing before me. I felt sick, remembering her trembling voice, her desperate plea for help in the courtroom. It had all been an act—a masterful, manipulative performance designed to get exactly what she wanted.

"You used me," I said, my voice rising. "You used all of us."

She tilted her head, as if considering the accusation. "*Used* is such a harsh word. Let's just say I gave you the narrative you wanted. You were so eager to believe me, to have your hero moment. All I had to do was give you the breadcrumbs."

"The women," I spat, the anger now outweighing the disbelief. "The ones you claimed Pierce killed. You let us think he was responsible. You let us build a case on lies."

"Not lies," she corrected smoothly. "Pierce played his part. The man's a coward, but he served his purpose. He kept the graves hidden and took the heat for years. But when he started cracking, when he thought he could get out of this and protect his family ..." Her eyes narrowed. "I'd given him the plane ticket. Told him to leave the country. Of course, the Feds would have been waiting for him, but he wouldn't take the bait. Something about his stupid daughter and wife and needing to protect them. That's when I knew it was time to let him take the fall."

My mind raced. "Whitaker was in on it, wasn't he?"

"Whitaker," Lydia sneered, the disdain in her voice sharp enough to cut. "The man's a useful pawn, nothing more. He thought he could clean up the mess and keep his hands clean, but we all have dirt under our nails, don't we?"

"That's why he was talking to Matthews and Ellis. He was trying to get ahead of things, wasn't he?"

Lydia's smirk widened, a glint of satisfaction in her eyes. "Exactly. He thought if he could spin the narrative just right, he'd be safe. But the thing about people like Whitaker is, they're always playing catch-up. He was panicking, trying to cover his own ass. And people like him? They're no good under pressure."

"You sent that email. You wanted to try to prevent Whitaker from going down because you knew he'd drag everyone else with him."

Lydia clapped her hands slowly, mock applause echoing in the cavernous space. "Bravo, Alex! You're sharper than I gave you credit for. Yes, I sent it. Whitaker's unraveling was inevitable. The moment he felt the noose tightening, he started looking for a way out. He was ready to turn on all of us. And I couldn't have that. Not after all the work I've put in."

"You're a coward," I said, my voice shaking with anger. "That's why you're doing all of this—because you couldn't handle him exposing you."

Lydia's laugh was cold, devoid of any real humor. "Coward? No, sweetheart. Whitaker's the coward. Always looking for someone else to clean up his messes. Always trying to run before the heat got too close. And you know what happens when you work with cowards? They make you weak."

Her eyes turned sharp, cutting into me like daggers. "If there's one lesson I've learned in all this, it's not to rely on cowards. They'll drag you down every time."

My breath hitched. Forcing my next words out, I wasn't sure I wanted the answer. "And my mother?"

Lydia tilted her head, a mockery of sympathy softening her features. Her voice, low and deliberate, dripped with cruel amusement. "Katherine Hayes got too close, just like you. Started asking questions, digging into places she shouldn't have. It was admirable in its own way—her determination, her belief that justice could prevail, even against us."

She leaned forward slightly, her tone shifting to one of cold finality. "But there's a cost to digging too deep. Your mother thought she was untouchable, that she could outsmart us. And for a while, she did. But she didn't understand the rules she was playing by. The deeper she went, the more dangerous it became."

My stomach churned, my fists clenching at my sides as I fought to stay composed. Every fiber of my being wanted to lash out, but I needed her to keep talking.

"So, we silenced her. It wasn't personal, you know. Just necessary." Her words landed like a physical blow. "She left us no choice. She knew too much, and she wasn't going to stop. We couldn't have someone like her running around, unraveling years of carefully built systems."

I swallowed hard, my voice trembling as I spoke. "What does that mean? You killed her?"

"What do you think, Alex? You're smart enough to figure it out. Or do you want me to spell it out for you?"

The air thickened around us, the silence that followed pressing down on my chest like a weight. I forced myself to hold her gaze, to not look away, even as my mind screamed at me to stop listening.

"You took her life because she was trying to save others," I said, my voice steadier now, fueled by anger. "She was trying to protect people like the ones you've destroyed. People like me."

Lydia's expression darkened, her feigned sympathy giving way to irritation. "And that was her mistake. She let her emotions cloud her judgment. She got sloppy."

Her words twisted in my gut, a sick mix of grief and fury rising in my chest. "You killed her, and now you think you can do the same to me? You think you'll be able to continue operating, if I'm gone?"

"Oh, Alex. You really don't get it, do you?" Lydia laughed, a hollow, joyless sound that echoed through the cavernous warehouse. Her eyes gleamed with a mix of disdain and amusement as she looked down at me. "This operation is bigger than you can imagine—bigger than one city, one state. It spans borders, crosses oceans."

Stepping closer, her voice dropped to a near-whisper, though it felt louder in the oppressive stillness of the room. "You could dedicate your entire life to this. Chase down every lead, prosecute every name I give you, and you'd still barely scratch the surface. For every one of us you take down, ten more will rise in our place."

Her words cut through me, sharp and cold, like a knife. I clenched my fists to keep my composure. Lydia leaned in slightly, her tone sharpening. "Your mother thought she could stop us too. She believed in justice, in the idea that people like you could tear this all apart. But the truth, Alex? We are everywhere. In your offices, your courtrooms, your police departments. The very systems you're trying to use against us—we've already corrupted them."

I swallowed hard, the weight of her words pressing down on me. But I forced myself to hold her gaze, refusing to show fear.

"You really believe there's no stopping this?"

Her smile turned cold, almost pitying. "I don't believe it, Alex. I know it." She gestured to the shadows surrounding us, as if the entire warehouse were a metaphor for the vastness of their operation. "This isn't just a machine—it's an empire. And you? You're just one person trying to fight it with a slingshot."

I bit back the retort on my tongue, the tension in the room tightening like a noose.

Her smirk widened as if she'd already won. "And now, just like her, you'll be silenced. Another unfortunate casualty in a fight you were never equipped to win."

The gun pressed harder against my skull, and my muscles tensed. Lisa whimpered from her corner, her wide eyes darting between me and Lydia.

"Don't worry," Lydia said, her voice dripping with mock comfort. "This will be quick. Cleaner than what we did to Katherine." She gave me one last, cruel smile. "Goodbye, Alex."

CHAPTER
FIFTY

THE COLD PRESS of the gun against the back of my head felt like the weight of inevitability. My breath came in shallow gasps as I stared at Lisa, her wide eyes filled with silent terror. Her bound hands twitched as if she wanted to reach out, to stop whatever was about to happen. The room closed in, the walls bending under the sheer force of my panic.

This was it. My luck was finally running out. My mind flickered back to the last time I was this close to death—the sharp crack of a gunshot, the fire in my shoulder, the endless nights of replaying it in my head. Back then, I'd told myself it wouldn't happen again. But here I was.

I tried to slow my breathing, to think past the fear hammering in my chest. The room smelled of rust and something sharper—metallic, acrid, and cloying. The faint drip of water still echoed somewhere in the distance, each drop ticking closer to what I thought might be my last moment.

Lisa's muffled protests dragged my attention back to her. Her eyes darted frantically to something behind me. Was she signaling me? I didn't have time to process it.

I closed my eyes for a split second, bracing for the shot. The sound of my own heartbeat filled my ears, deafening, drowning out every-thing else.

"Police! Drop your weapons!"

The shout was like thunder, reverberating off the walls of the warehouse. A cacophony of heavy boots followed, the stomp of authority that didn't leave room for negotiation. Bright beams of flashlight cut through the darkness, blinding in their intensity. Lydia flinched, drawing a gun from her own waistband and trying to train it on the uniformed men surrounding us.

The shift was enough. I twisted away from Scorpion, his curse loud and sharp in the chaos. The sudden movement sent me sprawling to the floor, the cold concrete scraping my hands.

"Drop it!" Turner's voice rang out, firm and unyielding.

I looked up to see him standing in the doorway, his gun trained squarely on Scorpion. His presence filled the space with authority, his jaw set in a way that brooked no argument. Behind him, officers continued pouring into the room, their weapons drawn, their commands overlapping in a chorus of control.

Lydia's face twisted into a snarl, but she didn't lower her weapon. "You think this changes anything?" she hissed, her voice cutting through the chaos like a dagger. She moved her gun to point at Lisa.

"Drop it!" Turner barked again, his tone sharp enough to cut steel.

Lisa was wriggling against her bonds, her muffled cries growing louder as she twisted in her restraints. My gaze darted between her and Lydia, my instincts screaming to do something, anything, but I was rooted to the spot. The room was suspended in time, the next second stretching into eternity.

Scorpion's gun clattered to the floor first. The sound was deafening in the sudden silence. He raised his hands, his expression unreadable as two officers moved in to restrain him.

Lydia hesitated, her gaze flickering between Turner and me. The fight in her eyes burned bright, but she wasn't stupid. With a venomous glare, she slowly lowered her gun, tossing it to the ground with a hollow clunk.

Two officers rushed forward, pinning her arms behind her back as they snapped on cuffs. She didn't struggle but held her head high, a small, defiant smirk still playing on her lips.

Turner stepped forward, his eyes sweeping over the scene before settling on me. "Are you okay?" he asked, his voice steady but laced with concern.

Nodding, my throat too tight to speak, I pushed myself to my feet, my legs shaking as I crossed to Lisa. An officer was already cutting through her restraints, and the moment she was free, she threw her arms around me, her body trembling against mine.

"I thought …" Her voice broke, and she pulled back, her eyes brimming with tears. "I thought they were going to—"

"I know," I said, my voice firmer than I felt.

Lydia and Scorpion were led away first, the officers flanking them on either side as their handcuffs gleamed under the harsh warehouse lights. Lydia's smirk never wavered, her head held high like she was walking a red carpet rather than toward the back of a squad car. Scorpion slouched in defeat, muttering curses under his breath. The sound of their footsteps faded into the distance, leaving an almost eerie silence behind.

As I knelt beside Lisa, a man in a uniform rushed forward. I recognized him as Scott Cooper, Lisa's father. "Lisa!" he called, rushing to her side. His hands were on her shoulders in an instant, helping her sit up straighter as he pulled her into a fierce hug.

"Dad," she croaked, her voice breaking. Tears streaked her face, but she clung to him like a lifeline.

"Thank God. Are you hurt? Did they—?"

"No, I'm okay," she assured him, her voice trembling. "Just shaken."

He helped her to her feet, steadying her when she wobbled. "Let's get you checked out. Just to be sure."

She nodded, leaning into his support as he guided her toward the paramedics waiting just outside. She glanced back at me once, her lips parting as if to say something, but I gave her a reassuring nod. "Go," I said gently. "I'll handle the rest."

As they disappeared into the night, Turner stepped closer, his gaze narrowing. "Hayes," he began, his tone sharp, "what the hell were you thinking?"

"I—"

"I told you not to go in without backup." His voice was steady, but the frustration was clear. "And what did you do? You went in alone, with no plan, no support, and nearly got yourself killed."

"I didn't have a choice," I argued, though my voice lacked conviction. "Lisa was in here. What was I supposed to do? Wait around and hope for the best?"

"Yes. You were supposed to wait for me, for the team. That's why I told you not to go in. You think this is some solo crusade, but it's not, Alex. We're a *team*. You're not supposed to carry this alone."

His words struck harder than I expected, the truth of them settling deep in my chest. I looked down at my scuffed boots, trying to find the right words. "I couldn't just stand there, Turner," I said quietly. "Not knowing what might be happening to her. I couldn't."

Turner sighed, the tension in his shoulders easing slightly. "I get it. But you can't keep doing this, Hayes. One of these days, your luck is going to run out."

I met his eyes, the weight of his concern surprising me. "Thanks," I muttered. "For showing up when you did."

"Don't thank me yet," he said with a wry smile. "I'm not done giving you hell for this."

"You did good tonight, Alex," he said, his voice softer now. "But next time, try trusting the rest of us to have your back."

"I'll work on it," I said, not entirely sure I believed it. Trust didn't come easy. Not for me.

"On a more positive note, for once, Hayes, you didn't get yourself shot."

A shaky laugh escaped me, more relief than humor. "Guess there's a first time for everything."

Turner placed a hand on my shoulder, a rare moment of camaraderie. "You stayed alive. That's step one."

"Step two?" I asked, trying to lighten the mood.

He smiled faintly. "Step two is making sure this whole operation comes crashing down."

CHAPTER FIFTY-ONE

THE COURTHOUSE FELT HEAVIER than usual Monday morning, as though the air itself carried the weight of what was about to happen. Sunlight filtered through the towering windows in fractured beams, glinting off the polished wooden benches and dull brass railings. The jury box sat empty for now, a reminder of the people we'd soon be addressing, people we'd asked to weigh a man's fate based on a version of events that, as of last night, no longer held true.

Lisa and I walked toward the front, her steps slower than usual as she adjusted her blouse and winced slightly. She was still sore from being tied up in that warehouse, but she refused to let it show too much. A bandage peeked out from her sleeve, covering the raw marks left by the duct tape.

"How are you feeling?" I asked, keeping my voice low.

"Like I've been hit by a truck," she admitted with a half-smile. "But I'll live. More importantly, I'll be right here if you need me."

Lisa took a seat in the front row, and I continued forward.

I reached the counsel table, where Shaw was already waiting. He stood tall and composed in his dark suit, his briefcase in one hand and a file in the other. His face was calm, but I could tell from the tension in his jaw that he was carrying the weight of this decision as much as I was.

"You ready?" he asked, his voice neutral.

"Ready as I'll ever be."

My stomach churned, and I felt a pang of doubt. This wasn't just any case. This was a decision that could ripple through the DA's office for years to come. We were about to tell the judge—the world—that we'd been wrong.

The courtroom buzzed softly as people settled into their seats, the atmosphere charged with anticipation. Randall Pierce entered first, escorted by a bailiff, his sharp suit unable to conceal the exhaustion etched into his face. His shoulders were hunched, his hands clasped tightly in front of him as he took his seat at the defense table. For the first time, he looked more like a man caught in the tide of something beyond his control, than the cold and calculating figure we had painted him to be.

Ellis followed shortly after, carrying his briefcase with the same practiced poise as always. His expression was unreadable, but when his gaze met mine, I caught the faintest flicker of suspicion. He sat beside Pierce, speaking in low tones.

Then came the judge's entrance. We all rose as Judge Carter stepped into the room, her black robe flowing behind her. Her sharp eyes swept over the courtroom, her presence commanding silence. She adjusted her glasses and gave the room a measured look before taking her seat.

"Good morning," she said, her voice cutting through the quiet. "Counsel, are we ready to proceed?"

The jury entered last, filing in one by one. Their faces were a mix of curiosity and fatigue, some exchanging puzzled glances as they took their seats. They could feel it—the shift in the atmosphere, the sense that something unexpected was coming. I couldn't blame them. The tension was palpable, a weight that seemed to settle over every corner of the room.

I glanced at Shaw, who gave a small nod. It was time.

Shaw stood, his voice firm and clear. "Your Honor, the prosecution would like to address the court before we move forward."

Judge Carter raised an eyebrow, leaning back slightly. "Go ahead, Mr. Shaw."

He stepped to the center of the room, holding the file in both hands.

"Your Honor, after reviewing newly discovered evidence, the prosecution has determined that the first-degree murder charges against Mr. Randall Pierce should be dismissed."

A murmur swept through the gallery. I could feel the jury's confusion beside me, their collective silence heavy with unspoken questions.

Judge Carter's gaze sharpened. "Dismissed? On what grounds?"

Shaw nodded, his demeanor steady. "This case has taken several unexpected turns, and while I can't go into detail at this moment, I can say with certainty that we've come to an agreement with the defense. A plea arrangement has been reached on obstruction of justice charges, but the charges of first-degree murder will be dismissed."

The judge regarded him for a long moment, then glanced at Ellis, who rose with his usual air of calculated poise. "The defense agrees with the motion, Your Honor. And we believe it's in the best interest of justice."

Judge Carter's lips pressed into a thin line, her eyes flicking between the two attorneys. "Very well. The charges of first-degree murder are dismissed. The court thanks the jury for their service and dismisses them as well."

I turned slightly to watch the jurors, their expressions a mix of relief and bewilderment as they filed out. Some looked to Pierce, others to Shaw, but most seemed eager to leave. I couldn't blame them. Trials were exhausting, and this one had just taken a turn no one expected.

As the courtroom began to empty, Pierce stood, his movements slower, as if the weight of everything was finally settling on his shoulders. He exchanged a quiet word with Ellis, who nodded subtly before gathering his papers with practiced efficiency.

When Pierce stepped toward me, the bailiff moved instinctively, raising a hand to block his path. I held up my own hand, stopping him. "It's okay," I said, my voice steady but low.

The bailiff hesitated but stepped aside, his watchful gaze never leaving Pierce. He was, of course, a man still awaiting sentencing and would continue in custody until that time.

I noticed Ellis glance up briefly, his brow furrowed, but he said nothing, slipping a file into his briefcase as if distancing himself from the moment.

Pierce approached cautiously, his eyes meeting mine. Up close, I could see the exhaustion etched into his features, the lines of a man who had been to hell and back. What I had once taken as cold and unfeeling was now clearly something else entirely—resignation. Pain.

"Thank you," he said, his voice rough. "For seeing the truth."

I nodded, unsure what else to say. Words felt insufficient in the face of what this man had endured. "Take care of yourself," I said quietly. "And your family."

He offered the faintest of smiles before turning back to the bailiff, who led him out of the room. I watched until he disappeared through the double doors, the weight in my chest finally easing, just slightly.

———

As we stepped into the cool afternoon air, Lisa nudged me with her elbow. "You know what we need?"

"Sleep?" I suggested, my lips quirking into a faint smile.

"Pizza. And maybe a lot of wine."

I laughed, the sound surprising even me. "You're on."

We walked down the courthouse steps together, leaving the weight of the case behind us—for now. There would always be another fight, another case, another impossible decision to make. But tonight, for the first time in what felt like forever, I allowed myself to smile.

EPILOGUE

THE CEMETERY WAS QUIET, the kind of stillness that pressed against your chest. The late afternoon sun cast long shadows across the rows of headstones, their inscriptions weathered and softened by time. My father and I walked side by side, the crunch of gravel underfoot the only sound. We stopped at the modest granite marker engraved with my mother's name. *Katherine Hayes, Beloved Mother and Wife. Gone But Not Forgotten.*

I knelt down, brushing away the fallen leaves that had collected at its base. For years, this grave had felt like a cruel joke—an empty plot meant to provide solace when we had no body to bury, no answers to cling to. But now, at least we had answers.

Scorpion had folded quickly under questioning. It turned out that beneath all his bravado and violence, he didn't have much of a backbone when faced with actual consequences. He'd laid out everything in excruciating detail: how my mother had infiltrated the ring, posing as someone willing to help cover their tracks to gather evidence. How she got too close, discovered Slim's identity—Lydia's true role—and had been silenced for it. The details were horrifying, but they also gave me something I hadn't had before: the truth.

"She never stopped fighting," I said softly, the words barely louder than the rustling leaves around us. "She could've walked away, but she didn't."

My dad stood beside me, his hands buried deep in his coat pockets. "That was who she was. She believed in justice, even when it cost her everything."

I bent over with the small bouquet of white lilies I'd brought, laying them carefully at the base of the headstone. "I just wish we'd known. That we could've done something."

"You didn't know. And even if you had … Alex, you were just a kid. You can't carry the weight of what happened to her. It's not your fault."

I didn't respond immediately, letting his words settle over me. The weight of guilt and anger had been my constant companion for so long, it was hard to imagine life without it. But maybe he was right. Maybe it was time to let some of it go.

We sat in silence for a few moments, the cool breeze tugging at my hair and carrying the faint scent of earth and fallen leaves. My dad broke the quiet first.

"So," he said, his tone casual but tinged with concern. "What's next? Are you going to keep digging into this?"

I leaned back on my heels, staring at the name etched into the stone. "I don't know if I have a choice," I admitted. "This ring is too big, too dangerous to ignore." I hesitated, my voice faltering. "But I don't know how I do that while working for the DA's office. This is bigger than one city, bigger than Houston. It's everywhere."

He nodded thoughtfully, his gaze distant. "Then maybe it's time to think about something else. You've done good work here, but if this is as big as it seems, you need the right tools, the right backing."

I looked at him, frowning slightly. "What are you saying?"

"You should consider moving to the feds," he said simply, meeting my eyes. "You've got the connections, Alex. Your friend Erin—she's in, what, organized crime now? She'd get it. The federal level is where this fight belongs."

I swallowed, the idea catching me off guard. "The feds," I repeated, testing the word. "I don't know, Dad. That's a whole other world."

"It's a world where you could make a real difference. You've already got your foot in the door. And if this ring is as big as you say, you can't fight it alone."

I stared back at the headstone, my thoughts churning. Could I leave the DA's office? Leave the cases and the people I'd worked so hard for? The more I thought about it, the more it made sense. If I stayed where I was, I'd only ever scratch the surface of something this vast. The real fight would be waged somewhere else.

"I'll think about it," I said finally, standing and brushing off my knees. "Maybe you're right."

"I usually am," he said, a faint smile tugging at his lips. He pulled me into a hug, the kind of hug that said he knew I had a hard road ahead of me but that he believed I could handle it.

Later that night, I sat at the kitchen table, the glow of my laptop the only light. My mother's notes were spread out in front of me, familiar handwriting that now felt like a message from the past.

I reached for my phone, hesitating for just a moment before dialing. Erin picked up on the second ring.

"Alex," she said, her voice bright but surprised. "I was just thinking about you. What's up?"

I took a deep breath, gripping the edge of the table. "You always said I should come work with you."

There was a pause, then a sharp intake of breath. "Are you serious?"

"Yeah," I said, my voice firm despite the weight of the decision. "I think it's time."

Erin let out a low whistle. "Welcome to the big leagues, Hayes."

As we talked logistics, the enormity of the choice started to settle in. I wasn't just leaving one job for another. I was stepping into something far bigger than I'd ever imagined. But as I glanced at my mother's notes, the determination in her words clear, even after all these years, I knew I was ready.

This fight wasn't over. It was just beginning.

———

Alex's story continues in Buried Testimony (ALEX HAYES Book 3).
Click the link below to order now, or turn the page for a preview.

https://www.amazon.com/dp/B0F1Y889KL/

Join the LT Ryan reader family & receive a free copy of the Alex Hayes
story, *Trial by Fire*. Click the link below to get started:
https://ltryan.com/alex-hayes-newsletter-signup-1

BURIED TESTIMONY

CHAPTER 1

The lobby of the U.S. Attorney's Office smelled like fresh carpet cleaner and bureaucracy. Everything was sterile—polished floors, neatly framed portraits of past Attorneys General lining the walls, the eagle seal mounted above the security desk as if it were watching, judging. I adjusted my blazer, reminding myself that this was a step forward. A fresh start.

Not that I felt like celebrating.

The elevator ride to the Criminal Division was quiet, save for the hum of fluorescent lighting. I kept my eyes on the numbers blinking above the door, half-expecting someone to step in and ruin my moment of solitude. No one did. When the doors slid open on the seventh floor, the shift in energy hit immediately—phones ringing, the distant clatter of keyboards, hushed voices carrying the weight of deals being cut, cases being prepped. It wasn't Harris County anymore. The U.S. Attorney's Office was bigger, grander, but the undercurrent of tension remained the same.

At least here, I wouldn't have to worry about people whispering about the Martin case. Or about how I'd single-handedly exposed corruption in the mayor's office while simultaneously tanking the trial that should have been my career-making moment. No, here I was just another new hire.

I followed the hallway signs to **Criminal Division – Intake,** passing offices with glass panels that revealed their occupants—some deep in conversation, others buried in files. The whole place had the efficiency of a well-oiled machine. It was unsettling.

When I found my assigned office, I was surprised to see my name already mounted outside the door in a temporary placard. **ALEX HAYES, AUSA**. Seeing it in print didn't make it feel real.

Inside, the office was sparse—just a desk, a government-issued chair that looked as uncomfortable as it probably was, and a tall bookshelf lined with the *Federal Rules of Criminal Procedure* and the current year's Sentencing Guidelines. The essentials. I dropped my bag on the desk, eyeing the computer that had a "Welcome to the Department of Justice" login screen glowing at me.

I was about to sit when a sharp knock sounded at the door.

Erin Mitchell leaned against the frame, arms crossed, her smirk firmly in place. "You look like someone who just realized they joined a machine bigger than they can break."

"Nice to see you, too," I said.

She stepped in and took a slow look around, nodding in approval. "Not bad. You're already ahead of where I started—my first office didn't have a window."

I smirked. "I get a stunning view of the parking garage, so I think we're even."

I still considered Erin a friend. At least, in the way you could be friends with someone who once used you as a pawn to take down a dirty cop. She'd had her reasons—I understood that now. But it didn't make it any easier to forget the way she'd maneuvered around me, steering me right where she needed me to go while keeping her own agenda close to the chest. It had worked. Andrews had gone down. And I'd been left to pick up the pieces. And a bullet wound. But it only hurt when the weather drastically changed these days.

Erin had apologized, in her own way, and I wasn't holding a grudge. Not really. But I wasn't naïve either. The trust we had before the Martin case? That was gone. Now, I kept one eye open, even with people I liked. Especially with people I liked.

"So," I said, bracing myself, "what's my first case? Racketeering? Drug cartel?"

Erin's smirk widened. "Oh, you sweet summer child."

She handed me a file.

I flipped it open. Habeas petitions. Post-conviction appeals. Inmate filings from prison. My stomach sank.

Habeas corpus—the so-called last hope of the damned. In theory, it was a noble concept. The great safeguard of justice, the mechanism by which the wrongfully convicted could claw their way out of a prison cell and back into the world. In reality? It was 99% bullshit.

Most of these petitions were just stacks of wasted paper filed by inmates who had nothing but time and a battered copy of *Federal Criminal Procedure for Dummies*. They'd scrawl out half-baked claims of ineffective assistance of counsel, constitutional violations, newly discovered evidence that conveniently didn't exist when they were actually on trial. Some of them even argued that the court had no jurisdiction over them in the first place—sovereign citizen nonsense written in all caps with red ink like that somehow made it legally binding.

I'd seen it before. Back when I worked at the DA's office, the state version of these filings had landed on my desk from time to time, and they were all the same: desperate, sloppy, and almost always meritless. An endless cycle of grasping at legal technicalities, hoping some poor overworked judge would be too exhausted to deny it outright.

"You're kidding, right?" I flipped to the first page. Some guy out of USP Beaumont claiming his defense attorney had been incompetent— failure to investigate witnesses, failure to object at trial, failure to present mitigating evidence. Classic. Every inmate swore their lawyer was an idiot after the fact. They never mentioned whether they'd taken a plea after being caught on security footage waving a gun around like it was a party favor.

"Welcome to the big leagues," Erin said, clapping a hand on my shoulder. "Hope you like reading handwritten legal filings on notebook paper, because you're about to drown in them."

I closed the file with a snap. "I didn't leave the DA's office to do post-conviction work."

"You didn't leave the DA's office at all," Erin pointed out. "You were recruited. Now you're here, and guess what? Everyone starts in habeas. Even me."

I shot her a look. "How long until I can actually do real work?"

"That depends." She grinned. "How fast can you prove you're not just another former state prosecutor trying to play federal?"

Before I could respond, another voice cut in. "Hayes?"

I turned to see a man in his early forties standing in the doorway, sleeves rolled up, tie slightly loosened, the type who looked like he'd been here long enough to know everyone's mistakes before they made them.

"This is Nathan Callahan," Erin said. "Your new supervisor."

Callahan didn't waste time on pleasantries. "Just making sure you found your office."

"I did." I kept my expression neutral. "Thanks."

"Good." He glanced at the files in front of me. "Habeas cases. Get through them fast. We'll see where you land after that."

I didn't miss the way his tone made it clear—I was here to prove myself, not to make demands.

Message received.

"Understood," I said, thumbing the files on my desk like I hadn't already considered tossing it in the trash.

Callahan gave a curt nod. "Welcome to the USAO." And just like that, he was gone.

Erin let out a low whistle. "Whew. You passed the Callahan test. He didn't look like he wanted to murder you."

"I'll consider that a win," I muttered. "Is that the benchmark around here? If your supervisor doesn't immediately fantasize about strangling you, you're doing great?"

"Pretty much," Erin said, smirking. She checked her watch. "I've got a debrief with Organized Crime in ten. Want to grab drinks after work? You're gonna need them."

I sighed, nudging the file on my desk like it personally offended me. "Yeah, probably." I gestured to the box tucked around the side of my desk, stacked high with even more habeas petitions. "And what happens when I finish this one? I assume I just...move on to the next pile of hopeless dreams?"

Erin's smirk widened. "That's the spirit." She patted my shoulder like I was a lost cause. "Oh, and don't worry—when you finish those, they'll just bring you more."

I groaned. "Of course they will."

With one last amused glance, Erin strode off, leaving me alone with my not-so-glamorous first assignment—and the soul-crushing box of appeals waiting to remind me of my place in the system.

I sat at my desk, flipping the file open again. The words "Petition for Writ of Habeas Corpus" stared back at me.

Not exactly what I'd envisioned for my first day at the U.S. Attorney's Office.

But if they wanted me to prove myself?

Fine.

I'd play the game. For now.

BURIED TESTIMONY

CHAPTER 2

I looked at the first file on my desk, bracing myself for the mind-numbing legalese inside.

PETITION FOR WRIT OF HABEAS CORPUS

THE UNITED STATES DISTRICT COURT

SOUTHERN DISTRICT OF TEXAS

Another federal inmate with a last-ditch attempt to get out of prison.

I skimmed the first few paragraphs. The petitioner—one Jerome L. Barlow, Reg. No. 48219-179—was serving forty years for drug trafficking and firearms offenses. According to him, his entire conviction was a miscarriage of justice. His attorney had been incompetent, the judge biased, and the government had conspired against him.

The usual greatest hits.

I flipped to the next page and saw the real reason I had to deal with this mess—a court order directing the government to file a response.

Lovely.

Here's how it worked. Any inmate could file a habeas petition, arguing that their conviction or sentence violated the Constitution. Most of them were summarily denied, meaning the judge tossed them without bothering to ask for the government's input. But every so often, a judge decided a petition warranted further review—hence the order on my desk.

That meant I had work to do.

I skimmed the court's directive:

ORDERED that the United States Attorney's Office shall file a response within 30 days addressing the petitioner's claims regarding ineffective assistance of counsel.

Translation: *Alex, welcome to the USAO. Here's some homework.*

The judge wasn't saying the claim had merit, just that it wasn't immediately laughable. The threshold for that was painfully low. If an inmate managed to string together a few coherent sentences and reference the Sixth Amendment, the court was basically obligated to take a second look.

I sighed and flipped back to Barlow's actual argument.

His claim? His lawyer never objected to certain testimony at trial, and if he had, the jury might have ruled differently. Specifically, a key witness—one of his former associates who had flipped on him—had allegedly misrepresented their own plea deal while testifying. Barlow was arguing that his lawyer should have called this out, that the jury had been misled, and therefore, his entire conviction was invalid.

Didn't matter that the guy had been caught with twenty kilos of cocaine, a firearm, and enough cash to buy a small island. He was hanging his hopes on one witness's plea agreement.

I checked the docket number and pulled up the case history on my computer. The trial transcripts would tell me whether his lawyer had, in fact, screwed the pooch or if this was just another inmate fishing for a loophole. If I had to bet, I'd say the latter.

Before I could dive in, a soft knock at my door pulled me out of my haze.

A man in his mid-thirties stood in the doorway, dressed in the standard prosecutor uniform—gray suit, blue tie, the harried expression of someone perpetually juggling too many cases.

"Hey, you must be Hayes," he said. "I'm Jason Ruiz, Criminal Division. Just wanted to introduce myself."

I sat up and extended my hand. "Nice to meet you."

"Welcome to the grind," Ruiz said, shaking my hand. "You settling in?"

I glanced at the towering stack of habeas petitions next to me. "I think 'settling' is a strong word."

Ruiz laughed. "Yeah, they love breaking in the new hires with the fun stuff. Let me guess—post-conviction appeals?"

"Bingo."

"Well, if you need a second opinion or just someone to confirm that a petition is, in fact, total garbage, I'm down the hall."

"Appreciate it."

Ruiz nodded and stepped out. Before I could return to Barlow's tragic tale of judicial betrayal, another figure appeared in the doorway.

A woman this time—blond, early forties, polished but no-nonsense. She held a travel mug of coffee in one hand and a stack of marked-up case files in the other.

"I'm guessing you're the new AUSA," she said. "Alex Hayes?"

"That's me," I said. "And you are?"

"Maggie Cohen, Appellate Division." She gave me a once-over, assessing. "You're coming from the DA's office, right?"

"Yeah."

Cohen smirked. "Welcome to federal. Hope you like paperwork."

I motioned to the stack on my desk. "I'm getting that impression."

She chuckled. "Let me guess—habeas petitions?"

"Are they always this bad?"

"They're worse," Cohen said. "But you'll get the hang of it. Let me know if you need any help deciphering the nonsense. Most of these cases have been appealed and denied so many times, they should come with a greatest-hits playlist."

"Duly noted."

She raised her coffee in a mock toast and walked off.

The parade of introductions continued throughout the day. More faces, more names, most of which I'd already started forgetting.

Before I knew it, my stomach was growling, and my inbox was full. I glanced at the time and realized I hadn't left my desk once. Not even for lunch.

The day had vanished.

I logged out of my computer, stacked the files into something resembling order, and grabbed my bag.

Time to meet Erin for that drink.

I swirled the last of my scotch in my glass, watching the amber liquid catch the dim bar light. Erin leaned against the counter, elbow propped up, her expression expectant.

"So," she said, taking a slow sip of her whiskey. "Are you gonna keep brooding, or are you actually gonna tell me what's eating at you?"

I exhaled through my nose, setting my glass down with a dull *clink*. "It's not that bad, really. I just...this isn't what I thought it would be."

Erin raised an eyebrow. "You mean you didn't dream of spending your days drowning in habeas petitions? Shocking."

I shot her a look, but the amusement in her eyes softened it. "I didn't expect to be thrown onto organized crime on day one or anything, but I thought maybe I'd be working actual cases. Instead, I'm sifting through stacks of long-shot appeals, filing response briefs no judge is actually going to read, and pretending that this is important work."

"It *is* important work," Erin said, tilting her glass toward me. "It just happens to be soul-crushingly boring."

I smirked. "Exactly."

She leaned back against the bar, studying me. "But that's not really what's bothering you, is it?"

I hesitated. Erin might have maneuvered around me during the Martin case, but she wasn't stupid. She knew me too well to buy the surface-level complaints.

I sighed, rubbing a hand across my forehead. "I thought maybe...maybe this would put me closer to figuring out what happened to my mother. That taking this job would give me more resources, better access to research the trafficking ring. But instead, I'm buried in the paperwork graveyard of federal prosecution."

There. I'd said it.

Erin's expression didn't shift, didn't turn patronizing or dismissive. Instead, she nodded, her gaze steady. "I get it."

I looked up at her, surprised.

She shrugged. "You want to *do* something. You want to pull at the threads, dig into whatever she was investigating before she died. But instead, they've got you shuffling through procedural motions like a glorified law clerk. That's frustrating as hell."

"Exactly." I let out a breath, staring at the rim of my glass. "It's been years, Erin. And now I've finally got my foot in the door at the feds, and it's like I'm still stuck on the sidelines."

She tapped her fingers against her glass, thoughtful. "It won't be forever."

I scoffed. "Easy for you to say. You're working real cases."

She smirked. "That's true. But you *will* get there, Alex. The USAO isn't like the DA's office. They don't just throw you into the fire. You've gotta prove yourself first. Which, let's be real, you'll do *annoyingly* fast."

I snorted, shaking my head. "That's generous."

"It's the truth." She took a sip, then gestured toward me with her glass. "Look at it this way—this is the first time in years you don't have a huge trial breathing down your neck, no hearings to sprint to, no cops demanding arrest warrants like you're some kind of vending machine for probable cause."

I smirked at the image.

"I know it's not what you wanted," she continued. "But this time? You get to breathe. No pressure, no public scrutiny, no media outside the courthouse waiting for you to screw up. Just you, some badly written petitions, and time."

"Time," I echoed, rolling the word around like it was something foreign.

"Yeah," Erin said. "Time to dig, time to put your own pieces together." She eyed me. "You're gonna keep looking into it, aren't you?"

I nodded. "Yeah. I have to."

Erin didn't argue. She just nodded. "Then use this time wisely. The big cases will come. In the meantime, don't waste the breathing room."

I let out a slow breath, some of the weight on my chest loosening. She was right. It wasn't the role I wanted, but that didn't mean I couldn't *use* it.

She changed the subject smoothly. "You still living at home with your dad?"

"Yeah," I said, finishing off the last of my scotch. "The commute's not much different since I managed to get a spot here in the Houston office. So, for now, it works."

Erin nodded thoughtfully. "Makes sense. I moved down here officially a few months back myself, so I get it."

I raised an eyebrow, slightly surprised. "Really?"

"Yeah," Erin said, smiling faintly as she stirred her drink. "Made the jump a few months ago. The Houston office needed another senior AUSA, and I figured why not."

I smiled softly. "Looks like we're both settling in."

She chuckled. "Something like that."

We fell quiet for a moment, sitting comfortably in the gentle lull of the conversation, the clinking of glasses and low hum of voices around us.

Erin glanced at the time on her phone. "Alright, I should head out before I start regretting tomorrow morning."

"Same," I said, stretching my arms. "First full day of government work really takes it out of you."

She smirked. "Yeah, yeah. You'll adjust. And when you do? You're buying the next round."

I laughed. "Deal."

We parted outside the bar, Erin heading off in the direction of her place while I made my way toward my car. The night air was crisp, carrying the distant hum of the city.

I exhaled, my mind turning over everything we'd talked about.

She was right—for once in my life, I had time.

BURIED TESTIMONY

CHAPTER 3

I rubbed my eyes, glancing at the clock in the corner of my monitor. It was creeping toward noon, and I had already knocked out four reply briefs this morning—four nearly identical responses explaining, in slightly different ways, why yet another federal inmate wasn't entitled to relief.

I stretched my arms, rolling out the tightness in my shoulders, then leaned back in my chair and stared at the box of petitions still looming at the side of my desk.

Each folder was practically identical. Same formatting, same desperate handwriting scrawled in margins. If I blurred my eyes, I wouldn't have been able to tell one from the next.

Sifting through them was depressing.

A few caught my eye for a second—claims about ineffective assistance, prosecutorial misconduct, newly discovered evidence—but I had already learned not to get too invested. The bar for actual relief was absurdly high, and most of these were grasping at straws.

I flipped past one claiming that an inmate's lawyer was "asleep" during trial. Another argued that the judge was *secretly colluding* with the prosecution. One had the ever-popular sovereign citizen rambling, which I tossed aside without another glance.

I was already flipping to the next file when something caught my eye.

Brady violation.

My pulse ticked up a notch.

I flipped the file open, scanning the pages. Gabriel Ortega was serving life without parole for felony murder. According to his petition, a key witness statement had been buried—a statement that, if disclosed, could have undermined the state's entire case against him, among the other standard claims like ineffective assistance of counsel.

The more I read, the tighter my jaw got.

The witness statement had been suppressed by the prosecution. Not lost. Not misplaced. Deliberately buried.

A Brady violation, in its simplest form, was when the prosecution failed to turn over exculpatory evidence to the defense—evidence that could have helped the defendant at trial. The term came from *Brady v. Maryland*, a 1963 Supreme Court case that basically laid down a simple rule: prosecutors don't get to play dirty.

If the government had something that could prove you weren't guilty, or even something that just made their case weaker, they had to turn it over. Period.

The reality? Prosecutors didn't always follow that rule.

And when they didn't, convictions got overturned. Cases fell apart. Careers were ruined.

I scanned Ortega's petition again. His claim wasn't just another inmate swinging blindly—it had specificity, details. He wasn't saying evidence *might have existed*. He was saying that a specific witness statement had been intentionally hidden. And he wasn't the one who had discovered it—a retiring prosecutor had come forward, admitting it had been buried.

That stopped me cold.

Anonymous tips in habeas petitions weren't unheard of. But a former prosecutor? Admitting to misconduct? Attaching his name to it? That wasn't normal.

I flipped to the court order attached to the petition. The judge had already ordered a preliminary response.

Which meant this wasn't just a shot in the dark—the judge thought it had enough weight to demand an explanation from the government.

I pulled up Ortega's trial records on my screen.

Felony murder. That meant he hadn't actually pulled the trigger but had still been convicted of murder under Texas's felony murder rule—basically, if you were committing a serious felony and someone died, you were just as guilty as if you had killed them yourself.

His case stemmed from a botched robbery. The prosecution had argued that Ortega had been part of a crew that held up a liquor store in Houston. The store owner pulled a gun, shots were fired, and a man ended up dead.

Ortega had always claimed he wasn't even there.

But the state had witnesses—one of Ortega's former associates, who had turned on him in exchange for a deal. His testimony had been the cornerstone of the case.

And now, I was looking at a claim that another witness—one the jury had never heard from—had contradicted the prosecution's version of events.

A witness the state had known about.

And hidden.

I exhaled slowly and leaned back in my chair, staring at the petition spread out in front of me.

If this was true, it wasn't just bad—it was disastrous.

I glanced at the clock again. I had other petitions to get through. Other reply briefs waiting.

But this?

This wasn't one I could ignore.

I grabbed my legal pad and started making notes.

I needed to track down the case files, pull the old court records, and find out who had prosecuted Ortega's trial. If this witness statement had been suppressed, I wanted to know who buried it—and why.

I tapped my pen against my desk, still staring at Gabriel Ortega's petition, when my calendar notification popped up on my screen.

Meeting with AUSA Daniel Wexler – Habeas Unit Chief.

Damn.

I was supposed to be in his office in five minutes. Ortega would have to wait.

I grabbed my notepad, straightened my blazer, and made my way through the maze of hallways to Wexler's office. He oversaw all habeas petitions filed against the government—a gatekeeper of lost causes, as I had started calling it in my head.

When I got to his door, I knocked lightly.

"Come in," a deep voice called.

I stepped inside and found AUSA Daniel Wexler behind his desk, sleeves rolled up, his head down in whatever file he was currently working on. He was in his mid-fifties, with a thick head of salt-and-pepper hair and the kind of posture that suggested he'd spent too many years hunched over case files. His office was lined with shelves of thick federal law books and case binders, but it was unnervingly neat—not a stray paper out of place.

He glanced up as I walked in and offered a small, practiced smile.

"Ah, Hayes. Come in, sit." He gestured to the chair across from him. "How are you settling in?"

I slid into the seat, setting my notepad on my lap. "It's been good so far. Still getting my bearings, but I think I'm getting the rhythm of things."

He nodded approvingly. "Glad to hear it. First few weeks are always an adjustment. Government work moves at its own pace—sometimes it feels like a slow crawl, sometimes it's like drinking from a firehose."

That sounded about right.

"I appreciate you making time," I said. "I know you're busy."

"Of course," Wexler said, lacing his fingers together. "Let's talk about your caseload. You've been moving through the petitions pretty efficiently—walk me through what you've handled so far."

I flipped open my notepad and ran down the list.

• Jerome L. Barlow – Claimed ineffective assistance of counsel. Argued his lawyer should have objected to testimony about a cooperating witness's plea deal. No merit—the judge even asked Barlow if he was satisfied with his attorney on the record.

•Tyrone Mitchell – Claimed actual innocence based on a "mystery witness" who conveniently never came forward at trial. No merit—no affidavits, no supporting evidence, just a rehash of trial arguments.

• Leonard Torres – Fourth habeas petition. This time arguing the

jury instructions were unconstitutional. No merit—he had already liti-
gated this on direct appeal and lost.

●Samuel Ross – DNA claim. But the "new evidence" he cited had
been available at trial, and his own lawyer had decided not to test it
because it was more damaging than helpful. No merit.

Wexler listened without interrupting, nodding occasionally. When I
finished, he leaned back in his chair.

"Sounds like you're doing great work," he said. "Habeas petitions
can be tedious, but you're moving through them quickly. Appreciate
the efficiency."

I hesitated for half a second.

He was about to wrap up the meeting. I could see it in the way he
shifted, reaching for the file on his desk as if this conversation was
over.

But I wasn't done yet.

"There's one more I'm looking into now," I said. "Gabriel Ortega."

Wexler froze.

For the first time in the meeting, he actually looked up from his
notes and studied me.

I watched his brows knit together, his expression shifting from
neutral to something else entirely—something that looked a lot like
concern.

"Ortega?" Wexler repeated, shaking his head slightly. "That conviction was twelve years ago."

I nodded. "That's right."

He leaned forward, resting his elbows on the desk. "You know the
statute of limitations for habeas petitions, don't you?"

I did.

"The standard deadline is one year from when a conviction
becomes final," I said. "After that, it's barred unless there's an exception—like newly discovered evidence or government interference."

Wexler nodded, but his brows stayed furrowed.

Twelve years was way past the statute. By all accounts, Ortega's
petition shouldn't even be getting a reply—it should have been
summarily denied as untimely.

Which made it all the more strange that Wexler immediately knew the case.

I didn't press. Not yet.

I kept my voice even. "Yes, it's well beyond the statute. But the court has ordered a response, so we're past the point of dismissal on timeliness. And if the claim is a Brady violation, that's a recognized exception."

Wexler's jaw tightened. "A Brady claim?"

I nodded. "There's an alleged tip from a retired prosecutor saying a witness statement was buried. It's the basis for the court order."

For a moment, he didn't say anything.

Then, he straightened his posture and exhaled through his nose. "Why don't you hand that case over to me?" he said casually. "I'll take a look at it."

My stomach dropped slightly.

I kept my face neutral, but inside, something felt off.

"Respectfully," I said carefully, "I'd like to see it through."

Wexler smiled, but it was just a little too tight. "I understand, but these more complicated petitions—ones that go beyond standard reply briefs—are usually better handled by senior attorneys."

I hesitated. "Is there some reason you don't want me working on it?"

There was a beat of silence.

Then, just like that, his entire demeanor shifted—his face smoothing out, his tone turning lighter. "No, of course not," he said with an easy chuckle. "Just didn't want you getting too buried in the weeds your first few weeks."

I didn't fully buy it, but I didn't push. Not yet.

I gave a short nod. "I appreciate that. I'll still take a look at the files and let you know what I find."

Wexler smiled again, but it didn't quite reach his eyes. "Sounds good. You can talk to my assistant, Cynthia, if you need any additional case files. She can pull anything that's not in the system."

I stood, smoothing out my blazer. "Thanks, I'll do that."

Wexler nodded, already looking back at his notes.

I left the office, closing the door behind me, and walked down the hall with a new weight settling in my gut.

That was weird.

I had been at this job for less than a week, and yet the moment I brought up Ortega's name, Wexler knew exactly who I was talking about.

A twelve-year-old conviction.

A Brady violation.

A retired prosecutor making a confession.

And now, my supervisor was suddenly very interested in taking this case off my plate. I had walked into Wexler's office expecting this to be just another meeting. Instead, I walked out feeling like I had just stepped onto something bigger than I understood.

And I had no intention of letting it go.

———

Preorder book Book 3 here!
https://www.amazon.com/dp/B0F1Y889KL/

Join the LT Ryan reader family & receive a free copy of the Alex Hayes story, *Trial by Fire*. Click the link below to get started:
https://ltryan.com/alex-hayes-newsletter-signup-1

ALSO BY L.T. RYAN

Find All of L.T. Ryan's Books on Amazon Today!

Deadline

End Game

Noble Ultimatum

Noble Legend

Noble Revenge

Never Look Back

Bear Logan Series

Ripple Effect

Blowback

Take Down

Deep State

Bear & Mandy Logan Series

Close to Home

Under the Surface

The Last Stop

Over the Edge

Between the Lies

Caught in the Web

Rachel Hatch Series

Drift

Downburst

Fever Burn

Smoke Signal

Firewalk

Whitewater

Aftershock

Whirlwind

Tsunami

Fastrope

Sidewinder

Redaction

Mirage (Coming Soon)

Mitch Tanner Series

The Depth of Darkness

Into The Darkness

Deliver Us From Darkness

Cassie Quinn Series

Path of Bones

Whisper of Bones

Symphony of Bones

Etched in Shadow

Concealed in Shadow

Betrayed in Shadow

Born from Ashes

Return to Ashes

Risen from Ashes (Coming Soon)

Blake Brier Series

Unmasked

Unleashed

Uncharted

Drawpoint

Contrail

Detachment

Clear

Quarry

Dalton Savage Series

Savage Grounds

Scorched Earth

Cold Sky

The Frost Killer

Crimson Moon

Dust Devil (Coming Soon)

Maddie Castle Series

The Handler

Tracking Justice

Hunting Grounds

Vanished Trails

Smoldering Lies

Field of Bones

Beneath the Grove (Coming Soon)

Affliction Z Series

Affliction Z: Patient Zero

Affliction Z: Abandoned Hope

Affliction Z: Descended in Blood

Affliction Z : Fractured Part 1

Affliction Z: Fractured Part 2 (Fall 2021)

Alex Hayes Series

Fractured Verdict

11th Hour Witness

Stella LaRosa Series

Black Rose

Red Ink

Black Gold

Avril Dahl Series

Cold Reckoning

Cold Legacy (Coming Soon)

Savannah Shadows Series

Echos of Guilt

Receive a free copy of The Recruit. Visit:

https://ltryan.com/jack-noble-newsletter-signup-1

ABOUT THE AUTHORS

L.T. RYAN is a *Wall Street Journal* and *USA Today* bestselling author, renowned for crafting pulse-pounding thrillers that keep readers on the edge of their seats. Known for creating gripping, character-driven stories, Ryan is the author of the *Jack Noble* series, the *Rachel Hatch* series, and more. With a knack for blending action, intrigue, and emotional depth, Ryan's books have captivated millions of fans worldwide.

Whether it's the shadowy world of covert operatives or the relentless pursuit of justice, Ryan's stories feature unforgettable characters and high-stakes plots that resonate with fans of Lee Child, Robert Ludlum, and Michael Connelly.

When not writing, Ryan enjoys crafting new ideas with coauthors, running a thriving publishing company, and connecting with readers. Discover the next story that will keep you turning pages late into the night.

Connect with L.T. Ryan
Sign up for his newsletter to hear the latest goings on and receive some free content
➜ https://ltryan.com/jack-noble-newsletter-signup-1

Join the private readers' group
➜ https://www.facebook.com/groups/1727449564174357

Instagram ➜ @ltryanauthor

Visit the website ➜ https://ltryan.com
Send an email ➜ contact@ltryan.com

———

LAURA CHASE is a corporate attorney-turned-author who brings her courtroom experience to the page in her gripping legal and psychological thrillers. Chase draws on her real-life experience to draw readers into the high-stakes world of courtroom drama and moral ambiguity.

After earning her JD, Chase clerked for a federal judge and thereafter transitioned to big law, where she honed her skills in high-pressure legal environments. Her passion for exploring the darker side of human nature and the gray areas of justice fuels her writing.

Chase lives with her husband, their two sons, a dog and a cat in Northern Florida. When she's not writing or working, she enjoys spending time with her family, traveling, and bingeing true crime shows.

Connect with Laura:

Sign up for her newsletter: www.laurachaseauthor.com/

Follow her on tiktok: @lawyerlaura

Send an email: info@laurachase.com

———

Printed in Great Britain
by Amazon

61362420R00167